HE STAYED AT SEA

First edition. June 24, 2025.

Copyright © 2025 Wallace Berry.

ISBN: 979-8990123670

Written by Wallace Berry.

I0676044

Table of Contents

Chapter 1

Theo leaned against the railing, as the early morning sun climbed higher. His mind drifted back to the predawn drive from his apartment in Rockport, streets empty except for shrimp boats heading out and the occasional delivery truck.

He'd driven that coastal road countless times, but this morning it felt different. The familiar silhouettes of wind-bent oaks had watched over his journey like old guardians, their twisted forms barely visible in his headlights. Past the bait shops and seafood restaurants, places that marked the rhythm of life in a town where the Gulf dictated everything.

At one curve in the road, he'd slowed where his father always pointed out the spot where, decades ago, a hurricane had pushed water clear across the peninsula. "Nature reminds us who's boss," Dad would say, the same man who'd taught him to respect the sea but never fear it.

The memory of those early fishing trips flooded back—Dad's calloused hands showing him how to bait a hook, the weight of his first catch, the pride in his father's eyes when he named every species in the bay by age nine. Back then, Theo had been more interested in what lived beneath the surface than what he could pull from it.

Theo smiled, watching a brown pelican glide alongside the boat. His aunt Clara would appreciate the sight. She'd been the one who showed him how coastal plants adapted to saltwater, how to identify edible seaweed, how nature's cycles connected land and sea. Between his father's practical knowledge and his aunt's scientific curiosity, his path had been set early.

He breathed deeply, filling his lungs with the briny air that felt more like home than any house ever had. Today wasn't just another dive. It was a homecoming to a place he'd only visited in textbooks—the underwater forests and meadows that sustained the Gulf's complex ecosystem.

The familiar anxiety before a dive mingled with something deeper—a sense that he was exactly where he belonged. Not just in Rockport, but here, poised between worlds, ready to slip beneath the surface and into the realm that had called to him since childhood.

Theo Mercer squinted against the glare of sunlight dancing across the water as he adjusted the straps on his diving mask. The rubber pressed firmly against his face, creating the watertight seal he'd need once beneath the waves. Around him, Fisherman's Wharf hummed with morning activity—charter boats loading eager anglers, the Jetty Boat preparing for its first run to San Jose Island, and seafood vendors arranging their fresh catches.

"First time diving the Gulf?" A weathered boat hand passed him an air tank.

Theo nodded, checking the pressure gauge with methodical precision. "Been diving since I was sixteen, but always in smaller spots. Nothing like this."

The vastness of what awaited below the surface sent a current of nervous energy through his body. Years of studying aquatic plant life in textbooks and controlled environments hadn't prepared him for the wild ecosystem he would soon witness firsthand. His fingers trembled slightly as he secured his weight belt.

Three boats down, a group of fishermen hoisted their equipment aboard a charter, their laughter carrying across the marina. Theo watched them for a moment, remembering countless mornings with his father casting lines from Rockport's shores. But where they sought to extract from the ocean, he aimed to understand it.

He ran through his mental checklist again. Regulator, backup regulator, dive computer, underwater camera specially fitted with macro lenses for capturing detailed images of marine vegetation. Each piece of equipment represented years of saving, planning, and dreaming of this moment.

The dive boat captain called for final boarding. Theo gathered his gear and stepped aboard, finding a spot at the stern where he could continue his preparations. As the engine rumbled to life, he gazed back at the Wharf growing smaller behind them.

What would he find down there? The question had kept him awake most of the night. Seagrass meadows, perhaps, or flowering aquatic plants that few had documented properly. The potential discoveries made his heart race faster than the anxiety of the dive itself.

"You look like a kid on Christmas morning," remarked an older diver securing her tank nearby.

Theo smiled. "Better than Christmas. Been waiting for this my whole life."

The boat picked up speed, cutting through the morning waters as Fisherman's Wharf receded into the distance. Ahead lay the diving site and beneath it, a world Theo had only glimpsed in his dreams.

"Alright folks, final equipment checks in five!" Marcus called out, moving toward the stern.

A stocky man with a shock of sun-bleached hair bounded over to where Theo stood, energy radiating from him like heat from summer asphalt. He extended a calloused hand.

"Danny Reeves. Heard you talking about plant biology. First time on Seven and a Half?"

Theo nodded, shaking the offered hand. "Theo Mercer. Yeah, first dive here."

"Man, you're in for a treat!" Danny's eyes widened with genuine excitement. "Last month I spotted three loggerheads cruising the southern edge. One old girl must've been pushing three hundred pounds, barnacles on her shell like she'd been swimming since the dinosaurs."

He pantomimed the turtle's size with outstretched arms, nearly knocking over another diver's tank in the process.

"Sorry, Marissa!" Danny called out with a grin that suggested this wasn't an uncommon occurrence. Turning back to Theo: "And the rays, brother. The rays will glide right under you, close enough to touch—though Marcus would have my hide if I tried."

Theo felt his anxiety loosening its grip, replaced by Danny's infectious enthusiasm.

"You study the plants, huh? The sea grasses down there are something else after that restoration project. Waving like wheat fields." Danny made undulating motions with his hands. "Been diving twenty years and still get butterflies every single time."

He nudged Theo with an elbow. "Bet your textbooks don't capture that feeling when a school of spadefish parts around you like you're Moses or something."

A laugh escaped Theo, surprising himself. "No, they definitely don't cover that."

"Stick with me if you want. I know where the good stuff hides." Danny winked, then lowered his voice conspiratorially. "Marcus keeps the best spots for regulars, but I'm feeling generous today."

Around them, the boat hummed with pre-dive activity—tanks clanking, regulators being tested, the soft rustle of neoprene. But in Danny's orbit, Theo felt a momentary connection to something beyond his academic interest—the pure joy of discovery shared.

"I'd like that," Theo said, meaning it.

Theo joined the small cluster of divers gathered around a weathered man with salt-and-pepper hair and skin tanned to leather by decades under the Gulf sun.

"Seven and a Half Fathom Reef might not look like much on your fancy maps," Marcus gestured to the GPS unit, his voice carrying the slight rasp of someone who'd spent years shouting over boat engines, "but she's got stories to tell for those willing to listen."

Marcus Delgado had been running dive expeditions in these waters for twenty years. His hands, adorned with faded tattoos of nautical symbols, moved expressively as he spoke, commanding attention without demanding it.

"The reef we're visiting today started as a freshwater lake during the last ice age. Now it's home to some of the most diverse marine ecosystems in the northwestern Gulf."

Theo leaned forward, notebook forgotten in his hand. Unlike the other divers checking equipment or half-listening, he hung on every word.

"We'll see sponges that filter thousands of gallons of water daily. Bryozoans building colonies that look like lace. And if we're lucky," Marcus's eyes twinkled, "maybe a loggerhead or two passing through."

A woman in a faded wetsuit raised her hand. "What about fishing pressure? I've heard these reefs are getting hammered."

Something flickered across Marcus's face—a shadow of concern quickly masked by his professional smile. "That's why education matters. Why what you all do after today matters." His gaze lingered on Theo. "Some folks just see what they can take. Others see what they can learn. What they can protect."

The conversation shifted to dive plans and buddy assignments, but Theo noticed how Marcus seemed to know things about each of them—commenting on the university logo on Theo's gear bag without having been told he was a student.

As the others dispersed to prepare their equipment, Marcus approached Theo. "First time at this reef?"

"Yes, sir. I've been studying marine plants, but—"

"Books and tanks are different worlds." Marcus nodded toward the water. "The Gulf doesn't give up her secrets easily. You have to earn them." He paused. "Something tells me you're here for more than just sightseeing."

Theo felt strangely transparent under the older man's gaze, as if Marcus could see past his casual interest to the deeper currents of his ambition.

"Excuse me, you are marine biologist, yes?" A woman's voice with a distinct German accent cut through the background noise of clanking equipment.

Theo turned to find a couple in matching royal blue wetsuits approaching him. The woman had her blonde hair tied in a practical braid, while her partner—taller with wire-rimmed glasses—adjusted an expensive-looking underwater camera.

"I'm still a student, actually," Theo said, extending his hand. "Plant biology."

"Martina Brauer," she said, giving his hand a firm shake. "And this is my husband, Klaus. We are from Munich."

Klaus lowered his camera and grinned. "Third reef this trip! We have done Flower Gardens last week. Very beautiful, very colorful."

Their enthusiasm was infectious. Unlike some of the more serious divers who approached the expedition with solemn determination, the Germans radiated pure joy.

"Is this your first time at Seven and a Half?" Theo asked.

Martina nodded vigorously. "We collect dive sites like others collect stamps. Klaus has spreadsheet—very organized, very German," she laughed at her own joke. "What about you? Many dives?"

"Mostly local spots," Theo admitted. "Nothing as impressive as your list."

Klaus waved dismissively. "Every dive is special. We are not professionals, just..." he searched for the word.

"Enthusiasts," Martina supplied.

Around them, the boat hummed with pre-departure energy. A deckhand called instructions, while Marcus consulted with the captain. Laughter erupted from a group of college-aged divers taking selfies near the stern.

"What do you hope to see today?" Theo asked.

Klaus adjusted his glasses. "Everything! The small things especially. Last dive, I spent thirty minutes with one tiny nudibranch. Martina had to drag me away."

"He forgets time underwater," Martina explained. "I am timekeeper, or we would need rescue!"

Their laughter joined the symphony of sounds on deck—the mechanical rumble of the engine, waves slapping against the hull, excited chatter in various accents. Each person carried different expectations into the water. The serious conservationists, the thrill-seekers, the scientists, the tourists—all drawn to the same mysterious world beneath the waves.

As the boat's horn signaled their imminent departure, Theo realized how this diverse group mirrored the reef itself—separate individuals forming a temporary, vibrant ecosystem of human curiosity.

The engines growled beneath their feet, vibrating through the deck as the captain eased the throttle forward. With a churning wake of white foam, the dive boat pulled away from Fisherman's Wharf, leaving the shoreline behind. Gulls circled overhead, their cries fading as the vessel picked up speed.

Theo made his way to the bow, gripping the railing as the boat sliced through the morning chop. Salt spray misted his face, and he closed his eyes briefly, savoring the transition. Behind him, divers settled into their chosen spots—some chatting excitedly, others quiet with anticipation or slight nervousness.

The Texas coastline receded, its familiar contours blurring into a thin line between sea and sky. Ahead lay nothing but the vast expanse of the Gulf, punctuated by distant oil platforms rising like industrial islands from the water. Their metal frameworks caught the strengthening sunlight, glinting like beacons.

"First time heading out this far?" The captain's voice carried over the wind as he emerged momentarily from the wheelhouse.

Theo shook his head. "Used to fish these waters with my dad. Never dove them, though."

The captain nodded with understanding before returning to his post. The comment lingered in Theo's mind—how strange to return to these same waters with such different purpose. Where he once helped pull life from the sea, he now sought only to observe it.

Several dolphins appeared alongside the boat, riding the bow wave with effortless grace. Their sudden presence drew excited shouts from the other passengers, who rushed to the railings with cameras. Theo watched as they darted beneath the surface, reappearing moments later in perfect synchronization.

The horizon seemed endless, the water's blue deepening as they moved farther from shore. Somewhere beneath them lay Seven and a Half Fathom Reef—unseen but waiting. The knowledge of its presence shifted something in Theo's chest, a tightening of anticipation.

He glanced back at his fellow divers—strangers united by a common desire to explore the hidden world below. They were crossing a threshold, leaving behind the familiar for something ancient and mysterious. The boat pushed onward, carrying them all toward an adventure that would unfold in slow-motion, in the hushed blue realm beneath the waves.

The pod expanded from three to seven dolphins, their sleek bodies carving through the water alongside the boat. Sunlight caught their movements, transforming each splash into a shower of diamonds. The divers clustered at the railings, cameras and phones capturing the impromptu performance.

"Look how they're drafting off our bow wave," Marcus called out, his weathered face bright with childlike enthusiasm. He pointed to the lead dolphin, a larger specimen with a distinctive notch in its dorsal fin. "They're conserving energy while showing off for us. Smart creatures."

Theo leaned over the rail, transfixed by their effortless coordination. The dolphins rolled sideways, their eyes seeming to meet his with ancient intelligence. One leapt clear of the water, performing a perfect arc before slicing back beneath the surface with barely a ripple.

"It's a good sign," Marcus continued, addressing the group but keeping his gaze on the water. "In all my years guiding, the best dives often follow dolphin escorts. Like they're welcoming us to their world."

Danny whooped as two dolphins crossed paths in perfect synchronization. "Man, I never get tired of this!"

Even Klaus and Martina had abandoned their equipment checks to watch, their matching wetsuits forgotten as they pointed and murmured to each other in rapid German.

The captain throttled back slightly, allowing the moment to stretch. The boat's engine hummed at a lower pitch, as if in deference to the natural symphony playing out around them. Waves slapped rhythmically against the hull, keeping time with the dolphins' dance.

A sense of communion settled over the diverse group of divers. Strangers minutes before, they now exchanged glances of shared wonder, temporary barriers dissolved by collective awe. Theo felt it too—this unexpected gift from the Gulf binding them together before they'd even submerged.

"They're wild, you know," Marcus said quietly, now standing beside Theo. "Not trained, not expecting anything from us. Just playing because that's what they do. Reminds you why we come out here in the first place."

Theo nodded, understanding. The dolphins weren't performing; they were simply being. And in their natural joy, they offered something beyond entertainment—a glimpse of connection to something larger, something ancient and unbroken.

The lead dolphin made one final spectacular leap before the pod veered away, disappearing into the vastness of the Gulf as suddenly as they had appeared, leaving behind a boat full of humans with uplifted spirits and a shared anticipation for what awaited below.

The dolphin magic faded as the boat pushed deeper into the Gulf. The horizon tilted, then righted itself, then tilted again. The captain adjusted their course, cutting through swells that had appeared seemingly from nowhere.

"Weather's shifting faster than forecast," he called back to Marcus. "Nothing dangerous, but we're in for some chop."

Theo's stomach lurched with the next wave. The pleasant warmth of excitement cooled into something less comfortable. He gripped the railing tighter, focusing on the distant line where sky met water, willing his equilibrium to stabilize.

Around him, the group's reactions varied. Danny laughed each time the bow slapped down against the water, treating the roughness like an amusement park ride. Klaus and Martina sat side by side on a bench, their faces impassive behind matching sunglasses. The woman who had earlier questioned Marcus about fishing pressure now looked distinctly green, her hand pressed against her mouth.

"First time in rough water?" Marcus appeared beside Theo, his stance wide and knees bent, body naturally compensating for the motion.

Theo swallowed hard. "Not exactly. Used to fish with my dad, but—" The boat dropped suddenly, his stomach rising into his throat. "Been a while."

"Breathe through your nose, out through your mouth. Keep your eyes on the horizon." Marcus patted his shoulder. "Ginger candy in the cabin if you need it."

Another wave struck the port side, sending spray across the deck. The salt water felt cold against Theo's face, a stark contrast to the heat building behind his eyes and the cold sweat forming at his temples.

He'd imagined this moment differently—standing confidently at the bow, prepared for scientific discovery. Instead, he fought the urge to vomit over the side while more experienced divers moved around the pitching deck with practiced ease.

"Seven and a Half's just ahead," the captain announced. "Water's calmer over the reef structure."

Theo nodded weakly, hoping it was true. The thought of donning his gear and slipping beneath these angry waves now seemed daunting rather than exciting. His body, which had felt so connected to the sea earlier, now rebelled against its motion.

He closed his eyes briefly, remembering his purpose. The discomfort was temporary. The discovery waiting below—that was worth enduring a little seasickness. Theo straightened, took a deep breath, and focused on the horizon once more.

The boat pitched forward, then rolled sideways. Theo's knuckles whitened against the railing as another wave slapped the hull. His earlier determination wavered with each lurch of his stomach.

"You're looking rough, buddy." Danny appeared at his side, somehow maintaining perfect balance despite the rolling deck. "First day jitters or genuine seasickness?"

Theo couldn't risk opening his mouth to answer. He nodded weakly, unsure which option he was confirming.

Across the deck, the other divers had adapted to the motion. Klaus and Martina remained seated, swaying in unison with the boat's movement. The captain stood at the wheel, legs braced wide, his posture suggesting this turbulence barely registered as noteworthy. Even the woman who'd looked ill earlier now sipped water, her color returning.

Only Theo remained caught in misery's grip. Cold sweat beaded on his forehead while heat flushed through his chest. The horizon—his anchor point—blurred and doubled. His biology training offered unwanted clarity about what was happening: his inner ear's vestibular system sending conflicting signals to his brain, triggering the nausea response.

Understanding the mechanism provided no relief.

Marcus approached, his experienced eyes assessing Theo's condition. "Deep breaths. We're almost to calmer water."

The boat crested another wave, hanging suspended for a terrible moment before dropping. Theo's resolve crumbled. He lurched toward the railing, bent double, and surrendered his breakfast to the Gulf.

"There you go. Better out than in." Marcus's voice held no judgment, only matter-of-fact compassion.

Shame burned hotter than the nausea. Theo had spent years studying marine ecosystems, dreaming of this moment—and now he couldn't even handle the journey to the dive site.

"Sorry," he managed, wiping his mouth with the back of his hand.

"Nothing to apologize for." Marcus handed him a water bottle. "Happens to the best. Rinse and spit."

Theo followed instructions, the cool water momentarily clearing the acid taste from his mouth. Surprisingly, his stomach felt marginally better after emptying itself.

"Ten minutes to the site," the captain called.

Theo straightened slowly, testing his equilibrium. The waves still rolled beneath them, but something had shifted—either the water was indeed calming as they approached the reef, or his body had finally surrendered to the motion.

"Think you can manage the dive?" Marcus asked quietly.

Theo nodded, finding his voice. "I didn't come this far to turn back now."

Theo retreated below deck, each step deliberate as he navigated the narrow stairs. The cabin offered respite from the wind and spray, though the motion remained—a constant reminder of the boundary between worlds he straddled. He sank onto a bench, elbows on knees, head hanging low.

The hatch opened, sending a shaft of sunlight across the cabin floor. Martina descended, her movements fluid despite the boat's pitch. Unlike her husband's boisterous energy, she carried a quiet competence that seemed to steady the very air around her.

"You are having the bad time, yes?" Her accent thickened her words, but the sympathy in them needed no translation.

Theo managed a weak smile. "That obvious?"

"The green face gives away much." Martina settled beside him, unzipping a small pouch on her utility belt. "First deep water dive?"

"First Gulf dive. I've done some bay dives, but nothing..." He gestured vaguely upward, where waves continued their assault on the hull.

Martina nodded, extracting a small tin from her pouch. "The North Sea, where Klaus and I learned, it was much worse. My first three dives, I fed the fish before even reaching the water." She pried open the tin, revealing small amber-colored candies. "These helped. Still do."

She extended the tin toward him. Theo hesitated, then selected one.

"Ginger," she explained. "Old remedy, but effective. Not miracle, but helps."

The candy's spicy sweetness spread across his tongue, warming his throat. Theo closed his eyes, focusing on the sensation rather than the boat's movement.

"Thank you."

"We divers, we look after each other." Martina's pragmatic tone carried no sentimentality, yet conveyed genuine concern. "The sea does not care about our comfort. Only our respect."

Theo nodded, recognizing wisdom that echoed his father's teachings.

"Take time. Breathe. The reef has existed for centuries. It will wait five more minutes." She patted his shoulder, then rose. "When you are ready, come up. But do not rush. The dive is already challenging enough without stomach rebellion."

As she climbed back toward the deck, Theo felt the ginger working its subtle magic. Beyond the physical relief, something else had shifted—a reminder that he wasn't facing this journey alone. The sea might be indifferent, but those who ventured upon it formed their own ecosystem of support.

The ginger's warmth faded too quickly. Theo's momentary relief dissolved as the boat pitched sideways, sending his stomach lurching against his ribs. Above deck, Marcus's voice carried through the floorboards—the dive briefing had begun. Fragments of information filtered down: "current patterns," "visibility expectations," "buddy system protocols." Each word represented knowledge Theo needed but couldn't bring himself to pursue.

"I should be up there," he muttered, pressing his palms against the cool metal wall.

The cabin's confines seemed to shrink with each passing minute. Maps of the Gulf Coast adorned the walls, their laminated surfaces catching the dim light from the single porthole. Faded photographs of record catches and smiling divers surrounded him—evidence of countless successful expeditions that had launched from this very vessel.

Theo closed his eyes, but the darkness only intensified the swaying. He'd prepared for every aspect of this dive—researched the reef's ecosystem, memorized fish species, practiced camera settings—yet had never considered his body might betray him so completely.

Footsteps thundered overhead. Laughter erupted, followed by Marcus's booming instructions. The community Theo had glimpsed earlier continued forming without him, connections strengthening through shared anticipation.

"First rule of field research," he reminded himself, recalling Professor Harmon's words, "is knowing when to adapt your methodology."

He pulled out his notebook, determined to salvage something from this setback. The pencil trembled against the page as he attempted to document his experience, but the words blurred together. Even this small act of scientific discipline proved beyond his current capabilities.

The boat's engine throttled down. They had reached the dive site.

Theo pictured the others preparing their gear, checking tanks, adjusting masks—the ritualistic choreography he'd hoped to join. Danny would be bouncing with excitement. Klaus and Martina would move with practiced efficiency. And he remained below, separated from it all by nothing more substantial than his own physiology.

"Some marine biologist," he whispered to the empty cabin. "Can't even handle the surface of the water."

The irony wasn't lost on him—that he felt most at home in the depths yet couldn't navigate the threshold to reach them. The sea had always represented possibility and discovery. Now it presented a humbling lesson in limitations, one that no amount of academic preparation could have prevented.

The ceiling above Theo's head became a membrane through which the excited voices of the divers filtered down. Words broke through in fragments—"visibility better than expected," "northern quadrant," "sponge formations." Each snippet heightened his sense of disconnection.

"—never seen coral this healthy in the Gulf—" That was Danny's voice, enthusiasm bubbling through the deck planks.

"—keep an eye on your depth gauges near the drop-off—" Marcus's authoritative tone, followed by murmurs of acknowledgment.

Theo's pulse quickened. The dive briefing contained critical information he was missing—information that might never be repeated. Seven and a Half Fathom Reef was unfolding in descriptions above him while he lay trapped in his misery below.

He pressed his ear against the ceiling, straining to catch more details.

"—possible current shift from the southeast—"

"—maintain visual contact with your buddy at all times—"

The sounds of equipment being checked followed—the metallic clank of tanks, the hiss of regulators tested, the snap of mask straps adjusted. A symphony of preparation that Theo should have been part of.

His research notes lay scattered beside him—pages detailing the reef's unique ecology, the convergence of currents that created a biodiversity hotspot, the remnants of what was once a freshwater lake during the last ice age. Knowledge that remained theoretical without firsthand observation.

Someone laughed overhead—Klaus, probably—followed by Martina's gentle admonishment. The camaraderie felt tangible, even through the barrier separating them.

Theo's stomach had settled somewhat, the worst of the nausea receding like a tide pulling back from shore. But had it improved enough? The thought of donning his gear, of facing the water again, sent a ripple of uncertainty through him.

Yet beneath that uncertainty lay something stronger—a current of determination that had carried him through years of study, through countless hours of preparation for moments exactly like this one.

The reef waited below—ancient, patient, indifferent to his personal struggle. It had witnessed the rise and fall of sea levels, the transformation from lake to marine habitat, the slow evolution of its ecological community. It would remain whether he visited it today or not.

But Theo might never get this chance again.

Above, a voice called out: "First team, gear up!"

The moment of decision had arrived.

Chapter 2

Theo's eyes fluttered open to an unfamiliar stillness. No engine rumble. No voices. No footsteps overhead. Just the gentle lapping of waves against the hull and the occasional creak of wood adjusting to the water's rhythm.

Something was wrong.

Golden morning light streamed through the porthole, casting a perfect circle on the cabin wall opposite his bunk. Dust motes danced in the beam, undisturbed by human movement. The air hung heavy with silence.

"Hello?" His voice sounded foreign in the emptiness, bouncing off the wooden panels before dissolving into nothing. No response came.

Theo pushed himself upright, wincing at the stiffness in his neck. His watch read 6:42 AM. He'd slept through the night—but where was everyone else? The last thing he remembered was the call for divers to gear up, his internal debate about joining them, and then...nothing.

Had he passed out? The embarrassing possibility crossed his mind as he swung his legs over the edge of the bunk. His stomach felt settled now, the nausea replaced by a hollow hunger.

He stood, steadying himself against the gentle rocking of the boat. His research notes remained scattered across the small table where he'd left them, but something about them seemed wrong—the pages had yellowed slightly at the edges, as though days rather than hours had passed.

The boat wasn't moving. Not the normal drift and bob of a vessel at anchor, but a peculiar stillness that suggested it hadn't moved in some time.

Theo moved to the porthole, peering out at water that glittered under the morning sun. The coastline was visible in the distance, but not where it should have been. The silhouette was wrong—sharper, more defined than the flat Gulf shores he knew.

"Marcus?" he called out, louder this time. "Danny?"

The silence that answered carried weight, pressing against his eardrums like the pressure of deep water.

Theo reached for the cabin door, his hand hesitating on the handle. Beyond this room lay answers, but something in his gut warned that he might not want to hear them.

The handle turned with a resistance that suggested disuse. Theo pushed the door open, wincing at the protesting creak of its hinges. The sound carried across the deck, unnaturally loud in the morning stillness.

He stepped onto the main deck, blinking against the brightness. The sun hung low in the eastern sky, casting long shadows across the weathered planks. Salt crystals had formed along the railings, a fine white crust that spoke of days without being wiped clean.

"Hello?" Theo called again, his voice swallowed by the vastness surrounding him.

The boat—the same vessel that had been crowded with eager divers just yesterday—lay completely deserted. Dive gear that should have been stowed neatly was scattered across the deck: a regulator here, a weight belt there. A single fin rested against the port railing, its partner nowhere in sight.

Theo moved slowly toward the bow, his footsteps echoing. The captain's cabin stood open, charts still spread across the navigation table, a half-filled coffee mug sitting beside them. The liquid inside had evaporated, leaving only a dark ring at the bottom.

The horizon stretched in every direction, unbroken by land or other vessels. The coastline he'd glimpsed from the porthole was nowhere visible now, as if it had been a mirage that disappeared with his emergence onto the deck.

A chill ran down Theo's spine despite the warming air. Where was Marcus with his enthusiastic briefings? Where was Danny's infectious excitement? What about Klaus and Martina with their matching wetsuits and quiet competence?

He checked the emergency radio—dead. The boat's log lay open, the last entry dated the previous day, noting their arrival at Seven and a Half Fathom Reef.

"This isn't possible," he whispered, running his hand through his hair.

A plastic water bottle rolled across the deck with a hollow sound as the boat shifted slightly. Theo caught it reflexively, noticing the label had faded as if left in the sun for weeks rather than hours.

Something fluttered near the stern—a dive flag, still attached to its line, whipping gently in the breeze. Below it, the water darkened to a deep blue, suggesting unfathomable depth where the reef should have been.

Theo gripped the railing, a cold knot forming in his stomach. He was alone, adrift on an empty boat, with no explanation for how or why.

Theo's breathing quickened as the full weight of his situation crashed over him like a wave. Alone. Adrift. Abandoned. The vastness of the Gulf stretched in every direction, a prison of endless blue.

His knees weakened, forcing him to grip the railing tighter as his vision narrowed to a pinpoint. The gentle rocking of the boat, once nauseating, now felt like the only tether to reality in a world gone mad.

"Think, Mercer. Think." His voice sounded foreign even to himself, thin and fragile against the immensity of silence.

Survival statistics from a coastal safety course flickered through his mind. Three minutes without air. Three hours in extreme conditions without shelter. Three days without water. Three weeks without food. The boat had water tanks—if they still contained anything—but how long had he truly been here? The yellowed notes and faded bottle suggested days, not hours.

Beneath him, the water shifted, dark and impenetrable. Seven and a half fathoms—approximately forty-five feet—but it might as well have been the Mariana Trench for all he knew of what lay below. The reef that should have been teeming with life appeared absent, replaced by an unsettling emptiness.

Sweat beaded on his forehead despite the morning chill. His aunt Clara's voice echoed in his memory: "Panic is the mind-killer, Theo. When lost in the wild, S.T.O.P. Stop, Think, Observe, Plan."

He forced himself to inhale deeply, counting to four, holding for seven, exhaling for eight. The technique slowed his racing heart marginally.

The boat had to have emergency provisions. A radio that could be fixed. Flares, perhaps. Something to signal passing ships—if any ever passed this forsaken spot.

But underneath the practical concerns lurked deeper, more primal fears. What had happened to the others? Why couldn't he remember anything after the dive call? Had he somehow slept through an evacuation? An accident?

Or was something else at work here—something beyond rational explanation?

The sun climbed higher, burning away the morning mist and revealing nothing but more empty ocean. No ships on the horizon.

No land in sight. No answers to the questions hammering at his consciousness.

Theo sank to his knees, the metal deck warm against his palms. He was a student of marine biology, not a sailor. Not a survivor. Just a young man suddenly, terrifyingly alone with the sea.

The rhythmic slap of waves against the hull eventually pulled Theo back from the edge of despair. He pushed himself upright, muscles stiff from tension. Survival required clear thinking, not panic.

He moved toward the helm, each step more deliberate than the last. The captain's station remained as abandoned as the rest of the vessel, but the navigation instruments might still offer answers. Theo's fingers trembled as he retrieved the compass from its housing.

The needle swung lazily before settling on north. At least some constants remained in this nightmare. He studied the instrument, its brass casing worn from years of handling by experienced hands. Unlike those hands, his own lacked the calluses of a seasoned sailor, but they possessed the precision of a scientist.

Theo closed his eyes, reconstructing their journey from memory. They had departed Fisherman's Wharf heading southeast toward Seven and a Half Fathom Reef. If the boat had drifted, prevailing Gulf currents would likely have pushed them... where?

He squinted at the horizon, methodically scanning each quadrant. The morning light revealed something he'd missed earlier—a dark smudge to the west, barely distinguishable from the boundary between sea and sky.

"Land," he whispered, the word carrying more weight than any scientific term he'd ever memorized.

Impossible to tell how far. Ten miles? Twenty? The hazy outline offered no details, but its mere existence sparked something within him—a fragile hope taking root where panic had reigned moments before.

Theo leaned against the helm, feeling the solid structure support his weight. The boat's controls remained intact, untouched since whoever had piloted it last. The key hung in the ignition.

"One problem at a time," he murmured, channeling his aunt's practical approach to challenges. He needed to determine if the engines still functioned, if enough fuel remained, if the navigation systems could guide him toward that distant shore.

His academic mind, trained to classify and categorize, began creating mental lists: resources available, knowledge gaps, potential actions. The process itself provided comfort, transforming overwhelming chaos into manageable components.

Theo's gaze returned to the distant landmass. Whatever had happened—whatever explanation waited to be discovered—that smudge of darkness represented his best chance of survival.

Theo descended the narrow steps to the galley, steadying himself against the wall as the boat rocked beneath him. The small kitchen space appeared untouched yet somehow aged—a time capsule of the last normal moments before whatever calamity had befallen the vessel.

He pulled open the first cabinet, revealing stacks of plastic plates and cups. Useless. The second yielded better results: six unopened bottles of water. Theo gathered them into the crook of his arm, the cool plastic against his skin a small comfort in the surreal situation.

"Water first, then food," he muttered, moving methodically through the remaining storage spaces.

A drawer beneath the sink contained emergency supplies—a flashlight with batteries corroded at the terminals, waterproof matches, and a first aid kit. Theo examined the kit, noting the antiseptic wipes and bandages within. The expiration dates on some items had passed, yet another unsettling indication of time's distortion.

The refrigerator hummed softly—still operational, though the interior light failed to illuminate when he opened the door. Inside, Theo found packages of lunch meat with dates three weeks in the future, an impossibility that sent a chill through him despite the Gulf heat.

"Don't think about it. Just survive," he told himself, setting aside questions that had no immediate answers.

A pantry revealed his best find: energy bars, canned beans, tuna, and crackers. Theo calculated mentally—enough sustenance for several days if rationed properly. He gathered the supplies into a weathered canvas bag he found hanging on a hook.

As he worked, Theo's mind remained clear, focused on the immediate task rather than the terrifying unknowns. His aunt Clara's voice seemed to guide him: "The wild doesn't care about your feelings, only your actions."

Theo paused at a small sink, turning the tap experimentally. A trickle of water emerged, then stopped. He tried again with the same result. The boat's water tank was nearly empty—another reason to reach land soon.

He arranged his salvaged provisions on the galley table, taking inventory. Water, food, basic medical supplies. It wasn't much, but it transformed his situation from hopeless to merely desperate.

Through the small porthole, the distant shoreline remained visible—a promise of answers if he could reach it. Theo zipped the canvas bag closed with newfound determination. He would not become another mystery of the Gulf.

Theo climbed back onto the deck, the canvas bag of supplies slung over his shoulder. The afternoon sun beat down mercilessly, casting harsh reflections across the water that made his eyes water. He squinted toward the western shoreline, calculating how long it might take to reach it if he managed to start the boat's engine.

The silence of the open water pressed against his eardrums, making the sudden distant rumble all the more startling.

Theo froze, his hand gripping the railing. The sound was unmistakable—an engine, growing steadily louder. His heart quickened as he scanned the horizon, searching for its source.

"Hello!" he called out, voice cracking from disuse. The word seemed to vanish into the vastness, swallowed by the endless blue.

The engine noise intensified, coming from the southeast. Theo rushed to the port side, shielding his eyes against the glare. A dark speck appeared, bouncing across the water's surface. As it drew nearer, it resolved into the distinct shape of a speedboat, cutting a white wake through the Gulf waters.

Relief flooded through him, followed immediately by caution. In his isolated state, any human contact represented both salvation and unknown risk.

"Who are you?" he whispered to himself, watching the boat's approach.

The vessel changed course slightly, heading directly toward the abandoned dive boat. Theo could make out two figures now—one piloting, another standing at the bow. Neither wore the bright colors of Coast Guard rescue.

Theo ducked below the railing, peering over the edge. Something in their deliberate approach triggered a primal warning in his mind. These weren't random boaters who'd spotted a stranded vessel. They moved with purpose, as if they knew exactly what they were looking for.

He retreated from the edge, crouching behind a stack of dive tanks. The speedboat's engine throttled down as it circled the larger vessel. Male voices carried across the water, though Theo couldn't make out their words over the idling motor.

The question of what had happened to Marcus, Danny, and the others suddenly seemed more urgent, more ominous. Had these men been involved?

Theo clutched the canvas bag to his chest, breath shallow, as the speedboat bumped gently against the dive boat's hull.

The speedboat bumped against the dive boat once more before a rope flew over the railing, landing with a soft thud on the deck. Theo pressed himself deeper into the shadow of the dive tanks, making himself as small as possible. His heart hammered against his ribs as a familiar voice cut through the air.

"Easy on the starboard side, Ricky! You'll scratch her paint job worse than she already is."

Marcus. The diving instructor's voice was unmistakable, but his tone carried none of the professional warmth Theo remembered. Instead, it rang with casual authority, the voice of someone accustomed to being obeyed.

Heavy footsteps landed on the deck as three men climbed aboard. Theo held his breath.

"Nobody's been here," a second voice announced—deeper, with a slight accent Theo couldn't place. "Everything's just like we left it."

"You sure about that?" Marcus asked, footsteps moving across the deck. "Check below. I don't want any surprises."

Laughter erupted from the third man. "Like last time with that Coast Guard rookie? Man, I thought Vince was gonna have a heart attack."

"That wasn't funny, Sal," Marcus replied, though his voice betrayed amusement. "Vince nearly shot the kid."

The three men moved with the easy familiarity of long acquaintance. Theo peered through a gap between tanks, catching glimpses of Marcus—dressed now in dark clothes rather than his diving instructor's gear—directing the others with subtle gestures.

These weren't colleagues from a diving operation. These men shared something deeper, darker—the silent communication of those who'd faced danger together, who kept shared secrets.

"We got about four hours before the drop," Marcus said, checking his watch. "Vince will be here with the main boat by sunset."

"Plenty of time for a beer," Sal replied, producing a can from his pocket.

The camaraderie between them stood in stark contrast to Theo's isolation. While he'd been stranded and confused, these men had been operating with purpose, following some hidden agenda.

Theo's earlier question about what had happened to the other divers took on new, disturbing dimensions. Had the entire dive been a cover for something else? And if Marcus noticed him now, what would happen?

Theo's muscles cramped as he maintained his position behind the dive tanks. When the men moved toward the cabin, he seized his opportunity, slipping below deck through the secondary hatch. Finding a narrow maintenance closet near the galley, he wedged himself inside, leaving the door cracked just enough to hear the conversation floating down from above.

The men settled around the small table in the main cabin, their boots scraping against the floor. Ice clinked in glasses as they poured drinks.

"Vince says this is the last run for a while," Marcus said. "Heat's coming down after that Coast Guard interception near Corpus."

"They didn't get shit," Sal replied. "Just an empty boat."

"They got close enough." The third man—Ricky—spoke with a gravelly voice. "Too close."

Theo's breathing slowed as he concentrated on their words. The closet smelled of mildew and cleaning chemicals, but he dared not move.

"This package is different anyway," Marcus continued. "Not the usual merchandise. High value, special handling. That's why we're using the dive boat as the transfer point."

"How high value we talking?" Sal asked.

"High enough that if anything goes wrong, we disappear. Permanently." Marcus's voice hardened. "That's why I don't want any mistakes. No witnesses, no evidence."

A chill ran through Theo's body. No witnesses. The words hung in the air like a death sentence.

"What about those tourists from yesterday?" Ricky asked. "They see anything?"

Marcus laughed. "Those idiots? They were so seasick they barely knew which way was up. We dropped them back at the dock before heading out to the meeting point. They never saw a thing."

The other divers were safe. Relief washed over Theo, quickly followed by the stark realization of his own precarious situation. He was alone on a boat with smugglers—drug runners, maybe worse—with no way to call for help.

"Sunset's in three hours," Marcus said. "Vince brings the package, we transfer it to the buyers, then we sink this boat. Clean break."

Sink the boat. Theo's mouth went dry. Whatever happened at sunset, he needed to be off this vessel before then. His life depended on it.

The sun sank toward the horizon, painting the sky in violent shades of orange and crimson. Theo's legs had long since gone numb in the cramped maintenance closet, but fear kept him motionless. He'd crept out only once to grab a water bottle before returning to his hiding spot.

A distant engine growl broke the evening stillness. Theo's heart hammered against his ribs as footsteps thundered across the deck above. He abandoned his closet sanctuary and crawled toward the small observation hatch near the stern—a circular window barely six inches across that offered a partial view of the deck.

"They're here," Marcus called out. "Get ready."

A sleek black vessel approached, its hull riding low in the water. Two men stood at its bow, faces obscured by the lengthening shadows. As it pulled alongside the dive boat, Theo glimpsed a third figure—a heavyset man with a salt-and-pepper beard who seemed to command the others with silent gestures.

"That's Vince," Ricky muttered, just loud enough for Theo to hear through the thin bulkhead.

The boats bumped together, ropes flying between them. Metal cases—three of them, matte black with reinforced corners—transferred from one vessel to the other. Theo's stomach knotted as he recognized the unmistakable hallmarks of a drug transfer. The diving expedition, the friendly guide persona—all of it had been cover for this moment.

"Count it," the bearded man ordered as Marcus opened one case.

Even from his limited vantage point, Theo could see the tightly wrapped packages inside, dozens of them stacked in neat rows. Marcus pulled one out, sliced it open with a pocketknife, and dipped his finger in the white powder before tasting it.

"Pure as promised," Marcus confirmed, nodding to the others.

The bearded man handed over a satellite phone. "Coordinates for the pickup are programmed in. Midnight. Don't be late."

As the black vessel pulled away, Theo sank back from the hatch, cold sweat trickling down his spine. This wasn't just some small-time operation—the quantity he'd seen represented millions in street value. And in less than three hours, these men planned to sink the boat with all evidence aboard.

Including, Theo realized with growing horror, any witnesses.

Theo collapsed against the bulkhead, his breath coming in shallow gasps. The satellite phone's midnight deadline echoed in his mind like a death knell. Three hours. Three hours until these men would destroy the boat—with him on it, if he didn't act.

His academic brain, normally so analytical and measured, spiraled into frantic calculations. The coastline he'd spotted earlier lay at least five miles west. Even if he could swim that distance—a monumental if—the water temperature would sap his strength within an hour. Hypothermia would claim him long before he reached shore.

The speedboat that had brought Marcus and his crew offered another possibility, but it remained tethered to the dive boat's starboard side, visible from nearly every angle of the deck. He'd be spotted before he could untie it.

Footsteps creaked overhead. Theo froze, holding his breath as dust particles drifted down from the ceiling.

"We'll need to move the tanks," Marcus's voice filtered through. "Too much evidence."

"What about the logbook?" Sal asked.

"Everything goes down. Clean break."

The realization crystallized in Theo's mind with terrifying clarity: he wasn't just witnessing a crime—he was a loose end. If discovered, his fate wouldn't involve arrest or threats. These men had too much at stake.

Aunt Clara's voice surfaced in his memory: "When you're lost in the woods, don't panic. Assess what you have, not what you lack."

Theo forced himself to inventory his assets: knowledge of the boat's layout, a few supplies, the element of surprise. Not much against three armed men, but it was something.

He needed a plan—not just to hide, but to escape. The dive gear scattered across the deck presented a possibility. If he could secure a tank, regulator, and wetsuit without being seen, perhaps he could slip overboard and swim beneath the surface, away from watchful eyes.

Darkness would be his ally. The sun had nearly set, and with it came his best chance for survival.

Theo clenched his fists, a cold determination replacing his fear. He would not become collateral damage in someone else's criminal enterprise. Not today. Not in these waters that had once felt like home.

The Gulf's dark waters lapped against the hull, each wave a whispered invitation to the depths below. Theo crouched at the stern, hidden in shadow, his wetsuit half-zipped and the weight of the oxygen tank pressing against his spine. His fingers trembled as he secured the mask around his face, fogging the glass with quick, panicked breaths.

Twenty feet away, Marcus and his crew huddled around the satellite phone, plotting coordinates for their midnight rendezvous. Their laughter carried across the deck—the easy confidence of men who believed themselves alone and unobserved.

Theo's mind raced through every potential outcome. The tank contained enough air for forty minutes underwater—maybe an hour if he controlled his breathing. Not enough to reach shore, but perhaps enough to find somewhere to hide until daylight. The alternative was waiting for discovery, for the moment when Marcus's eyes would widen with recognition before narrowing with deadly intent.

I'm not a diver. Not really. Just a student who took a certification course.

The thought paralyzed him. Beneath his feet stretched countless fathoms of black water, home to creatures that had evolved in darkness while mankind still huddled in caves. What waited in that abyss terrified him more than the men on deck.

He closed his eyes, feeling the weight of the regulator in his mouth. Salt air filled his nostrils—perhaps for the last time. He thought of Aunt Clara, of his father, of the coastal ecosystems he'd studied with such passion. Would anyone ever know what happened to him?

The boat rocked suddenly as one of the men moved toward the bow. Time had run out.

Theo tightened the strap on his mask, checked his regulator one final time, and edged toward the water. The Gulf opened below him like a mouth, patient and eternal. In its darkness lay both salvation and doom.

Three seconds, he promised himself. *Count to three, then jump.*

One. His muscles tensed.

Two. He visualized the descent, the quiet envelopment of water.

Three—

The sound of approaching footsteps froze him in place.

The footsteps grew louder. Theo's heart hammered against his ribs, each beat a countdown to discovery. No more hesitation. No more choices. Just action.

He slipped over the edge.

The Gulf swallowed him whole. Water rushed past his ears as he plunged beneath the surface, the sudden cold shocking his system into hyperawareness. Bubbles erupted around him, silver ghosts rising toward the boat's hull silhouetted against the night sky.

Theo kicked hard, angling away from the vessel, his movements awkward with fear. The regulator hissed with each breath, unnaturally loud in the underwater silence. He fought the instinct to surface, to seek the comfort of air and light. Instead, he forced himself deeper, where darkness concealed him.

Ten feet down. Twenty. The pressure built in his ears.

Above, a beam of light cut through the water—a flashlight scanning the surface. Had they heard him? Seen him? Theo froze, suspended in the black water, waiting for the moment a face would appear at the rail, for shouts of alarm.

The light swept past, continuing its casual arc across the waves. They hadn't noticed.

He exhaled slowly, watching the stream of bubbles disappear into the darkness above. The crushing weight of terror began to lift, replaced by a strange, crystalline clarity. In this alien realm, with death hovering above and below, Theo found himself strangely centered.

The water held him, neither friend nor enemy, simply existing. Like the coastal ecosystems he'd studied, the Gulf operated by its own ancient rules—indifferent to human concerns, yet offering sanctuary to those who understood its ways.

Theo checked his depth gauge, his compass. Shore lay west, beyond his reach with this limited air supply. But a series of natural gas platforms dotted the horizon to the northwest. He'd studied their locations for a class project on artificial reefs.

He oriented himself, feeling the current's gentle push against his body. For the first time since waking on the abandoned boat, Theo had a plan. He had a direction. The water no longer felt like a tomb but a path.

With measured kicks, he began to swim, each stroke carrying him further from the boat where men plotted destruction, and closer to whatever waited beyond this night.

Chapter 3

The sun crested the horizon, spilling gold across the waters of the Gulf. Miles from where he had first entered the water, Theo emerged from the foaming surf. His legs trembled beneath him as he staggered onto the pristine sands of Matagorda Peninsula, each step a victory against exhaustion. The diving equipment that had saved his life now hung from his body like dead weight, the empty tank a hollow reminder of how close he'd come to not making it.

Salt water streamed from his wetsuit, creating dark patches in the sand beneath him. His lungs burned with each breath, raw from the exertion and the occasional gulp of seawater when his regulator had failed in the final stretch. But he was alive.

The beach stretched before him, untouched and indifferent to his ordeal. No footprints marred its surface, no structures interrupted the clean line where sand met scrubby vegetation. Just endless shoreline curving away in both directions, beautiful in its emptiness and terrifying in its isolation.

Theo collapsed onto his knees, then rolled onto his back. The sky above him was impossibly vast, cloudless blue meeting the horizon in every direction. His mind, which had maintained laser focus during his desperate swim, now scattered in a thousand directions. Questions bubbled up like the sea foam still clinging to his ankles: Where exactly was he? How far to civilization? What had happened to the other divers—Danny, Klaus, Martina? Had they been part of Marcus's operation, or victims of it?

The warmth of the morning sun contrasted sharply with the chill that had seeped into his bones during the night swim. He had navigated by stars and instinct after the platform he'd aimed for proved to be further than he'd calculated. When his air ran dangerously low, he'd been forced to surface, alternating between swimming and floating on his back through the remainder of the night.

Theo pushed himself up on his elbows, scanning the shoreline. No boats on the water. No buildings visible. Just the rhythm of waves meeting shore—a sound that had once brought him comfort but now carried an undercurrent of menace.

Theo unzipped the small waterproof bag strapped to his waist, his fingers still trembling from cold and exertion. He'd grabbed it instinctively during his escape, a final act of foresight before plunging into the Gulf. Now, as gulls wheeled overhead with their piercing cries, he methodically laid out his meager possessions on the sand.

"Not much," he muttered, arranging the items in order of importance.

Three protein bars, slightly crushed but sealed. A half-liter water bottle, miraculously full. His wallet containing seventy-three dollars, a useless credit card, and his student ID. A multi-tool with pliers, knife, and screwdriver attachments. His phone—dead and waterlogged despite the bag's protection. A small compass that had guided him through the darkness. The waterproof notebook with his research notes, pages warped but legible.

The tide pushed higher up the beach, foam hissing as it retreated over the sand. Theo calculated his position based on his swim trajectory and the currents he'd battled. He could be anywhere along a thirty-mile stretch of the Matagorda Peninsula—a barrier island with limited access points and fewer inhabitants.

"Aunt Clara would say start with the basics," he told himself, channeling the woman who had taught him to navigate wilderness areas with little more than observation and common sense.

He tore open one protein bar, rationing it into three pieces. The sweet, dense nutrition hit his empty stomach like concrete, but he forced himself to eat slowly. One-third now, the rest for later. Water was more precious—a single cautious sip to combat dehydration.

Theo shrugged off the dive tank and weight belt, keeping only the wetsuit for protection against the strengthening sun. The morning air warmed rapidly, promising scorching heat by midday. His aunt's voice echoed in his memory: assess your surroundings, identify water sources, find shelter.

The dunes behind the beach offered minimal protection, but might conceal freshwater pools. Inland meant possible civilization, but also exposure and uncertainty. The coastline would be easier to navigate but offered little shade or water.

Theo repacked his supplies, mind clearing as he focused on immediate problems rather than the enormity of his situation. He couldn't control what had happened on the boat, but he could control what happened next.

Theo rose to his feet, brushing sand from his wetsuit. His scientific mind kicked in as he surveyed the landscape stretching before him. The beach gave way to a series of low dunes crowned with sea oats, their slender stalks swaying in the Gulf breeze. Beyond lay the coastal prairie, a patchwork of textures and colors that spoke to him like an open book.

"Spartina alterniflora," he murmured, identifying the cordgrass that dominated the salt marsh. The tall, reed-like plants formed dense clusters, their presence indicating regular tidal flooding.

Further inland, patches of shorter Spartina patens created a mosaic of tan and green against the darker mud.

A great blue heron stalked through the shallows of a distant tidal creek, its deliberate movements telegraphing the presence of fish. Theo noted how the bird's path revealed the hidden channels cutting through the seemingly uniform marsh—natural waterways that could either guide him to safety or lead him deeper into the wetland maze.

The tide had begun to ebb, exposing mud flats where fiddler crabs scuttled sideways, males waving oversized claws in territorial displays. Their presence confirmed what Theo already knew—this was a healthy ecosystem, but one with precious little freshwater.

"Glasswort and saltwort," he noted, spotting the succulent plants growing in the transition zone. Their presence indicated high soil salinity, challenging conditions for most plants—and humans. The sight of sea purslane brought a flicker of hope; its fleshy leaves stored water and could be chewed to relieve thirst in an emergency.

Theo shaded his eyes against the strengthening sun, searching for signs of human presence. No power lines or buildings interrupted the horizon, only the distant shimmer of heat rising from the prairie. A turkey vulture circled lazily overhead, a reminder of nature's indifference to his plight.

He recognized both opportunity and danger in this landscape. The same ecological knowledge that allowed him to identify edible plants also warned him of the disorienting sameness of the marsh, the deceptive depths of mud that could trap an unwary traveler, and the rapid temperature changes as day would eventually surrender to night.

Adjusting his pack, Theo faced the decision that would determine his survival: follow the coastline or risk cutting across the marsh toward civilization.

Shadows stretched across the sand like grasping fingers as the sun began its descent toward the western horizon. Theo stood at the boundary where beach met vegetation, caught between two unappealing options. The open expanse of beach offered visibility but left him exposed to the elements, while the dense coastal vegetation promised shelter but harbored unknown dangers.

He glanced back at his footprints trailing behind him, already being erased by the persistent Gulf breeze. Soon there would be no trace of his passage, as if the beach itself conspired to erase his presence.

"Staying in the open means dealing with temperature drops," he muttered, mentally calculating the rapid heat loss that would occur once the sun disappeared. His wetsuit would provide minimal insulation against the night chill, and the wind sweeping unimpeded across the flat beach would sap his body heat mercilessly.

Theo's gaze shifted to the tangle of vegetation. Salt cedar and yaupon holly formed dense thickets that could block the wind. Yet those same sheltering branches could conceal snakes, spiders, or even larger predators. The shadows between the trees deepened as he watched, transforming the inviting shelter into something more ominous.

"Aunt Clara would say to follow the four priorities," he reminded himself. "Shelter, water, fire, food."

The decision crystallized with unexpected clarity. The beach offered none of these essentials, while the coastal forest at least promised windbreak and the possibility of materials to construct a rudimentary shelter.

He recalled a fragment of wisdom from a wilderness survival manual: exposure kills faster than thirst. The night would bring dropping temperatures, possibly dew, and the risk of hypothermia even in this subtropical climate.

Theo adjusted his pack and stepped decisively toward the vegetation line. The sand gave way to firmer soil beneath his feet, the transition as clear as his resolve. Something rustled in the underbrush ahead, freezing him momentarily before a small marsh rabbit darted away.

"At least there's life here," he whispered, drawing a strange comfort from the encounter.

As he pushed through the first screen of vegetation, the wind's howl immediately diminished. The setting sun cast long shadows through the trees, transforming the landscape into a maze of light and darkness. Theo pressed forward, each step taking him deeper into unknown territory, away from the certainty of the open beach and toward the possibility of survival.

The coastal brush closed around Theo like a living entity, sea oats whispering against his legs as he pushed forward. Each step required deliberate effort—lifting his feet higher than normal to clear the tangled undergrowth, balancing on uncertain terrain that shifted between sand, mud, and the occasional hidden pool. Salt-resistant shrubs crowded his path, their branches scratching against his wetsuit.

The setting sun painted the landscape in amber hues, transforming ordinary vegetation into fiery sculptures. Above him, clouds gathered, absorbing the day's final light in deep pinks and purples. Behind him, the rhythmic crash of waves grew fainter, replaced by the subtle symphony of rustling leaves and occasional bird calls.

"Just keep moving inland," Theo told himself, wiping sweat from his brow despite the cooling air. "Find higher ground before full dark."

The scent of the marsh intensified as evening approached—a complex bouquet of brine, decomposing vegetation, and the clean, sharp note of wild sage crushed beneath his feet. He paused, breathing deeply, his biologist's mind automatically cataloging the plants around him. Wax myrtle. Yaupon holly. Baccharis. The familiar scientific classification grounded him, transforming the alien landscape into something comprehensible.

A stand of salt cedar blocked his path, forcing him to veer northward. The detour led to firmer ground, a slight rise that lifted him above the wettest parts of the marsh. His steps grew more confident as his body found its rhythm in this new environment.

Twenty minutes into his trek, Theo encountered a game trail cutting through the brush—a narrow corridor where animals had trampled the vegetation into submission. Relief washed over him as he followed this natural pathway, his progress suddenly doubling in speed.

The exertion warmed his core despite the cooling evening air. His muscles, initially tense with anxiety, now worked with purposeful efficiency. The weight of the dive gear and his meager supplies settled into a manageable burden across his shoulders.

As twilight deepened around him, Theo's pace steadied into a determined stride. The chaos of his situation—the abandoned boat, the drug runners, the desperate swim—all receded behind the immediate challenge of navigation. One foot after another. One obstacle at a time. The beach behind him and whatever lay ahead were problems for another moment. Right now, there was only the path, the growing darkness, and his will to survive.

The rustling came from his left—sharp, deliberate, and much too large to be the wind. Theo froze mid-step, his body instantly rigid. The sound repeated, closer this time, accompanied by the snap of a twig.

His mind flashed through Texas coastal predators—coyotes, bobcats, maybe even the occasional alligator this close to the marshland. The wetsuit that had protected him in the Gulf now felt like a second skin of vulnerability, offering no protection against teeth or claws.

Theo's breath caught in his throat as he scanned the darkening landscape. The tall grasses swayed in patches where no breeze touched, betraying movement beneath their cover. Purple coneflowers and seaside goldenrod stood like silent sentinels around him, their colors muted by encroaching night.

"Stay calm," he whispered to himself, the sound barely audible even to his own ears.

The darkness thickened between the vegetation, shadows stretching and merging until distinct shapes became suggestions rather than certainties. Another rustle, followed by a low grunt that Theo couldn't immediately identify.

He reached slowly for his multi-tool, the only potential weapon he possessed. The metal felt cold and inadequate in his palm as he eased it from his pocket.

A flash of movement caught his eye—something substantial pushing through a stand of cordgrass twenty feet ahead. Theo crouched lower, making himself smaller while straining to see through the dim light.

The creature emerged from the grass—a wild hog, its dark bulk surprisingly graceful as it paused to test the air. Behind it, two smaller forms followed—juveniles, staying close to their mother. The sow's head lifted, nostrils flaring as she caught Theo's unfamiliar scent.

Their eyes met across the clearing, a moment of mutual assessment. Theo had heard enough stories about wild hogs to know their unpredictability, their potential for aggression when threatened or cornered.

The sow pawed the ground once, a warning. Her piglets huddled closer to her flanks.

Theo remained motionless, barely breathing, acutely aware that he stood in her territory, an intruder at dusk. The standoff stretched for seconds that felt like minutes, predator and prey roles uncomfortably ambiguous in this twilight encounter.

The sow's dark eyes never left Theo's as she retreated with her piglets, backing slowly into the brush until they vanished completely. Only the subtle rustling of grass marked their departure. Theo remained frozen for several heartbeats longer, his muscles coiled tight, ready to flee if necessary.

When he finally exhaled, the sound seemed unnaturally loud in the twilight stillness. But as his own breathing steadied, he became aware of another sound—different from the hogs' movement, more rhythmic and deliberate. It came from beyond a dense thicket to his right, where briars formed an impenetrable wall topped by swaying sea oats.

Theo crouched lower, pressing his body against the cool earth. His scientific mind began categorizing the sound, separating it from the background noise of the coastal ecosystem. Not the scurrying of small mammals. Not the wind. Something larger, with purpose.

Approximately seventy kilograms minimum, he estimated, based on the displacement of vegetation. *Bipedal gait. Consistent stride length.*

The realization struck him: human footsteps.

His heart rate accelerated again, but Theo forced himself to think methodically. The footfalls lacked the cautious quality of someone stalking—more like someone walking with determination, unaware they were being observed.

Could it be a park ranger? A fellow hiker? Or perhaps one of Marcus's crew searching for him?

Theo pressed himself deeper into the tall grass, careful not to disturb the surrounding vegetation. The coastal prairie that had seemed so exposed moments ago now provided perfect camouflage, its varying textures and heights creating natural blind spots.

He remembered his aunt Clara's lessons about the prairie ecosystem—how indigenous peoples had used these natural features for both hunting and hiding. Now he was doing the same, becoming part of the landscape rather than moving through it.

The footsteps grew closer, accompanied by the soft jingle of metal—keys or tools, perhaps. Theo calculated the trajectory based on sound alone, estimating the person would pass within fifteen feet of his position.

As darkness settled more firmly across the landscape, Theo made a critical decision. Rather than fleeing, he would observe. Knowledge was survival, and he needed to know who else walked these coastal trails as night approached.

Darkness settled over the coastal prairie like a heavy blanket, transforming the landscape into a canvas of deep blues and blacks. The temperature dropped several degrees, bringing with it a silence that seemed to amplify every sound. Somewhere in the distance, an owl called out, its hollow question echoing across the peninsula.

Theo remained motionless in the grass, his breath shallow and controlled. The footsteps he'd been tracking had faded away, moving parallel to his position before disappearing altogether into the night.

Just as he considered his next move, a sharp crack from behind sent a jolt through his system.

A massive feral hog—not the sow from earlier but a solitary boar—emerged from the thicket. Its dark silhouette cut an imposing figure against the twilight sky, shoulders hunched and head lowered. The creature paused, snout twitching as it sampled the air.

Theo took a sharp breath and held it. The boar was easily twice the size of the sow, with yellowed tusks curving upward from its lower jaw. Even in the dim light, Theo could make out the bristled ridge along its spine, raised in alertness.

Every cell in his body screamed at him to run, but his rational mind knew better. Running would trigger the chase response. Instead, he pressed himself deeper into the earth, willing his body to become part of the landscape.

The boar took another step forward, hooves crushing the undergrowth with surprising delicacy for such a large animal. No more than twenty feet separated them now. Theo could smell the creature's musky scent, could hear the low, rumbling breath from its snout.

In that moment, the abstract knowledge of coastal wildlife that he'd studied in textbooks crystallized into visceral understanding. This was the raw, unfiltered nature of survival—predator and prey locked in an ancient dance, each assessing the other's threat.

The boar's head swung toward him, dark eyes reflecting what little light remained in the sky. It stamped one hoof against the ground, testing, challenging. Theo's muscles coiled tighter, ready to spring if necessary, though he knew his chances against such a creature were slim.

The standoff with the boar stretched into what felt like hours but lasted mere minutes. The creature snorted once more, pawed at the earth, then turned and disappeared into the thicket with surprising grace for its bulk. Theo released a breath he hadn't realized he'd been holding, his lungs burning with relief.

Night fell across the peninsula with alarming speed. The blue-black of twilight deepened to an impenetrable darkness punctuated only by the first stars appearing overhead. The temperature continued to drop, and Theo's wetsuit—designed to insulate in water—now clung to him uncomfortably, trapping the day's sweat against his skin.

"Shelter," he whispered to himself, the word hanging in the still air. "Priority one."

He rose to his feet, muscles stiff from prolonged stillness. The coastal prairie offered little natural protection—no caves, no overhangs, nothing but low vegetation and scattered trees. Without a tent or even a tarp, he faced exposure to whatever elements the Gulf might throw at him overnight.

Theo scanned the horizon, where the last purple light faded to black. The darkness pressed in from all sides, transforming familiar shapes into looming threats. Every rustle in the undergrowth, every snap of a twig became amplified in the night air.

His aunt's voice echoed in his mind: *In a survival situation, you work with what you have, not what you wish you had.*

The wetsuit would provide some thermal protection, but not enough. The coastal wind picked up, cutting through his damp clothes with knife-like precision. Shivering, Theo moved forward, hands outstretched to navigate the darkness.

A cluster of gnarled live oaks appeared as darker shadows against the night sky. Their twisted branches reached outward like arthritic fingers, but beneath them lay the promise of some protection from dew and wind.

Theo picked his way carefully toward the trees, aware that each step could bring an ankle-twisting hole or another encounter with wildlife. The soil beneath his feet changed from sandy to more compact as he approached the oak stand.

Time was running out. Each passing minute robbed him of precious moonlight he needed to construct even the most rudimentary shelter. The stars multiplied overhead, beautiful but indifferent to his plight as Theo raced against the deepening night.

The moon rose, a sliver of silver against the vast canvas of night, casting just enough light for Theo to navigate through the tangle of live oak roots. He moved toward the edge of the salt marsh, where land and water engaged in their ancient negotiation of boundaries. The air hung heavy with brine and decomposition—life and death mingling in the coastal ecosystem.

Theo's legs trembled with exhaustion. Each step required conscious effort as he pushed through cordgrass that whispered against his wetsuit. The temperature continued to drop, and the wind carried a chill that penetrated to his bones.

Then he saw it—a chaotic assemblage of driftwood, palm fronds, and plastic debris washed up during some long-ago storm. Nature and human waste had formed an accidental architecture against the base of a dune. Larger pieces of driftwood created a framework, while smaller debris had caught in the gaps, forming a crude but recognizable shelter.

"Thank God," Theo whispered, approaching the structure cautiously. He knelt and peered inside, wary of animal occupants. Finding it empty, he allowed himself a moment of pure relief.

The shelter wasn't perfect—gaps between the driftwood would let in wind, and the floor was nothing but sand—but it offered protection from the elements that the open prairie couldn't provide. Theo crawled inside, his muscles finally releasing their tension as he settled against the back wall.

Outside, the marsh came alive with night sounds: the chirp of insects, the distant splash of something entering water, the rustle of nocturnal creatures emerging to hunt. Inside his driftwood sanctuary, Theo felt removed from immediate danger for the first time since leaping from the boat.

He unpacked his meager supplies, placing them within arm's reach. The protein bars and water bottle represented life itself now—sustenance that would have to last until he found civilization. His fingers brushed against his notebook, and he considered documenting the day's events but decided to conserve his energy instead.

As Theo's breathing slowed, his mind drifted to the others—Danny with his enthusiasm, Klaus and Martina with their quiet competence. Had they escaped? Were they searching for him? Or had they met a darker fate at Marcus's hands?

The questions swirled in his mind as exhaustion pulled him toward sleep, temporary safety found amid the wreckage of things discarded and forgotten.

Theo rearranged the smaller pieces of driftwood around the entrance to his shelter, creating a windbreak against the persistent coastal breeze. His fingers, stiff with cold and fatigue, fumbled with the weathered wood. October on the Gulf Coast brought a deceptive chill—tourists imagined Texas warmth year-round, but locals knew better. The nights turned surprisingly cold, especially for someone trapped in a damp wetsuit with no fire.

He settled back into his makeshift home, drawing his knees to his chest. The shelter smelled of salt, decay, and something indefinably primal—the breath of the marsh itself. Outside, night creatures conducted their symphony: the rhythmic chirping of crickets, the occasional splash from the water's edge, the distant hoot of an owl hunting in darkness.

Stars punctured the blackness above, visible through gaps in his shelter's roof. Theo found Polaris, the North Star, his gaze automatically seeking the celestial constant as his father had taught him years ago. The stars appeared impossibly bright, undiminished by city lights, their ancient patterns unchanged despite the chaos of his day.

"What the hell happened?" he whispered to the darkness.

The events replayed in his mind: the dive boat, his seasickness, Marcus's betrayal, the drug deal, his desperate swim, and now this—crouched in driftwood and debris on a peninsula that felt more wilderness than the civilized coast he knew. It seemed impossible that yesterday morning he'd been a graduate student whose biggest worry was completing his thesis research.

A hollow feeling expanded in his chest. His academic knowledge of coastal ecosystems had helped him identify edible plants and navigate the terrain, but textbooks hadn't prepared him for the cold reality of survival. Or for witnessing a crime that had nearly cost him his life.

He thought of Danny's enthusiasm about the reef, Klaus and Martina's quiet competence. Were they innocent tourists caught in Marcus's web, or had they been part of the operation all along? The uncertainty gnawed at him.

Theo pulled his notebook from the waterproof bag. Even in darkness, the familiar weight of it in his hands provided comfort. Tomorrow would bring new challenges—finding water, seeking help, avoiding Marcus if he came looking—but tonight, in this fragile shelter, he had survived.

Theo clicked on his small flashlight, the beam barely penetrating the darkness of his shelter. The light flickered, a reminder of its limited battery life. He angled it downward, creating a small pool of illumination on the sandy floor where he arranged his meager supplies in neat rows.

Three protein bars lay side by side—his only food. The half-empty water bottle stood like a sentinel beside them, its contents more precious than gold in this coastal wilderness. His multi-tool gleamed in the artificial light, its metal surfaces reflecting tiny constellations back at him. The compass, wallet, and waterproof notebook completed his inventory.

Outside, the coastal prairie had transformed into an alien landscape of shadows and sounds. Waves crashed rhythmically against the distant shore while unknown creatures rustled through the undergrowth. The temperature continued to drop, and Theo shivered as a gust of wind found its way through his makeshift windbreak.

"Shelter, water, food," he whispered, reciting Aunt Clara's survival mantra. "Then signals and rescue."

He had the first one covered, however temporarily. Tomorrow would bring the challenge of finding fresh water and stretching his limited food supply. The wetsuit that had saved his life during his escape now clung uncomfortably to his skin, trapping the day's salt and sweat against his body.

Theo reorganized his supplies, placing the most critical items—water, compass, multi-tool—within easy reach. He folded his notebook and tucked it safely away, protecting the pages that might soon hold the key to his survival.

The flashlight dimmed momentarily, prompting Theo to switch it off. Darkness enveloped him again, but rather than panic, he felt his other senses heighten. The sound of the wind through the cordgrass, the distant call of a night bird, the subtle shift of sand beneath him—all became clearer in the absence of sight.

He leaned back against the curved wall of his shelter, allowing his muscles to relax for the first time since his desperate plunge into the Gulf. Whatever tomorrow brought—whether rescue or further challenges—he would face it with the same determination that had carried him through this day.

"One problem at a time," Theo murmured, settling into the darkness. "Just like any ecosystem. Everything connects."

Chapter 4

The first fingers of dawn reached across the Gulf, painting the horizon in smears of orange and pink. Theo stirred in his crude shelter, consciousness returning in painful increments. Each muscle in his body protested as he shifted position, the night spent on packed sand and driftwood leaving him stiff and aching. Salt clung to his skin where the wetsuit had dried, creating a gritty friction with every movement.

He blinked against the growing light filtering through the gaps in his shelter. For one merciful moment, disorientation clouded his mind—perhaps he was waking in his apartment, or on a camping trip with friends. Reality crashed back as his eyes focused on the weathered driftwood above him.

"Still here," he whispered, his voice raspy from thirst.

The cordgrass outside his shelter swayed in the morning breeze, their shadows dancing across the sand. Theo ran his tongue over cracked lips, the salt sting a sharp reminder of his dehydration. His stomach contracted painfully, demanding sustenance beyond the meager protein bar he'd allowed himself yesterday.

Theo reached for his water bottle, lifting it to gauge the contents. Less than a quarter remained. He permitted himself the smallest sip, just enough to moisten his mouth without truly satisfying his thirst. The tepid liquid barely registered against his parched throat.

Outside, the coastal prairie awakened. A distant bird called across the marsh, its voice carrying in the still morning air. The tide had receded during the night, exposing mud flats that would soon steam under the Texas sun. The world continued its rhythms, indifferent to the stranded biologist in its midst.

Theo eased himself up to sitting position, wincing as his muscles complained. His wetsuit, still damp in places, clung uncomfortably to his skin. The protective layer that had saved him in the Gulf now felt like a prison, trapping heat and restricting movement.

"Water first," he murmured, organizing his priorities. "Then shelter improvement, then signal."

He peered through the entrance of his makeshift home, surveying the landscape that would either sustain or defeat him in the coming days. The vastness of the peninsula stretched before him, beautiful and merciless in the growing light.

Theo stepped out from his shelter, the morning sun already asserting its dominance across the coastal landscape. He clutched the plastic water bottle, holding it up to the light. The remaining liquid barely covered the bottom—perhaps three ounces at most. His throat constricted at the sight, a physiological response to the knowledge that this meager supply stood between him and severe dehydration.

"Twelve hours," he calculated, squinting at the bottle. "Maybe eighteen if I'm careful."

The coastal breeze carried salt and heat rather than relief. Sweat had already begun to bead along his hairline, his body's cooling system activating despite the water deficit he faced. Theo unscrewed the cap and allowed himself another minimal sip, just enough to wet his lips. The precious liquid disappeared into his parched mouth, leaving him wanting more.

He tucked the bottle carefully into his bag and surveyed the landscape with a biologist's eye. The cordgrass and salt marsh vegetation suggested brackish conditions—water present but likely too saline for consumption. Beyond the immediate marsh, stands of live oak might indicate fresher groundwater. The coastal prairie stretched inland, undulating with patches of vegetation that hinted at varying moisture levels.

"Look for green depressions," he muttered, recalling Aunt Clara's lessons. "Animals. Birds circling. Morning dew collection points."

The sun climbed higher, its heat intensifying with each passing minute. Theo felt the first signs of dehydration already—slight dizziness when he turned his head too quickly, a dull headache forming at his temples. His wetsuit trapped the heat against his skin, accelerating his body's water loss.

Somewhere in this landscape, water existed. It had to. The vegetation proved it. The question was whether he could find it before his body surrendered to thirst.

Theo reached for his compass, orienting himself. The morning light revealed more detail in the landscape than he'd been able to see the previous evening—a deeper depression to the northwest where vegetation grew thicker, possibly indicating a seasonal creek or pond. Birds circled in the distance, another promising sign.

He shouldered his meager supplies. Time was his enemy now, each hour without water diminishing his strength and clarity of thought. The morning stretched before him, filled with promise and threat in equal measure.

The coastal prairie unfurled before Theo like a botanical textbook come to life. As he moved from the higher ground toward the depression, the landscape shifted through subtle microhabitats, each hosting its own specialized plant community. Despite his thirst and the growing heat, a flicker of professional interest sparked in his mind.

"Salicornia virginica," he murmured, kneeling beside a patch of succulent stems. Glasswort—or sea asparagus as Aunt Clara called it. He pinched off a segment and placed it on his tongue. The salty burst flooded his mouth, both satisfying and aggravating his thirst. But beneath the saltiness lay nutrients his body desperately needed.

Theo harvested a handful, tucking them into his bag. The plants' high water content might provide minimal hydration, though the salt content made them a double-edged sword.

Twenty yards further, the sandy soil gave way to a slightly more sheltered depression. Here, sprawling vines with heart-shaped leaves caught his attention.

"Ipomoea pes-caprae." Beach morning glory. Theo traced the vine to its root system and began carefully digging with his multi-tool. The thick storage roots could contain valuable moisture. He extracted one, brushed off the sand, and sliced into it. A faint dampness appeared at the cut surface. Not enough to drink, but perhaps enough to suck on later if desperation mounted.

The scientist in him catalogued each discovery, momentarily displacing the stranded survivor. This was his element—the language of plants spoke clearly to him even as human connections had failed.

A cluster of dark beans caught his eye, scattered beneath wind-twisted vegetation. Sea beans—drift seeds carried by ocean currents. Theo collected several, recognizing their potential food value once properly prepared.

"Saltwort," he identified another succulent plant, its segmented stems reminiscent of the glasswort but with a different growth pattern. He harvested some, noting its slightly less salty taste when he tested a small piece.

The sun climbed higher, beating down on his shoulders. Sweat trickled down his back inside the wetsuit, precious moisture wasted. His headache intensified, a persistent reminder of his body's increasing water debt.

Yet as Theo moved through this harsh landscape, his confidence grew. Plants were speaking to him, revealing their secrets. His years of study hadn't prepared him for this specific scenario, but they'd given him a framework for understanding—for survival.

Theo paused, wiping sweat from his brow. Something had changed—subtle but unmistakable. The vegetation around him was shifting in composition, growing denser and more vibrant than the surrounding prairie. Where salt-tolerant species had dominated, freshwater-loving plants began to appear.

"Typha latifolia," he whispered, recognizing the distinctive silhouettes of cattails swaying in the breeze. His pace quickened despite his fatigue.

The cattails grew thicker, forming a natural barrier. Theo pushed through them, ignoring the scratches on his arms as the plants' rough edges caught his skin. A sweet, earthy smell replaced the brackish scent of the marsh—the unmistakable perfume of fresh water.

The ground beneath his feet softened, squelching slightly with each step. His heart raced with anticipation as he forced his way through the final stand of vegetation.

There, in a small depression where the prairie met the marsh, water bubbled up from the sandy soil—a natural seep where groundwater reached the surface. Sunlight danced across its surface, turning the small pool into a mirror of hope.

Theo dropped to his knees, trembling. The universe had offered him a gift.

He bent close, inhaling deeply. No sulfurous odor, no brackish smell. Using his cupped hand, he lifted a small amount to his lips, letting just a drop touch his tongue. The water tasted clean, with only the faintest mineral undertone.

"Thank you," he breathed to no one and everyone.

With reverent care, Theo uncapped his water bottle and submerged it in the pool, watching as bubbles escaped and clear water replaced emptiness. He waited for the disturbed sediment to settle before capping it tightly.

Only then did he allow himself a proper drink directly from the source, cupping his hands and bringing them to his parched lips. The water was cool and sweet against his salt-crusted mouth. Each swallow felt like life itself flowing back into his body, easing the pounding in his temples.

As he drank, a red-winged blackbird called from atop a nearby cattail, its distinctive conk-la-ree! seeming to celebrate alongside him.

For the first time since washing ashore, Theo felt the weight of hopelessness lift. His knowledge had led him here—to this life-sustaining treasure hidden in plain sight. If he could find water, he could find his way home.

Theo knelt by the seep, carefully pouring water through his t-shirt into the bottle. The improvised filter caught bits of sediment and plant matter, leaving cleaner water behind. The simple act felt like a victory—small but significant.

A sudden shift in the air made him pause. The gentle breeze that had cooled his skin all morning vanished, replaced by an unnatural stillness. Theo's muscles tensed instinctively before his mind fully registered why.

He looked up from his task, scanning the horizon. There, building over the Gulf, a wall of dark clouds gathered strength. Charcoal gray at the bottom, fading to an ominous purple-black at the top, the formation was unmistakable to anyone who'd grown up on the Texas coast.

"That's coming fast," he muttered, capping his bottle.

The air pressed down on him with increasing weight—the telltale drop in barometric pressure that preceded severe weather.

Distant thunder rolled across the water, vibrating in his chest. Theo estimated the storm was still miles offshore, but Gulf systems moved with frightening speed, especially in October when cold fronts collided with warm coastal air.

Seagulls screeched overhead, flying inland—nature's first responders evacuating ahead of danger. The temperature dropped several degrees in minutes, raising goosebumps on Theo's arms despite the lingering humidity.

He gathered his supplies quickly, mentally calculating his options. The driftwood shelter wouldn't withstand what was coming. The depression that held his precious water source would likely flood, becoming a hazard rather than a haven.

"Higher ground," he decided, securing his possessions in the waterproof bag.

Lightning flashed in the distance, followed by another deeper rumble of thunder. The storm was accelerating, feeding on the warm Gulf waters. Theo had perhaps thirty minutes before the full force hit.

His newfound confidence wavered. Just when he'd solved one survival problem, nature had introduced another. The water he'd found—his greatest triumph—now threatened to become part of a larger danger.

Theo took one last drink directly from the seep, then stood and faced inland, toward the dunes and oak mottes that might offer shelter. The coming storm would test everything—his knowledge, his resourcefulness, his will.

"Come on then," he challenged the approaching clouds, shouldering his bag. "Let's see what you've got."

The first strong gust hit Theo as he crested the tallest dune, nearly knocking him sideways. The wind carried salt and electricity, promising the storm's imminent arrival. Dark clouds now dominated half the sky, swallowing the afternoon sun and casting premature twilight across the peninsula.

Theo surveyed his surroundings with renewed purpose. Where others might see only danger in the approaching tempest, he recognized opportunity. Rain meant water—clean, fresh water that could sustain him for days if properly collected.

"Work with what you have," he muttered, echoing Aunt Clara's pragmatic wisdom.

He emptied his waterproof bag and spread it wide, creating a makeshift catchment. Using driftwood stakes and cordgrass, he fashioned a frame that held the bag open, its waterproof material forming a perfect basin. Theo positioned it in a clearing where nothing would block the rainfall, weighing down the corners with smooth stones.

The wind intensified, bending the coastal grasses in violent waves. Theo's fingers worked quickly, tying knots and adjusting angles to ensure maximum collection. Each gust threatened to undo his work, but he persisted, making adjustments and reinforcements.

Next, he turned to his shelter. The natural depression beneath the oak needed reinforcement against flooding. He dug a small trench around the perimeter, creating a channel to divert water away from his sleeping area. Using fallen branches and palmetto fronds, he built a stronger windbreak on the Gulf-facing side.

Lightning flashed closer now, followed almost immediately by a crack of thunder that vibrated through the ground. The storm's leading edge had reached the shoreline.

Theo gathered his foraged plants—the salicornia, sea beans, and ipomoea roots—and tucked them into a protected nook within his shelter. These hard-won resources represented meals for tomorrow and beyond.

As the first heavy raindrops struck his face, Theo felt an unexpected surge of satisfaction. He'd transformed potential disaster into resource, threat into opportunity. The storm that might have broken another person's spirit instead offered him salvation.

"Come on," he said to the darkened sky, watching as the first raindrops splashed into his collection bag. "Fill it up."

The heavens obliged, opening with tropical intensity as Theo ducked into his reinforced shelter, listening to the rhythm of survival drumming all around him.

The first raindrops quickly multiplied into sheets of water as the storm announced itself with authority. Theo's hands moved with surprising dexterity, weaving flexible strands of marsh grass between the driftwood supports of his shelter. Each gust of wind tested his work, revealing weaknesses he hadn't anticipated.

"Not good enough," he muttered, remembering a field expedition to the Louisiana bayou where their research camp had nearly washed away. Professor Harmon's voice echoed in his memory: *Structure follows function, and function follows need.*

Theo repositioned the main support beam, angling the entire shelter to present its narrowest profile to the Gulf-facing winds. Rain plastered his hair to his forehead as he worked, but he barely noticed. His world had contracted to this immediate challenge—the intersection of physics, available materials, and the relentless elements.

The drainage trench he'd started earlier needed expansion. Using a flat piece of driftwood as a makeshift shovel, Theo dug deeper, creating a channel that would carry water away from his sleeping area. Mud caked his hands and forearms, but each scoop represented protection against the rising puddles forming across the dune base.

Lightning split the sky, illuminating his work in stark relief. In that flash, Theo saw his shelter as if from above—a primitive yet purposeful structure, born of necessity and shaped by understanding. It wasn't pretty, but it was functional.

"Aunt Clara would be proud," he said, patting another handful of grass into place.

He'd always been the academic in the family—the one who could identify plants but needed help starting campfires. The one who could explain coastal ecosystems but struggled to tie proper knots. Yet here he was, building something with his hands that might mean the difference between comfort and misery.

The rain intensified, but water now flowed around his shelter rather than into it. Inside, a relatively dry patch remained where he could wait out the worst of the storm. Theo crawled inside, watching his handiwork hold against the wind's assault.

For the first time since washing ashore, Theo felt a quiet pride that had nothing to do with academic achievement. This was different—primal and satisfying in ways that laboratory success never quite matched.

The storm unleashed its full fury as twilight descended over the peninsula. Sheets of rain pummeled Theo's shelter, each gust of wind testing the limits of his craftsmanship. Thunder cracked overhead—not just sound but physical sensation, a pressure wave that Theo felt reverberate through his ribcage.

He pulled his knees to his chest, creating a smaller target for the cold that seeped through his still-damp wetsuit. Outside, the world had transformed into chaos, but inside this fragile pocket of relative dryness, Theo fought to maintain order in his thoughts.

"Just water and wind," he whispered, though the words vanished instantly beneath the storm's roar.

A small rivulet of water found its way through the upper corner of his shelter, tracking down the interior wall. Then another. Despite his careful construction, the sheer volume of rain overwhelmed his defenses. Water began pooling at the lowest point of his shelter floor.

Theo shifted position, moving away from the growing puddle. The space felt increasingly claustrophobic—protection and prison simultaneously. He closed his eyes, focusing on the steady rhythm of his breathing against the storm's irregular percussion.

In through the nose, out through the mouth. Four counts in, six counts out.

His mind wandered to the water collection system he'd rigged outside. By now, his bag should be filling with precious freshwater—if the wind hadn't destroyed it. Each lightning flash illuminated his shelter in stark white, followed by deeper darkness that made the space feel smaller still.

"The storm is an opportunity," he reminded himself, thinking of his nearly empty water bottle. "This is exactly what you needed."

A particularly violent gust sent a spray of water through the entrance. Theo wiped his face and laughed—a short, defiant sound. There was something liberating about being this exposed to elemental forces, stripped of technology and comfort. Here, success was measured in the simplest terms: staying dry, collecting water, enduring.

He thought of the university lab with its climate control and predictable experiments. Nothing there had prepared him for this raw confrontation with nature. Yet somehow, he wasn't afraid anymore. The storm's intensity matched something within him—a determination that had been there all along, waiting to be discovered.

The storm's final grumbles retreated across the Gulf, leaving behind an eerie stillness punctuated only by the rhythmic dripping of water from saturated vegetation. Theo emerged from his shelter, stretching cramped muscles and blinking in the strange, golden light of the storm's aftermath. His collection system had worked—the waterproof bag hung heavy with rainwater, nearly two liters of life-sustaining liquid.

"Not bad for a plant biologist," he murmured, carefully transferring some of the water to his bottle.

But as Theo surveyed his surroundings, triumph faded to confusion. The landscape had transformed completely. Where the coastal prairie had stretched in undulating waves of cordgrass and salt meadow hay, now a labyrinth of shallow pools reflected the darkening sky. Standing water submerged familiar markers—the distinctive clump of yaupon holly, the fallen driftwood log shaped like a serpent—all gone beneath a mirror of floodwater.

Theo checked his compass, orienting himself toward where the freshwater seep should be. He needed to confirm it was still viable after the deluge.

"Northwest, two hundred paces," he said, setting off with confidence.

But twenty steps in, a channel of knee-deep water blocked his path. He detoured east, then north again, trying to maintain his bearing. The fading light cast long shadows across the water's surface, creating illusions of depth where there was shallowness and solid ground where there was none.

"This isn't right," Theo muttered, stopping to reassess.

The sun hung low, a bloated orange disk bleeding into purple clouds. Dusk approached rapidly, stealing definition from the landscape. Birds called to one another—unfamiliar, urgent sounds that seemed to mock his confusion.

He turned a full circle, seeking any recognizable feature. The dune where he'd built his shelter was now just one of many similar mounds rising from the flooded plain. Even his footprints had vanished, swallowed by standing water.

A flutter of panic rose in Theo's chest. He'd survived the storm only to find himself more lost than before. The water he'd collected suddenly felt insignificant against this new challenge.

"Focus," he whispered, fighting the disorientation. "One problem at a time."

But as darkness thickened around him, the coastal prairie became an alien world, and Theo stood alone at its center, unsure which direction meant safety and which meant deeper trouble.

Darkness encroached from all sides, stealing definition from the flooded landscape. Theo's breathing quickened as he fought rising panic, his mind racing through worst-case scenarios. Then, a memory surfaced—Professor Harmon's voice during field ecology: "When you're lost, let the plants be your map."

Theo exhaled slowly. Plants. This was his domain.

He crouched, examining the vegetation around his ankles. Even in the fading light, he could distinguish the silvery sheen of saltbush from the darker green of sea oxeye. These weren't random assemblages—they were botanical breadcrumbs.

"Salt-tolerant species decrease as elevation increases," he murmured, tracing a finger along a saltbush stem. "And freshwater-dependent species increase."

Theo stood, scanning the horizon with new purpose. To his right, a patch of cordgrass gave way to clusters of marsh elder—a subtle but significant transition. He broke a stem and placed it pointing toward his destination, creating the first marker in what would become his trail.

"Higher ground is that way."

As he waded through ankle-deep water, Theo cataloged each plant community, noting the gradual shift from halophytes to glycophytes. Where sea lavender grew abundantly, he turned slightly north. Where goldenrod appeared among the grasses, he knew the soil contained less salt—a sign he was moving inland.

Every twenty paces, he broke another stem, creating a traceable path. The sky darkened to indigo, but Theo's confidence grew with each step. His botanical knowledge transformed from academic pursuit to survival tool, each plant a signpost in the gathering gloom.

"Groundsel bush," he whispered, fingers brushing the fuzzy white seed heads. "Upper marsh zone."

The water level dropped imperceptibly at first, then more noticeably. Mud gave way to damp sand. When Theo encountered a stand of yaupon holly, he knew he'd reached the upland transition zone.

Night had fully claimed the peninsula when Theo found a patch of ground elevated enough to be merely damp rather than submerged. Exhaustion weighed on him as he sank down, leaning against the trunk of a salt-pruned live oak.

He wasn't certain of his exact location, but he'd escaped the flood zone. Tomorrow would bring new challenges, but tonight, he'd found safety through the silent guidance of plants—organisms he'd studied for years but never appreciated quite this way before.

"Thanks, Professor," Theo whispered to the darkness, a tired smile crossing his face as he settled in for the night.

Chapter 5

Dawn arrived with hesitant fingers of light stretching across the coastal prairie. Theo had slept fitfully, his dreams filled with churning waters and Marcus's calculating eyes. He woke with a start, his body stiff from the damp ground beneath him.

The marsh awakened around him—marsh wrens trilling their morning songs, fiddler crabs emerging to scuttle across mud flats exposed by the receding floodwaters. For a moment, the world seemed perfectly ordinary, the violence of yesterday's storm erased by the gentle palette of sunrise.

Then he heard it. A mechanical growl, faint but unmistakable, cutting through the natural symphony of the wetlands.

Theo froze, instinctively pressing his body lower into the tall cordgrass. The sound came again—boat engines, their pitch rising and falling with the contours of the channels that wound through East Matagorda Bay.

"They're looking for me," he whispered, the words barely audible even to himself.

The engines grew louder, then softer, then louder again as they navigated the labyrinthine waterways. Theo's heart hammered against his ribs. He parted the grass with trembling fingers, trying to glimpse the source of the sound without exposing himself.

Nothing visible yet, but the mechanical intrusion felt like a violation of the marsh's tranquility. Gulls scattered overhead, their harsh cries adding to his sense of exposure.

A red-winged blackbird darted from a nearby cattail, startled by something Theo couldn't see. The engines surged, closer now. He calculated his options—run and risk being spotted in the open, or remain hidden and hope they passed by?

The rising sun cast long shadows across the sandy terrain, transforming each clump of vegetation into potential concealment or betrayal. Theo pressed himself deeper into the earth, feeling mud seep through his already salt-crusted wetsuit.

The mechanical drone paused, then resumed at a lower pitch. They were slowing down, perhaps searching more carefully. Did they know he'd survived the swim? Had they found his shelter from the night before?

Theo held his breath as the sound intensified, then gradually diminished, moving eastward along the bay. Not gone, just temporarily distant. The respite wouldn't last long.

The tranquil marsh had become a chess board, with Theo a desperate pawn evading capture. Somewhere beyond his sight, men who wouldn't hesitate to eliminate a witness were methodically searching the waterways, their engines echoing like a promise of violence to come.

Theo inched forward on his elbows, the mud cold against his skin as he navigated to a better vantage point. The cordgrass parted just enough to reveal the scene unfolding across the shallow waters of the bay.

Three boats cut through the morning mist—not Coast Guard vessels as he'd briefly hoped, but sleek, unmarked crafts with powerful outboard motors. The lead boat, a black fiberglass skiff, carried Marcus and another man Theo recognized from the dive boat. They moved with practiced efficiency, scanning the shoreline methodically.

"Check the high ground first," Marcus called to the second boat, his voice carrying clearly across the water. "He's a student, not some survival expert. He'll stick to what he knows."

The words sent a chill through Theo's body that had nothing to do with his damp wetsuit. They knew he was alive. Somehow, they'd tracked him here.

In the third boat, a man with binoculars swept the tree line while another worked a radio. Their coordination spoke of something far beyond a simple drug handoff. This was an established operation with resources, manpower, and clearly, connections that allowed them to operate so boldly in daylight.

"Sweep east through the channel, then circle back," the man with the radio instructed. "Sal, take the western inlet. We need to contain this before noon."

Theo ducked lower as the nearest boat veered toward his position. The morning sun glinted off something in the vessel—rifles, their barrels catching the light. These weren't men looking to capture a witness. They were hunters seeking to eliminate a problem.

His academic mind cataloged details even as fear tightened his throat—the boats' movements suggested intimate knowledge of the bay's hidden channels, the men's casual handling of weapons indicated experience, and their methodical search pattern revealed tactical training.

Theo's heart pounded against the muddy ground. The scope of what he'd stumbled into expanded with each passing second. This wasn't just about one drug deal—he'd witnessed a glimpse of something much larger, something with tentacles reaching far beyond a single dive boat operation.

He needed to move, to find higher ground and better cover. But first, he needed to understand exactly what he was running from.

As the boats dispersed to continue their search, Theo retreated deeper into the marsh grass. The tide had begun to recede, exposing mudflats that led toward a stand of scrubby pines. Through gaps in the vegetation, he spotted movement—figures unloading cargo from a weathered dock into a clearing beyond.

Crawling on his belly through the wet sand, Theo positioned himself at the edge of a natural depression that overlooked what could only be described as a smuggler's camp. Three canvas tents stood in a semicircle around a central area where wooden crates were stacked with military precision. Men moved between stations with practiced efficiency, some unpacking electronics while others transferred smaller packages into waterproof containers.

The operation was alarmingly professional. Two generators hummed steadily, powering satellite communications equipment and what appeared to be a sophisticated radar system. A man with a tablet tracked inventory while another used a handheld scanner on incoming packages. This wasn't some makeshift drop point—it was a distribution hub.

Theo counted eight men total, each armed with sidearms and moving with the alertness of those accustomed to danger. Near the water's edge, a camouflaged boat shed concealed what looked like two more vessels, ready for rapid deployment.

What caught Theo's attention most was a weather-beaten shipping container converted into a makeshift office. Through its open door, he glimpsed maps pinned to walls and what appeared to be schedules. That container held answers—information that might explain why they were so desperate to find him.

A sudden commotion erupted as one of the search boats returned. The men gathered, distracted by new instructions from a tall figure Theo hadn't seen before. The newcomer gestured emphatically toward the eastern marshes, redirecting their search efforts.

This was his chance.

Theo slid down the embankment, using the noise of the generator to mask his movements. The distance to the container seemed impossibly vast in the open, but the alternative—remaining ignorant of what he faced—seemed worse. He needed leverage, information that might keep him alive if caught.

Heart hammering against his ribs, Theo made his decision. He would circle behind the tents, using their canvas walls as cover, and make a dash for the container during the next moment of distraction.

Knowledge was survival, and right now, Theo needed both.

The morning sun climbed higher, casting harsh light across the smuggler's camp. Reflections danced off the water's surface, illuminating the scene with an unforgiving clarity that matched the brutality unfolding before Theo's eyes.

He never made it to the shipping container.

Halfway through his planned route, a commotion from the central area froze him in place behind a stack of empty fuel drums. Two men dragged a third figure into the clearing—a weather-beaten man in his fifties wearing torn fishing clothes. His face was bloodied, one eye swollen shut, and his hands bound behind his back with plastic zip ties.

"Found him near the north channel," one of the smugglers announced, shoving the fisherman to his knees. "Had a radio."

The tall leader approached, circling the kneeling man like a predator. "Where's your boat, Carlos?"

The fisherman—Carlos—spat blood onto the sand. "Sank it. Coast Guard was all over after your boys made a mess of things."

A vicious backhand sent Carlos sprawling. Theo pressed himself deeper into the shadows, heart hammering so loudly he feared they might hear it.

"Tell me about the Coast Guard patrols," the leader demanded. "Their new schedule. You promised information."

"I told you what I know," Carlos wheezed. "They've doubled shifts since Tuesday. New cutters deployed from Corpus."

Another smuggler stepped forward. "He's lying. We intercepted communications about a surveillance operation, but nothing about increased patrols."

The leader crouched beside Carlos, voice dropping to a dangerous whisper. "You're playing both sides. Did you think we wouldn't find out?"

Carlos's laugh was hollow, edged with resignation. "I survived twenty years on these waters. You think you're the first cartel to threaten me?"

Theo watched in horror as the leader nodded to his men. One produced a pair of pliers while another forced Carlos's mouth open.

"Last chance," the leader said. "The Coast Guard operation—what do they know?"

Theo closed his eyes but couldn't block out the scream that followed. When he looked again, blood streamed from Carlos's mouth, and something small and white lay in the sand before him.

The personal cost of this world crashed over Theo like a physical blow. These weren't just smugglers—they were monsters wearing human skin.

And if he didn't act soon, he might be next.

Carlos's screams faded into whimpers as the smugglers dragged him toward a tent. Blood trailed across the sand, marking his path like a grotesque breadcrumb trail. Theo remained frozen behind the fuel drums, pulse thundering in his ears.

Then a familiar voice cut through the camp's commotion.

"Enough with the theatrics. We're on a schedule."

Marcus Delgado strode into view, no longer the affable dive instructor but a commander in his element. Gone was the easygoing smile, replaced by cold efficiency as he surveyed the operation with calculating eyes. He wore cargo pants and a lightweight tactical vest, a far cry from his diving gear.

Theo's stomach twisted into knots. The man who had checked his equipment, who had offered him ginger candy for seasickness, now directed armed smugglers with practiced authority.

"Status report," Marcus demanded, checking his watch.

A burly smuggler approached. "Three boats secured the perimeter. No sign of the student."

"He's out there," Marcus replied, his voice carrying across the camp. "Biology major. Smart kid. Don't underestimate him."

Theo shrank deeper into the shadows. Marcus knew he was alive. Knew he was nearby.

"What about the others?" someone asked.

Marcus waved dismissively. "The German couple were clean. Legitimate tourists. The rest were just cover. Only the kid matters now—he saw the exchange."

With clinical precision, Marcus directed the loading operation. Crates moved from tents to boats, equipment was dismantled, evidence erased. Throughout it all, Marcus remained composed, occasionally checking his satellite phone.

This wasn't just some local operation. The coordination, the equipment, the manpower—Theo was witnessing something far more organized than he'd initially feared.

A cold realization settled over him. Marcus had been playing a role from the beginning. The entire diving expedition had been a cover, with Theo and the others serving as unwitting props in a dangerous performance.

As Marcus turned in Theo's direction, sunlight caught his profile. For a moment, Theo could see both versions superimposed—the friendly guide and the calculating criminal—and understood with terrible clarity that his chances of survival were dwindling by the minute.

The smugglers' voices faded as they moved toward the shoreline. Theo counted thirty seconds of silence before daring to move. His body trembled—not from fear alone, but from hunger that had hollowed him out over the past day. The protein bars were gone. The foraged plants sustained him barely. He needed more.

He scanned the camp. Three tents, the shipping container, and a smaller storage shed stood unattended. The shed's door hung slightly ajar—an invitation or a trap. Either way, necessity outweighed caution.

Theo crept from behind the fuel drums, staying low. Each footfall calculated, each breath measured. The sand crunched beneath his feet as he crossed the fifteen yards of exposed ground. His wetsuit, once a symbol of adventure, now felt like a prison—constricting, conspicuous, impossible to blend in.

At the shed door, he paused. Voices carried from the shoreline where Marcus directed the loading operation. Theo slipped inside.

Darkness enveloped him. The musty interior smelled of salt, diesel, and something metallic. As his eyes adjusted, shapes emerged from shadow—stacked crates, canvas bags, and cardboard boxes labeled in Spanish.

Theo pried open the nearest box. Canned beans, tuna, and fruit cocktail gleamed in the dim light filtering through cracks in the wall. His mouth watered instantly.

He grabbed a canvas bag hanging from a nail and filled it methodically. Six cans of tuna. Four of beans. Three fruit cocktails. A box of crackers. Two bottles of water. A roll of duct tape. A folding knife. Each item weighed against its value and the space it consumed.

A shout from outside froze him mid-reach.

"Check the storage! We're missing a case!"

Footsteps approached. Theo looked frantically for an exit, finding none. He slid behind a stack of crates as the door swung wide.

Sunlight flooded the shed. A silhouette filled the doorway—broad-shouldered, weapon visible at his hip.

Theo held his breath, clutching his stolen provisions. The smuggler stepped inside, muttering curses as he rummaged through supplies mere feet from Theo's hiding place.

In that moment, Theo understood with perfect clarity what he'd become—not just a witness, not just a survivor, but a thief. The morality that once defined him blurred against the sharp edge of survival. Carlos's blood-streaked face flashed in his mind, reinforcing the stakes of discovery.

The smuggler grabbed a box and retreated, leaving the door ajar.

Theo waited ten heartbeats before moving again, his stolen lifeline secured against his chest.

Theo retreated from the camp with his canvas bag of provisions, heart hammering against his ribs. Every rustle of wind through cordgrass sounded like pursuit. He moved inland and upward, away from the smugglers and toward higher ground where he might gain perspective—both literal and figurative.

The limestone outcropping appeared suddenly, jutting from the coastal prairie like an afterthought of geology. Wind and rain had carved its face over centuries, creating a shallow overhang that deepened into shadow at its base. Theo approached cautiously, scanning for signs of animal habitation or human use.

"Perfect," he whispered, ducking beneath the rock shelf.

The space wasn't large—perhaps eight feet deep and twice as wide—but the ceiling rose high enough for him to stand. More importantly, it offered concealment from three sides while providing a commanding view of the bay and the smugglers' camp below. Nature had crafted an ideal observation post.

Theo set down his bag of stolen supplies and ran his hand along the limestone wall. It felt cool and dry despite yesterday's storm. Small pockets and natural shelves dotted the interior, ideal for organizing his meager possessions.

"Aunt Clara would approve," he murmured, remembering her lessons about natural shelters.

He arranged his supplies methodically. Water bottles in the coolest corner. Canned goods organized by type. The folding knife and duct tape placed where he could grab them quickly. His actions held purpose now, each movement deliberate and focused.

Outside, the afternoon sun cast long shadows across the coastal prairie. From his elevated position, Theo could track movement around the smugglers' camp while remaining hidden. He watched as men loaded crates onto boats, their voices carrying faintly on the breeze.

For the first time since washing ashore, Theo felt a flicker of control returning. This refuge wasn't just shelter—it was a strategic advantage.

He pulled out his notebook and began sketching the layout below, marking patrol patterns and access points. The knowledge of plants that had guided him through the marsh now helped him identify potential escape routes through the terrain.

"I'm not just surviving anymore," Theo realized. "I'm fighting back."

The limestone walls around him seemed to absorb his words, holding them like a promise.

The afternoon light shifted, sending a golden beam deeper into the limestone shelter. Theo paused in his sketching as the light illuminated something tucked into a crevice he hadn't noticed before—a folded square of weathered paper.

He reached for it cautiously, half-expecting it to crumble at his touch. The paper held firm despite its obvious age, unfolding to reveal a map of the Matagorda Peninsula. Faded blue and green inks showed coastal contours, marked trails, and notable landmarks. In the corner, a Texas Parks & Wildlife Department logo had partially survived years of exposure.

"Someone else found this place," Theo whispered, running his fingers over the brittle surface.

The map predated recent coastal developments, judging by the absence of certain structures he knew existed. Yet its fundamental geography remained unchanged—the peninsula's spine, the marshlands, the bay where smugglers now operated. Most importantly, a ranger station was clearly marked with a star, approximately seven miles northwest of his current position.

Theo compared it with his own crude sketch of the area. The station might still exist, possibly staffed or at least equipped with communication equipment. It represented more than shelter—it was a connection to the outside world, to authorities who could stop Marcus and his operation.

He traced potential routes with his finger, weighing options against known dangers. The most direct path crossed open terrain where he'd be exposed. An alternative route followed the coastline—longer but offering more cover and reliable navigation markers.

"Seven miles," he calculated. "I could make it by tomorrow afternoon if I pace myself."

Outside, the sun began its descent toward the horizon. The smugglers' boats had returned to the camp, figures moving with purpose as they secured their operation for the night. Soon darkness would provide cover for movement.

Theo folded the map carefully and tucked it into his waterproof bag. The discovery had transformed his thinking from mere survival to strategic escape. Knowledge—even in the form of an outdated map—had power. The same academic mind that had studied coastal ecosystems now plotted his path to freedom.

He would rest until nightfall, then begin his journey under cover of darkness. The ranger station beckoned like a lighthouse across an uncertain sea.

Theo gathered his supplies with methodical precision, mentally rehearsing his route to the ranger station. The map had injected new purpose into his movements, transforming fear into focused determination. Seven miles—a journey that would require stealth, endurance, and luck. He tucked the last of his provisions into the canvas bag and moved toward the cave entrance.

The setting sun cast long shadows across the limestone outcropping, painting the landscape in amber and deep purple. Theo paused at the threshold, scanning the terrain below for movement before making his exit. That's when he saw them—fresh boot prints pressed into the soft earth just outside the shelter.

His breath caught in his throat.

The prints weren't his own. The treaded pattern was distinctive—tactical boots, much larger than his wetsuit booties. They approached from the south, circled the entrance, then continued northward along the ridge.

Someone had been here. Recently.

Theo crouched lower, pressing his back against the cool limestone as his eyes darted across the landscape. The smugglers weren't just searching the coastline—they were systematically combing the high ground. His sanctuary had already been discovered, perhaps even while he slept.

His earlier confidence evaporated like morning dew. The map in his bag felt suddenly irrelevant against the immediacy of the danger. Theo's heart hammered against his ribs as he realized how close they had come—how close they might still be.

Below in the camp, figures moved with renewed purpose. Had they radioed back about finding signs of an intruder? Were they converging on his position even now?

Theo closed his eyes, fighting against the rising panic. The seven-mile journey to the ranger station now seemed impossibly distant, a gauntlet of exposed terrain with hunters tracking his every move.

"Think," he whispered to himself. "They know you're here, but they don't know you're leaving."

Night was falling rapidly. He had to move soon or lose his advantage of darkness. But rushing blindly into the open with smugglers nearby would be suicide.

The boot prints told a story—not just of danger, but of patterns. If he could decipher their search grid, perhaps he could slip between their lines.

Theo unfolded the map once more, his earlier plans now complicated by the knowledge that he wasn't just being hunted—he was being hunted by professionals who had already found his trail.

Theo retreated deeper into the cave, heart pounding against his ribs. Time was slipping away, but an urgent thought crystallized in his mind. If something happened to him—if Marcus and his crew caught up before he reached safety—someone needed to know what he'd witnessed.

He pulled out his waterproof notebook and a stubby pencil, hands trembling as he pressed the paper against a flat limestone surface. The dim light made writing difficult, but determination steadied his grip.

October 14th. Seven and a Half Fathom Reef dive was cover for smuggling operation. Marcus Delgado leading. Approx. 8 armed men. Coordinates...

Theo sketched a rough map of the camp layout, marking the shipping container, patrol patterns, and boats. He described the brutal interrogation of Carlos, the weapons he'd observed, and Marcus's transformation from dive instructor to criminal commander.

Cargo transfer happening tonight. Evidence of Coast Guard infiltration. Drugs, weapons, possibly human trafficking.

He paused, pencil hovering over the paper. This might be his last testimony. He added his full name, student ID, and contact information for Aunt Clara.

If found, please get this to authorities immediately.

Theo tore the pages from his notebook and folded them carefully, sliding them into a plastic bag from his supplies. He wedged the package into a narrow crevice in the cave wall, high enough to be overlooked by casual searchers but visible to anyone conducting a thorough investigation.

His uncle's Vietnam stories flashed through his mind—tales of jungle survival and improvised early warning systems. Working quickly, Theo gathered small rocks and balanced them precariously across the cave entrance. Anyone entering would send them clattering down, creating noise that might provide precious seconds of warning.

Satisfied with his trap, Theo shouldered his pack and took one final look at the shelter that had briefly protected him. The walls seemed to close in, no longer offering safety but threatening to become his tomb if he lingered.

Outside, darkness had fallen completely. The stars overhead offered navigation but no comfort. Theo oriented himself northwest, toward the distant promise of the ranger station, and slipped into the night like a shadow.

The hunt was on, but this time, he wasn't just prey. He was a witness with evidence that could bring down Marcus's entire operation—if he survived long enough to deliver it.

Chapter 6

D awn seeped through the coastal fog like watery paint bleeding across canvas. Theo crouched in a thicket of reeds, his muscles stiff from hours of movement through the night. The wetlands stretched around him—an alien landscape of sawgrass and shallow channels that both concealed and trapped him.

He'd made good progress since leaving the limestone outcropping, pushing northwest through terrain that shifted between mudflats and shallow water. The first hint of sunrise now revealed a narrow waterway cutting through the marsh before him, its surface mirror-smooth in the misty light.

A splash shattered the silence.

Theo dropped lower, pressing his body into the damp earth. Twenty yards away, a figure emerged from the water—a man with a weathered face and salt-and-pepper beard. Blood had dried along a deep cut on his cheek.

Carlos. The fisherman from the camp.

Theo's breath caught. The man had escaped his captors. But how? And why was he here, in this exact stretch of wetland?

Carlos dragged himself onto a muddy bank, his movements deliberate despite obvious pain. He scanned the surroundings with the practiced gaze of someone accustomed to reading landscapes. When he spoke, his voice carried clearly across the water.

"You can come out. They're miles behind us now."

Theo remained frozen, calculating possibilities. Carlos sighed and settled against a cypress knee, wincing.

"I saw you at the camp, boy. Behind those fuel drums. I didn't say nothing to them, and I ain't saying nothing now."

The morning mist swirled between them, ghostly tendrils connecting predator and prey—though Theo couldn't be certain which was which.

"Name's Carlos Mendoza. Been fishing these waters thirty years." He gestured at his battered face. "Until I saw something I shouldn't have."

Theo hesitated, then slowly rose from the reeds. Every instinct screamed caution, but isolation had worn at his resolve. Besides, the fisherman looked half-dead himself.

"Theo Mercer."

Carlos nodded, his dark eyes revealing nothing. "Biology student, right? Marcus mentioned you. Said you were too curious for your own good."

A chill ran through Theo that had nothing to do with his damp clothes.

"We need to move," Carlos said, standing with effort. "They'll sweep the waterways at first light. I know a place." He extended a calloused hand. "Trust is hard to come by out here. But sometimes it's all we got."

The mist thickened around them, obscuring the boundaries between land and water, truth and deception.

Morning light filtered through the cypress canopy, casting dappled patterns across the wetland path. Carlos moved with surprising agility for a man who had endured such brutality hours before. His steps were deliberate, each foot placement tested before committing his weight, leaving barely a trace in the soft earth.

"These wetlands been here longer than any of us," Carlos said, gesturing toward a stand of ancient cypress trees. "Some of these old sentinels were seedlings when the Spanish first sailed into the Gulf."

Theo followed closely, noting how Carlos navigated the landscape with intimate familiarity. The fisherman chose routes invisible to untrained eyes, following subtle rises in the terrain that kept them above the waterline.

"You seem to know this place well," Theo observed, ducking beneath a low-hanging branch.

Carlos's laugh was dry as kindling. "When you make your living from these waters, you learn their secrets or you don't survive." He paused at a narrow crossing, pointing to faint scratches on a cypress trunk. "See those marks? Alligator. Big male. Territory marker."

The sun climbed higher, burning away the morning mist and warming their sodden clothes. Carlos maintained a steady pace, occasionally sharing bits of knowledge that revealed years of observation.

"The Karankawa used these wetlands as hunting grounds for centuries," he said, indicating a slight rise ahead. "They'd build platforms in the trees during flood seasons. Smart people. Understood the rhythms here."

Theo absorbed each detail, his scientific mind cataloging the information while another part remained wary. How had this man escaped from Marcus? Why was he so willing to help?

"Over there—see those birds?" Carlos pointed to a cluster of white ibises probing the mud with curved bills. "They follow the tides. When they feed this far inland, means the tide's out for another four hours at least."

As they crossed a small clearing, Carlos knelt suddenly, examining something in the grass. "Fresh deer tracks. Good sign—means no humans been through here recently."

Theo watched the fisherman's weathered hands trace the impression, struck by the depth of knowledge displayed so casually. Whatever Carlos Mendoza might be—victim or something more complex—his connection to this environment was undeniable.

"We'll rest up ahead," Carlos said, rising. "There's a spot where we can see anyone coming from three directions."

He smiled, the expression transforming his battered face into something almost grandfatherly. "Don't worry, biology student. These wetlands protected my ancestors. They'll protect us too."

Midday heat pressed down on the wetlands like a physical weight. The air thickened with humidity, clinging to skin and filling lungs with each labored breath. Insects buzzed in frantic clouds around their faces as Carlos led Theo deeper into the marsh's heart.

"Watch your step here," Carlos warned, pointing to what looked like solid ground ahead. "That's a bog trap. Looks firm but swallows men whole."

Theo paused, studying the deceptive patch. Nothing visibly distinguished it from the surrounding terrain, yet Carlos had spotted it instantly.

"How can you tell?"

"See those pitcher plants?" Carlos indicated delicate red-veined cups nestled among the grasses. "They only grow where the ground's too soft to support weight. Nature gives warnings if you know how to read them."

They skirted the danger, Carlos choosing a narrower path that required balancing on cypress knees and fallen logs. Sweat streamed down Theo's face, stinging his eyes and soaking his already damp clothes. The oppressive heat made each step an effort of will.

"The Spanish moss," Carlos said, gesturing to the gray tendrils hanging from branches overhead, "it's not moss at all. It's related to pineapples."

Despite his exhaustion, Theo found himself drawn to the fisherman's knowledge. Carlos moved through the wetland with the ease of someone navigating his own home, identifying medicinal plants and pointing out a well-camouflaged cottonmouth before Theo could blunder into its territory.

"My grandmother could cure twenty ailments with plants from this marsh alone," Carlos said, breaking a stem and offering it to Theo. "Chew this. Helps with thirst."

The bitter taste spread across Theo's tongue, but the relief was immediate. He realized with growing unease how completely dependent he had become on this man—a stranger whose true nature remained a mystery.

When Carlos extended a hand to help Theo across a particularly treacherous stretch, the younger man hesitated for just a moment before accepting. The fisherman's grip was firm, reliable. Trustworthy.

"Almost there," Carlos encouraged, his eyes scanning the horizon. "There's a dry spot ahead where we can rest."

As they pressed on, Theo found himself caught in an unsettling calculation—weighing his growing reliance on Carlos against the nagging suspicion that the fisherman's story might not be entirely what it seemed. The marsh, with its hidden dangers and deceptive surfaces, felt suddenly like a perfect metaphor for his predicament.

They settled on a fallen cypress log beside a small pond, its surface mirroring the cloudless sky above. Water lilies dotted the edges with delicate white blooms while dragonflies darted across the surface, their iridescent wings catching the afternoon light. Carlos removed his tattered shirt to rinse it in the clear water, revealing a patchwork of scars across his back—some old and faded, others fresh and angry.

Theo uncapped his water bottle, taking a careful sip as he studied the fisherman. Something didn't quite add up.

"You mentioned the smugglers have three different routes through the marsh," Theo said, keeping his tone casual. "How does a fisherman know so much about their operations?"

Carlos wrung out his shirt, his movements deliberate. "When you live on these waters long enough, you notice patterns. Boats that move at night. Men who never bring back fish."

"And the safe houses? You pointed out two already."

The older man's eyes narrowed slightly. "The coast has eyes, Theo. Nothing happens here without the locals knowing."

A heron landed at the pond's edge, its reflection doubling its elegant form. It stood motionless, watching for prey beneath the water's surface with predatory patience.

"You knew exactly which trails the smugglers wouldn't patrol," Theo pressed. "That's more than casual observation."

Carlos pulled his damp shirt back on, his expression unreadable. "Maybe I've had reason to avoid them before today."

"Or maybe you know their routines because you're one of them."

The words hung between them, heavy as the humid air. Carlos didn't immediately deny it, which troubled Theo more than any protestation might have.

"We all make choices to survive," Carlos finally said. "Judge me when you've lived my life."

The heron struck suddenly, spearing a fish beneath the water. The peaceful scene shattered with the violence of nature's reality.

"I'm grateful for your help," Theo said carefully. "But I need to know who I'm following."

Carlos stood, scanning the lengthening shadows. "Right now, I'm the only friend you've got. The ranger station is still four miles northwest. You want to make that journey alone?"

Theo weighed his options, feeling the weight of his vulnerability. Trust was a luxury he couldn't afford, yet survival might depend on a man whose story had more holes than the Spanish moss overhead.

The harsh buzz of engines shattered the wetland silence before either man could respond. Carlos froze, his head snapping toward the sound with practiced recognition.

"Down!" he hissed, shoving Theo off the log.

They crashed into the mud as an airboat rounded the bend, its flat-bottomed hull skimming across the shallow water. A second followed close behind. The lead boat carried three men, their faces obscured by bandanas, weapons glinting in the afternoon sun.

"There!" One smuggler pointed directly at them, raising his rifle.

The first shots peppered the water mere feet from where they lay. Mud kicked up around them as bullets tore into the bank.

"Move!" Carlos grabbed Theo's collar, dragging him toward a dense stand of cattails. "Stay low!"

Theo's world narrowed to the sound of his own ragged breathing and the thunderous crack of gunfire. He crawled through muck on his elbows, the weight of terror pressing him into the earth. Behind them, the airboats curved in a wide arc, preparing for another pass.

"They found us," Theo gasped. "How did they—"

"Shut up and keep moving," Carlos snarled, his earlier gentleness vanished. He pulled a knife from his boot with practiced efficiency.

The airboats split, one circling to flank them from the north. Their engines howled across the open water, an unnatural intrusion in the ancient marsh. A great blue heron took flight, its wings beating frantically against the chaos below.

"Mendoza!" A voice called out across the water. "We know it's you! The boss wants a word!"

Carlos's face hardened at the name. His eyes, once warm with guidance, now calculated escape routes with cold precision.

"They know you," Theo whispered, realization dawning. "They called you Mendoza."

Carlos—or Mendoza—didn't deny it. Instead, he pointed toward a narrow channel cutting through the tall grass. "That way. When I create a distraction, you run and don't look back."

Before Theo could protest, Carlos broke cover, waving his arms. "I'm here! Come get me, you worthless dogs!"

The airboats immediately swung toward him, engines roaring with renewed purpose. In that moment, as bullets tore through the reeds around them, Theo glimpsed the truth—he'd been following a man who belonged to this violent world all along.

The crack of gunfire erupted from Carlos's hand as he pulled a compact pistol from beneath his tattered shirt. Three shots in rapid succession—precise and devastating. The first smuggler fell backward off the airboat, disappearing beneath the murky water with barely a splash.

"Get down!" Carlos shouted, shoving Theo toward a half-submerged wooden structure—the remnants of an old dock, its timbers green with algae and rot.

Theo stumbled forward, splashing through knee-deep water. The weathered planks offered meager shelter, but he pressed his body against them, heart hammering against his ribs. Through gaps in the wood, he watched Carlos move with lethal efficiency.

Gone was the injured fisherman. In his place stood a fighter—calculating, ruthless, and terrifyingly competent. Carlos rolled behind a cypress knee, fired twice more, then changed position before return fire could find him. His movements had the fluid precision of someone who had done this many times before.

"Flank him!" shouted one of the smugglers, his voice tight with panic.

The second airboat swung wide, its pilot struggling to navigate the narrowing channel. Carlos anticipated the maneuver, placing three shots into the engine housing. Black smoke billowed as the motor sputtered and died.

Across the marsh, birds took flight in panicked clouds. A gator slipped beneath the surface, disturbed by the unnatural violence invading its domain. The wetland itself seemed to recoil from the human conflict unfolding within its boundaries.

"You picked the wrong side, Mendoza!" The remaining smuggler fired wildly, bullets splintering the ancient cypress trees.

Carlos laughed—a cold, dangerous sound that sent chills down Theo's spine. "I always pick my own side."

From his hiding place, Theo saw everything with brutal clarity. The man who had guided him through the marsh, who had shared knowledge of plants and wildlife, who had spoken of the Karankawa with reverence—this same man now dealt death with practiced hands.

The remaining airboat attempted retreat, its pilot desperate to escape. Carlos tracked it with his pistol, squeezing the trigger with mechanical precision. The engine exploded in a ball of orange flame, sending black smoke spiraling into the cloudless sky.

In that moment, as the echoes of gunfire faded across the water, Theo understood with crushing certainty: he had allied himself with a predator far more dangerous than those pursuing them.

Smoke hung over the marsh like funeral shrouds, obscuring the carnage Carlos had left behind. Without a word, he grabbed Theo's arm and pulled him away from the dock, his grip unyielding.

"Move. They'll have heard the explosion." Carlos's voice carried no emotion, as if he hadn't just killed three men. Blood from his reopened wounds mingled with marsh water, trailing behind them in diluted crimson wisps.

Theo stumbled after him, mind reeling. The world had shifted beneath his feet once again. The man he'd followed—trusted, even—was something else entirely. Not victim. Not guide. Something darker.

They pushed through dense cattails toward higher ground where cypress trees gave way to pine and oak. The late afternoon sun filtered through the canopy, casting dappled shadows that danced across Carlos's tense features. Birds resumed their calls, indifferent to human conflict, while insects hummed their endless chorus.

A weathered wooden sign appeared through the foliage: MATAGORDA ISLAND WILDLIFE REFUGE - FEDERAL PROPERTY.

"In there," Carlos said, pointing toward the protected area. "Border patrol doesn't venture deep, and smugglers avoid federal land when possible."

Theo followed, watching Carlos's back with new wariness. "Who are you? Really?"

Carlos didn't break stride. "Someone who's survived longer than most in this business."

"You're one of them." It wasn't a question.

"Was. Now I'm a liability." Carlos checked his pistol's magazine before tucking it away. "Like you."

They crossed into the refuge, where the vegetation grew thicker and untamed. A deer and fawn startled at their approach, bounding away through golden shafts of sunlight. The irony wasn't lost on

Theo—this sanctuary designed to protect wildlife now sheltered men who brought violence with them.

As they reached a small clearing, Carlos finally stopped. Sweat and blood had soaked through his shirt, but his eyes remained alert, scanning their surroundings.

"We rest. Ten minutes." He settled against a tree trunk, wincing.

Theo stood apart, unwilling to sit. The sanctuary around them felt tainted now. Birds called overhead, a great blue heron stalked through nearby shallows, and somewhere in the distance, a wild hog rooted through underbrush—all continuing their existence while men hunted men just beyond the refuge boundaries.

"I trusted you," Theo said quietly.

Carlos met his gaze, unflinching. "That was your mistake."

Twilight bled across the sky as Carlos and Theo approached the abandoned ranger station. The structure stood in a small clearing, its weathered wooden exterior half-consumed by creeping vines and wild morning glory. Once a symbol of protection and order, it now slouched against the wilderness, surrendering to nature's reclamation.

"We'll stop here for the night," Carlos said, his voice barely audible above the evening chorus of cicadas and frogs.

Theo eyed the dilapidated building with suspicion. "How did you know this was here? It's not on any recent maps."

Carlos didn't answer, merely testing the warped door with his shoulder before forcing it open with a groan of rusted hinges. The sound scattered a family of mice into the underbrush.

Inside, the station was a museum of abandonment. Dust-covered filing cabinets stood against walls where faded posters of native wildlife curled at the edges. A desk remained in the center, drawers hanging open as if someone had left in a hurry. The air smelled of mildew, rodents, and forgotten purpose.

"Check those cabinets," Carlos instructed, moving toward a small kitchenette in the back. "Look for anything useful—maps, first aid supplies."

Theo hesitated, watching as Carlos methodically opened cupboards with his free hand, his other never straying far from the pistol at his waist. In the fading light filtering through grimy windows, Carlos looked more predator than prey, despite his injuries.

"Why are we really here?" Theo asked, remaining by the door.

Carlos paused, turning to face him. The shadows accentuated the hard lines of his face. "Because it's defensible, off the main trails, and has supplies if we're lucky."

"That's not what I meant."

A knowing look crossed Carlos's face. "You think I led you into a trap." It wasn't a question.

The evening light continued to dim, casting longer shadows across the room. Outside, a distant coyote called to its pack, the sound eerily human in its loneliness.

"I think," Theo said carefully, "that you know more than you're telling me."

Carlos nodded slowly, his expression unreadable. "Smart boy. Trust is a luxury neither of us can afford right now." He turned back to the cupboards. "But if I wanted you dead, you wouldn't be standing there questioning me."

The statement offered little comfort as darkness settled around them, transforming the abandoned station into a fortress of secrets neither man seemed willing to share.

Moonlight sliced through the broken blinds, casting prison-bar shadows across the ranger station's interior. Theo rummaged through a filing cabinet, the metal drawers protesting with each pull. His fingers traced over forgotten incident reports and wildlife surveys, all coated in the dust of abandonment.

Behind him, Carlos had spread something across the desk, his weathered hands moving with deliberate precision in the beam of a small flashlight he'd produced from his pocket. The light caught his profile—the sharp nose, the tightened jaw—as he studied whatever lay before him.

Theo turned, curiosity overcoming caution. "Find something useful?"

Carlos didn't look up. "Maybe."

Stepping closer, Theo saw it wasn't the station's standard-issue coastal map but something far more detailed—a waterproof chart with handwritten notations, coordinates, and times scrawled in the margins. Red lines snaked through the wetlands and across the bay, avoiding the regular Coast Guard patrol routes marked in blue.

"Those are smuggling routes," Theo said, the words hanging in the air between them.

Carlos's hand stilled. His eyes, dark and unreadable, lifted to meet Theo's. "They are."

The silence stretched, punctuated only by the distant call of a night heron. Outside, the wind picked up, rattling the loose window frames.

"You're not just some fisherman who got caught up in this," Theo said, understanding washing over him like cold Gulf water. "You know these routes because you use them."

Carlos folded the map with practiced movements, tucking it into his shirt. "What matters is that I know how to keep us alive."

"Us? Or just you?" Theo backed away, his mind racing through possibilities, each darker than the last. "Was everything a lie? The torture at the camp—was that staged?"

"Not everything is black and white out here." Carlos's voice remained steady, but something flickered across his face—perhaps regret, perhaps calculation. "Sometimes survival means playing both sides."

The revelation settled over Theo like a physical weight. The man he'd followed through the marsh, the man who'd killed to protect them both, wasn't a victim but a player in the very operation Theo had stumbled into.

"Who are you really?" Theo asked, the question barely audible above the creaking of the old building.

Carlos didn't answer immediately. When he did, his words carried the weight of a confession. "Someone who's in too deep to get out clean."

Moonlight painted silver patterns across the ranger station floor as Theo sat with his back against the wall, knees pulled to his chest. Carlos had stepped outside, claiming to check the perimeter, leaving Theo alone with the weight of his thoughts and the symphony of night creatures beyond the walls.

The wetlands came alive after dark—bullfrogs croaking their territorial warnings, insects chirping in relentless chorus, and somewhere distant, the splash of something heavy entering water. These natural sounds felt trustworthy, predictable. Unlike his companion.

Theo closed his eyes, mentally cataloging the day's revelations like specimens in a lab. Carlos's intimate knowledge of smuggling routes. His tactical precision during the airboat attack. The casual efficiency with which he'd taken lives. These weren't the actions of a simple fisherman caught in circumstances beyond his control.

He's playing a game I don't understand.

The floor creaked as Theo shifted position. His muscles ached from days of running, swimming, hiding. Physical exhaustion he could manage—it was the mental chess match that drained him now.

Why had Carlos saved him from the smugglers if he was one of them? What value did a marine biology student hold in this dangerous equation? The pieces refused to fit together in any configuration that made sense.

Aunt Clara's voice drifted through his memory: *"Trust isn't about what someone says, Theo. It's about what they do when they think no one's watching."*

He'd watched Carlos study that map with the familiarity of someone who'd used it many times before. Watched his eyes calculate distances and routes. Watched his fingers trace paths through waters where Coast Guard boats wouldn't follow.

Outside, an owl called—three haunting notes that hung in the humid air.

Theo opened his eyes, decision crystallizing. Whatever game Carlos played, whatever role he truly occupied in this coastal underworld, one truth remained clear: Theo needed to escape. Not just from the smugglers hunting them, but from Carlos himself.

The ranger station had a radio. It might work; it might not. There would be supplies, maps that weren't marked with criminal routes. Come morning, he would need to make his move.

Beyond the broken blinds, the coastal darkness waited, indifferent to human schemes. Theo listened to the night sounds, finding in their chaotic patterns a strange comfort. Nature, at least, never pretended to be anything other than what it was.

Chapter 7

The mist clung to the water's surface like a living thing, parting reluctantly as the aluminum boat sliced through the dawn-lit delta. Carlos sat at the stern, one hand on the small outboard motor's throttle, the other resting lightly on the tiller. His eyes never stopped moving—from the water's subtle ripples to the bending reeds that signaled hidden currents, to the distant treeline that most would see as uniform green but that he read like a map.

Theo huddled near the bow, shoulders hunched against the morning chill. Despite his misgivings about Carlos, he couldn't help but admire the man's skill. Where Theo saw only a confusing maze of identical channels and false passages, Carlos navigated with the casual confidence of someone returning home.

"The water tells you everything you need to know," Carlos said, breaking the silence that had stretched between them since leaving the ranger station. He pointed to a barely perceptible change in the water's texture fifty yards ahead. "Sandbar there. Would tear the bottom out of this boat."

Carlos eased the throttle back and adjusted their course, threading between cypress knees that rose from the water like ancient fingers. Spanish moss hung in gray-green curtains, occasionally brushing against Theo's shoulder as they passed.

"How did you find this boat?" Theo asked, unable to contain his curiosity any longer.

Carlos's face remained impassive. "I didn't find it. I left it. Years ago."

The implications of this statement hung in the air between them. This wasn't opportunistic survival—this was planned. Carlos had resources scattered throughout the delta, had moved through these waters often enough to leave insurance policies against the day things went wrong.

A great blue heron lifted from the reeds ahead, its massive wings beating slowly as it rose above them. Both men watched its ascent in silence.

"Beautiful," Theo murmured.

"And smart," Carlos added. "It knows when to leave."

The boat rounded a bend, revealing a channel so narrow that branches from either bank nearly touched overhead, creating a natural tunnel. Carlos guided them into this passage without hesitation, reducing their speed further.

"Nobody comes this way," he said, voice low as if the delta itself might be listening. "Too tight for most boats. Too many turns to remember. But it'll get us where we need to go."

Theo nodded, understanding growing with every mile. Carlos wasn't just surviving in this environment—he owned it. And that made him more dangerous than Theo had initially realized.

The mist began to burn away as the sun climbed higher, revealing the true complexity of the delta's arterial waterways stretching in all directions.

The sun climbed higher as they navigated deeper into the delta's maze. Heat shimmered above the water, transforming the morning chill into a heavy blanket of humidity. Sweat beaded on Theo's forehead while Carlos remained dry, as though the elements themselves had agreed to spare him their discomfort.

"Been on these waters since I was a boy," Carlos said, breaking their lengthy silence. He steered them around a half-submerged log with practiced ease. "My father taught me to fish when I was five. By twelve, I could navigate the entire coastline blindfolded."

Theo nodded, studying Carlos's weathered profile. The man's eyes remained fixed on the water ahead, but something in his tone suggested he was watching Theo's reaction from the corner of his vision.

"How'd you get mixed up with those men?" Theo asked, keeping his voice neutral.

Carlos sighed, a perfect performance of reluctance. "Not much choice for a fisherman when the catches get smaller every year. They approached me three years ago—just to transport some packages, they said." He shook his head. "Simple work, good money. By the time I realized what I was carrying, I was already in too deep."

The boat drifted into a narrow channel where mangroves created a canopy overhead, plunging them into green-tinted shadow. A turtle slipped from a branch into the water as they passed.

"Marcus and his crew—they control everything from Corpus Christi to Galveston. They needed someone who knew the waters." Carlos gestured at the labyrinthine channels surrounding them. "Someone who could find paths that don't exist on any map."

Theo wiped sweat from his brow. "You said three years ago. But earlier you mentioned knowing these routes for decades."

Carlos's expression didn't change, but his knuckles whitened slightly on the tiller. "I knew the waters. They showed me how to use them differently."

A bird called from somewhere in the dense vegetation—three sharp notes that echoed across the water. Carlos's head turned toward the sound with practiced precision before he seemed to catch himself.

"The authorities—they never caught on?" Theo asked.

"Coast Guard has their patrol routes. Predictable." Carlos laughed softly. "Though you mentioned earlier that your dive trip was your first time on the Gulf, but then you recognized Coast Guard patterns when we saw that patrol yesterday."

The observation hung between them, neither acknowledging the mutual catching of inconsistencies.

"Sometimes I transported people," Carlos continued, steering around another bend. "Desperate ones. Families. I told myself I was helping them." His voice lowered. "Other times, it was just packages. Better not to know what was inside."

The boat emerged into a wider channel where islands of tall grass rose from the shallow water. Carlos pointed to a distant cluster of cypress trees. "I was just a fisherman caught in their net. Not like Marcus—he built the operation from nothing. Started small, they say, running marijuana. Now it's bigger things. More dangerous things."

Theo noticed how Carlos's knowledge expanded and contracted—specific about operations when painting himself as peripheral, vague when details might place him at the center.

"We're all just trying to survive," Carlos said, eyes forward as the boat curved around another bend, taking them deeper into the delta's embrace. "Wouldn't you agree?"

The distant whine of engines cut through the delta's symphony of birdsong and rustling reeds. Carlos tensed, his hand flying to the motor's throttle and cutting power in a single fluid motion. The boat drifted forward on momentum alone as he pivoted, scanning the horizon with narrowed eyes.

"Get down," he hissed, already maneuvering their small craft toward a dense wall of vegetation along the eastern bank.

Theo dropped low, his heart accelerating as the sound grew louder—not one engine, but several, their high-pitched whines echoing across the water in dissonant harmony. Carlos worked with practiced efficiency, using a paddle to guide them silently into a pocket beneath drooping willow branches and tangled vines.

"Airboats," Carlos whispered, pressing the aluminum hull against the mud. "Three of them, moving in a search pattern."

The morning sun beat down mercilessly, eliminating the long shadows that might have concealed them earlier. Light filtered through the vegetation in dappled patterns across Theo's arms as he peered through gaps in their leafy shelter.

The first airboat appeared around the bend—a flat-bottomed craft with an enormous fan mounted on the back, allowing it to glide over the shallowest water. A man stood at the elevated helm, scanning the waterways with binoculars while another sat forward, cradling what was unmistakably a rifle.

Carlos's breathing slowed to near imperceptibility as two more airboats emerged, positioning themselves in a formation that effectively blocked any escape routes. The three vessels moved with military precision, maintaining visual contact while covering different channels.

"That's not Marcus's usual crew," Carlos murmured, so quietly that Theo barely caught the words. "Look at their movements—too coordinated."

Theo studied the methodical search pattern. These weren't disorganized thugs but professionals executing a carefully planned operation. The lead boat paused near a junction, and the helmsman made a series of hand signals that sent the other two vessels branching into separate channels.

"Who are they?" Theo asked, his voice barely audible over the distant engines.

Carlos didn't answer immediately. His eyes tracked the lead boat, his expression unreadable. "Someone with resources," he finally said. "Someone who wants us very badly."

The airboats continued their relentless sweep, moving closer to their hiding spot with each passing minute. Sweat trickled down Theo's spine as the realization settled over him: this wasn't just a local crew searching for escaped witnesses—this was something much larger, with far greater reach than he had imagined.

Carlos waited until the airboats' engines faded to a distant hum before easing their craft back into open water. Without a word, he steered them toward a seemingly impenetrable wall of mangroves that stretched across the horizon like a green fortress.

"There's nothing but trees ahead," Theo whispered, scanning the dense tangle of roots and branches.

Carlos's mouth twitched into something resembling a smile. "That's what everyone thinks."

He guided the boat directly toward the mangrove wall, maintaining speed until Theo braced for impact. At the last possible moment, Carlos made a sharp turn, revealing a narrow opening barely wider than their hull. The passage would have been invisible from even ten feet away, concealed by overlapping branches and the play of shadows on water.

"Welcome to the back door," Carlos murmured as they slipped into the green labyrinth.

Sunlight filtered through the dense canopy, creating an otherworldly emerald glow. The temperature dropped immediately, the air heavy with moisture and the rich scent of decomposing vegetation. Twisted roots rose from the brackish water like skeletal fingers, forming natural archways and tunnels that seemed to shift and change with each turn.

Carlos navigated without hesitation, reading the water's subtle currents and the patterns of light that most would overlook. He ducked beneath low-hanging branches without breaking stride, anticipating each twist in the hidden channel before it appeared.

"How do you know this place so well?" Theo asked, brushing aside a curtain of aerial roots.

"Years of necessity," Carlos replied, his eyes constantly scanning ahead. "Customs and Border Protection have radar, helicopters, fast boats. Nature provides better cover than technology ever could."

They emerged into a small clearing where four identical channels branched outward. Without pausing, Carlos chose the second from the right, though nothing distinguished it from the others.

"I've seen Coast Guard get lost in here for days," he continued. "The channels shift with the tides. What's open now might be closed in six hours."

Theo studied Carlos's profile, noting the ease with which he handled the boat, the absolute certainty in his movements. This wasn't knowledge gained from occasional fishing trips—this was expertise born from countless journeys through this aquatic maze, likely carrying cargo that couldn't bear scrutiny.

"You could find your way through here blindfolded, couldn't you?" Theo observed.

Carlos didn't deny it. "Sometimes, I had to."

They rounded a bend in the mangrove tunnel, emerging into a sun-drenched clearing where water met a narrow strip of mud-caked land. Carlos cut the engine, letting the boat drift to a stop. The sudden silence amplified the sounds of the delta—water lapping against roots, insects humming in the thick air, birds calling from unseen perches.

"Look there," Carlos whispered, pointing toward the bank.

A massive alligator lay sprawled across the mud, its prehistoric form motionless except for the occasional blink of a reptilian eye.

Fourteen feet of armored predator basked in the afternoon heat, jaws slightly parted to reveal yellowed teeth.

Twenty yards from the gator, a sounder of wild hogs rooted through the marsh grass—six adults and several striped piglets. The largest boar, scarred and tusked, kept raising his head to stare at the alligator before returning to his foraging.

"Neither moves on the other," Carlos observed. "Been that way since time began."

Theo watched the strange standoff, fascinated by the unspoken boundaries. "The gator could take one of the smaller hogs."

"And the boars could rush the gator if they coordinated." Carlos leaned back, sweat beading on his forehead in the oppressive heat. "But they don't. Each respects what the other can do."

A piglet strayed closer to the water's edge. The alligator's eye tracked the movement, but it made no attempt to lunge.

"Nature's neutral territory," Carlos continued, his voice taking on an unusual philosophical tone. "Out here, everything understands its place. The predators, the prey—they all face the same sun, the same storms, the same hunger."

The boar snorted, calling the piglet back from the water's edge.

"Marcus and his men, the Coast Guard, even me—we're no different from them." Carlos gestured toward the animals. "We each have our territory, our strengths. The delta doesn't care who's right or wrong."

Theo studied the alligator's unblinking patience, the hogs' nervous vigilance. "So which are we? Predator or prey?"

Carlos turned to him, his face carved with lines of experience. "Depends on the day. Sometimes you're the gator. Sometimes you're the hog. The trick is knowing which one you are before the other guy does."

The alligator suddenly slipped into the water, disappearing beneath the murky surface. The hogs, sensing the shift, retreated deeper into the brush.

"Time to move," Carlos said, restarting the engine. "The balance just changed."

They drifted into the shade of ancient cypress trees, waiting for the wildlife to clear from their path. The boat rocked gently beneath them as Carlos killed the engine once more. A peculiar stillness settled over the delta—the kind that existed between heartbeats, between breaths.

"My grandfather taught me to read these waters," Carlos said unexpectedly, breaking the silence. His weathered hands traced invisible patterns over the surface. "When I was seven, he'd take me out before dawn in a boat not much bigger than a bathtub."

Theo watched a transformation spread across Carlos's face—the hardened lines softening around his eyes, his vigilant posture easing.

"Abuelo could find fish where no one else could. He'd say, 'Carlos, the water speaks if you know how to listen.'" A smile touched the corners of his mouth, genuine and unguarded. "I thought he was magic."

A great blue heron landed on a nearby cypress knee, folding its wings with deliberate grace.

"We were poor—everyone was—but we never went hungry." Carlos dipped his fingers into the water, creating gentle ripples. "He showed me how to feel the current against my palm, how to spot the places where fish would shelter during storms."

Theo shifted, seeing Carlos not as the dangerous smuggler or the calculating survivor, but as a boy learning his grandfather's wisdom.

"What happened to him?" Theo asked.

Carlos's eyes darkened. "Hurricane took him when I was fifteen. Found his boat, never found him." He glanced up at the cloudless sky. "That's when everything changed. My mother couldn't manage alone. I started running packages across the bay for quick money."

The confession hung between them, neither accusation nor excuse.

"Started small. Just cigarettes, some liquor." Carlos shrugged. "You take one step, then another. Each one makes sense at the time."

The heron stabbed suddenly into the water, emerging with a silver fish wriggling in its beak.

"By the time I realized how far I'd waded in, the shore was too distant to swim back." Carlos watched the bird swallow its catch. "Sometimes I still hear Abuelo's voice when I navigate these channels. Disappointed."

The sun hung low in the western sky, casting long shadows across the water as Carlos guided the boat toward what appeared to be an impenetrable wall of mangroves. The afternoon light filtered through the dense canopy, dappling the water's surface with golden patterns that shifted with each gentle wave.

"Nothing but thick brush ahead," Theo observed, squinting at the tangled mass of roots and branches.

Carlos smiled—not the warm smile of his childhood memories, but one tinged with pride and secrecy. "That's what everyone thinks." He eased the throttle forward, angling the boat toward a specific point in the vegetation that looked identical to the rest.

At the last moment, Carlos turned the boat sharply, revealing a narrow channel barely wider than their craft. Branches scraped against the aluminum sides as they slipped through the hidden passage.

"I've maintained this entrance for eight years," Carlos said, ducking beneath a low-hanging branch. "Replaced some natural growth with cultivated mangroves that I can move when needed."

The passage twisted through the dense growth, each turn revealing another corridor that seemed to lead nowhere until suddenly they emerged into a sheltered cove. Theo's breath caught as the space opened before them—a perfect natural harbor hidden from the world.

A small wooden dock extended from a patch of solid ground where a weathered shed stood partially concealed by vegetation. Various containers and equipment were organized beneath camouflage netting.

"Welcome to my office," Carlos said, cutting the engine and letting the boat drift toward the dock.

Theo noted how the entrance they'd passed through was nearly invisible from this side as well—a perfect defensive position. The entire setup spoke of years of careful planning, of a man who had prepared for every contingency.

"How many people know about this place?" Theo asked, his voice tight.

"Alive?" Carlos secured the boat to a weathered cleat. "Just you and me now."

The implication hung in the air between them as Carlos stepped onto the dock. He moved with the confidence of a man on his own territory, while Theo remained in the boat, suddenly aware of how completely he had surrendered control by following Carlos this far from civilization.

"Come," Carlos gestured toward the shed. "The light won't last much longer."

Theo hesitated at the threshold of what Carlos had called a "shed." The weathered exterior had suggested something rudimentary—perhaps a simple shelter with basic supplies. What greeted him inside shattered that assumption completely.

Carlos struck a match, touching it to a kerosene lamp that cast warm light across an interior that more resembled a military command post than a fisherman's hideout. The single room extended deeper than the exterior suggested, with walls lined with metal shelving units bearing an arsenal that made Theo's blood run cold.

"Make yourself comfortable," Carlos said, lighting additional lamps that revealed the full extent of the cache.

Assault rifles—at least a dozen—stood in neat rows alongside handguns arranged by caliber. Boxes of ammunition were stacked and labeled with military precision. On the opposite wall, communication equipment hummed quietly—satellite phones, radio transmitters, and what appeared to be signal jammers.

A medical station occupied one corner, stocked not with basic first aid supplies but with surgical equipment, IV bags, antibiotics, and morphine—enough to treat gunshot wounds without hospital assistance. Behind a partition, food supplies were organized meticulously—canned goods, dried proteins, purified water—enough to sustain multiple people for months.

"This isn't a fisherman's stash," Theo said, his voice barely audible. "This isn't even what a smuggler's lieutenant would have."

Carlos watched him carefully, eyes reflecting the lamplight. "You're observant."

"You told me you were just moving packages," Theo continued, connecting pieces of a puzzle he wished he'd never seen. "That you were a minor player caught in something bigger."

"Everyone is caught in something bigger," Carlos replied, checking the satellite phone's battery with practiced efficiency.

The realization settled over Theo like ice water. "You're not running from Mendoza. You are Mendoza."

Carlos didn't confirm or deny, but his silence spoke volumes. He simply continued his inventory, allowing Theo to process the truth.

Outside, darkness had fallen completely. The mangroves that had seemed like protection now felt like prison walls. Theo understood with crushing clarity that he stood in the inner sanctum of the very operation he had been fleeing—not with an ally who had escaped, but with the architect of it all.

Carlos moved to the door with deliberate steps, sliding a heavy metal bar across it. The sound of the lock engaging echoed through the shelter with finality. He turned to face Theo, and in that moment, something fundamental shifted in his demeanor. The weary fisherman persona dissolved completely, replaced by something harder and more refined.

"Sit," Carlos said. Not a request but a command, his voice dropping an octave. He gestured to a metal folding chair beside the communications array.

Theo remained standing, calculating the distance to the nearest weapon. "I prefer to stand."

"And I prefer that you sit." Carlos straightened to his full height, shoulders squaring. The wounds that had seemed to pain him earlier now appeared inconsequential. "We have things to discuss, and I find conversation more productive when everyone understands their position."

The lamplight cast long shadows across Carlos's face, accentuating the scar on his cheek. His eyes, previously warm with camaraderie, had cooled to the calculating gaze of a predator.

"My position?" Theo asked, buying time as he scanned the room for options.

Carlos smiled thinly. "You're alive because I allow it. That's your position." He moved toward a cabinet, retrieving two glasses and a bottle of amber liquid. "But it needn't be unpleasant. We can be civilized."

The space seemed to contract around Theo. What had momentarily felt like sanctuary now revealed itself as a cage—one with Carlos Mendoza as its keeper.

"What happens now?" Theo asked, finally lowering himself into the chair, recognizing that resistance in this moment would be futile.

Carlos poured two fingers of whiskey into each glass, sliding one toward Theo. "Now we have an honest conversation. No more stories about fishing routes or childhood memories. You've seen what I built here. You understand who I am."

Outside, the swamp creatures fell silent, as if the natural world itself recognized the dangerous current flowing through the shelter. The kerosene lamps flickered, casting dancing shadows across the arsenal that surrounded them.

"And who exactly are you planning to be to me?" Theo asked, leaving the whiskey untouched.

Carlos's smile didn't reach his eyes. "That depends entirely on how useful you decide to make yourself."

Carlos finally left Theo alone in a cramped sleeping area partitioned off from the main room by a hanging tarp. The space contained nothing but a narrow cot with a thin mattress, a wooden crate serving as a nightstand, and a small battery-powered lamp casting weak yellow light against the walls.

"Get some rest," Carlos had said, his voice carrying that new authoritative edge. "We'll discuss your options in the morning."

Options. As if Theo had any.

He sat on the edge of the cot, the metal frame creaking beneath his weight. Outside, night creatures resumed their chorus after Carlos's departure, filling the darkness with chirps, croaks, and distant splashes. The sounds that had once seemed threatening now felt like the only connection to a world beyond Carlos Mendoza's control.

Theo ran his hands through his hair, still damp from the day's journey through the mangroves. His muscles ached from the tension of constant vigilance. The full weight of his situation pressed down on him like the humid air—he was utterly dependent on the man who had revealed himself to be the very criminal mastermind he'd been trying to escape.

The realization crystallized with cold clarity: Carlos hadn't rescued him; he'd collected him.

Theo took inventory of his circumstances with scientific detachment, as if analyzing data from a field study. He had no idea where in the delta they were located. The twisting, turning journey through the mangroves had disoriented him completely. Even if he managed to steal the boat, he'd likely become hopelessly lost in the labyrinth of waterways.

No phone. No radio. No flare gun. No one who knew where he was.

He thought of his aunt Clara, who would be expecting his call after the diving trip. How long before she reported him missing? And even then, would anyone connect his disappearance to this hidden outpost?

The lamp flickered as if emphasizing the precariousness of his position. Theo stared at the weapons mounted on the wall beyond the tarp—tools of death that represented both threat and potential salvation. He had never fired a gun in his life. The likelihood of successfully overpowering Carlos, a man who had dispatched trained killers with ruthless efficiency, approached zero.

His mind returned to the moment Carlos had revealed his true identity. "I am Mendoza." Not just involved with the operation—its architect. The fisherman story contained fragments of truth, carefully selected to manipulate Theo's trust. How much of Carlos's shared history was fabrication? The grandfather? The hurricane? The reluctant entry into smuggling?

Theo recalled the precision with which Carlos had navigated the delta, the cold calculation in his eyes when he'd fired his weapon, the network of resources evidenced by this hidden command post. This was no desperate man caught in circumstances beyond his control. This was someone who created circumstances, who bent reality to his will.

A new thought surfaced, pushing through Theo's fear: Carlos needed something from him. Otherwise, Theo would already be dead, another body feeding the alligators in the delta. That need—whatever it was—represented Theo's only leverage.

The predator and prey dynamic Carlos had described while watching the alligator and wild hogs took on new meaning. Survival wasn't about strength alone, but about understanding the rules of engagement. About patience. About waiting for the right moment.

Theo stretched out on the cot, eyes fixed on the ceiling. Tomorrow, he would begin the most important performance of his life—convincing Carlos Mendoza he was worth keeping alive.

The door swung open with a metallic groan, startling Theo from his troubled half-sleep. Carlos entered carrying a steel thermos and two tin cups. Outside, the delta had fallen into complete darkness, the kind that swallowed even the memory of light. No moon penetrated the dense canopy above the hideout, and no distant glow betrayed the existence of civilization. They might as well have been the last two men on earth.

"You look like hell," Carlos observed, pouring steaming coffee into both cups. The rich aroma filled the small space, momentarily masking the mustiness of the shelter. "But at least you're alive. Many wouldn't be, after what you've seen."

Theo accepted the cup without speaking, wrapping his fingers around its warmth. He watched as Carlos unrolled several maps across the makeshift table constructed from wooden crates and an old door. Red markers indicated locations across the Gulf coastline, with timestamps and notations in a precise, economical hand.

"Come," Carlos commanded, gesturing toward the table. "It's time you understood your position."

Theo approached cautiously, studying not just the maps but the man before him. Carlos had changed into dry clothes—a simple black t-shirt and cargo pants that somehow made him look more dangerous than before. The façade of the simple fisherman had been completely abandoned, replaced by the calculating presence of a man accustomed to command.

"Three days from now," Carlos said, tapping a location on the map, "a shipment arrives here. Very valuable. Very dangerous to lose." His finger traced a route through the waterways. "The Coast Guard has increased patrols after our last... disagreement. We need a new approach."

"And I'm supposed to help with that?" Theo asked, careful to keep his tone neutral.

Carlos smiled thinly. "You're a marine biology student. You have legitimate reason to be collecting samples, studying the ecosystem." He pulled out a laminated identification card and slid it across the table. "The University of Texas Marine Science Institute now has a new research assistant."

Theo stared at the forged ID. His photo, but with the name Thomas Morrow.

"Your boat will carry specialized equipment," Carlos continued. "Equipment that contains my cargo. You'll navigate these channels under the perfect cover of academic research."

"And if I refuse?" Theo asked, though he already knew the answer.

Carlos didn't bother responding to the question. Instead, he unfolded a detailed chart of Coast Guard patrol patterns. "I've lost men. Good men. The authorities are closing in, which means this is my final operation in this territory." His dark eyes fixed on Theo. "After this, I disappear. You can disappear too—with enough money to fund whatever research you want for years. Or you can disappear another way."

The threat hung in the air between them, unnecessary but clear.

"I'm offering you a partnership of convenience," Carlos said, his voice softening into something almost reasonable. "One job. Three days. Then freedom."

Theo nodded slowly, appearing to consider the offer while his mind raced through possibilities. Carlos was revealing too much—either he truly intended to let Theo live after the job, or he had already decided Theo would never leave the delta alive.

"When do we start?" Theo asked, meeting Carlos's gaze with manufactured determination.

Carlos smiled, satisfied with the apparent capitulation. "We prepare tomorrow. You'll need to memorize the route, learn to operate the equipment, practice your cover story."

Beyond the shelter walls, an alligator bellowed in the darkness, the sound echoing across the water like distant thunder—nature's reminder that in this place, only the strongest survived.

Moonlight spilled through a break in the clouds, casting a silver pathway across the delta waters. Carlos stood at the shelter's entrance, his silhouette sharp against the night. Theo joined him, feeling the weight of what remained unspoken between them. The air hung heavy with moisture and consequence.

"Beautiful, isn't it?" Carlos gestured toward the moonlit water. "Most people never see the delta like this. They miss its secrets."

Theo remained silent, watching the ripples disturb the moon's reflection. A night heron called somewhere in the darkness, its cry echoing across the water.

"Before we begin tomorrow, there's something you need to do tonight." Carlos reached into his pocket and withdrew a satellite phone. "Call the Coast Guard."

Theo's pulse quickened. "What?"

"Call them. Report a suspicious boat you spotted while camping." Carlos handed him the phone, its screen glowing blue in the darkness. "Coordinates are already programmed. Just press send."

The phone felt impossibly heavy in Theo's hand. "I don't understand."

"It's simple. We're redirecting their attention." Carlos pointed across the water to where the delta opened into the Gulf. "That location is twenty miles from our actual route. While they investigate nothing, we move our cargo."

Theo stared at the device. This wasn't just information; this was action. Pressing that button would cross a line he could never uncross.

"This is your moment, Thomas Morrow." Carlos used the fake name deliberately, a reminder of the new identity awaiting him. "Are you in, or are you out?"

A fish jumped nearby, breaking the water's surface with a quiet splash. The delta continued its nighttime symphony, indifferent to human dilemmas.

"If I make this call, I become part of this." Theo's voice sounded strange to his own ears.

"You already are part of this." Carlos's tone hardened. "The moment you stepped onto my boat, you chose a side. The only question now is whether you're an asset or a liability."

The ultimatum hung between them, as tangible as the mist rising from the water. Theo thought of Aunt Clara, of the principles she'd instilled in him. He thought of the ranger station they'd passed, of the path not taken. He thought of the weapons inside the shelter and the wilderness surrounding them.

"What happens to the Coast Guard when they arrive at these coordinates?" Theo asked.

"Nothing. They find nothing, file a report about a false alarm, and move on." Carlos shrugged. "No one gets hurt."

"This time."

"This time," Carlos agreed, making no promises about the future.

Theo's finger hovered over the button. One press would implicate him in Carlos's operation. Refusal would mark him as expendable.

"You have thirty seconds to decide," Carlos said quietly. "After that, I make the decision for you."

The sliver of moonlight caught the water, illuminating their reflections—two figures standing at the edge of darkness. One the predator, one the prey. Or perhaps both predators now, of different kinds.

"Twenty seconds."

Theo thought of the maps inside, the routes, the patrol patterns. Information that could be valuable if he ever escaped. If he lived long enough to use it.

"Ten seconds."

The satellite phone weighed heavy in his palm. A simple action with complex consequences. The moment stretched between heartbeats, between breaths.

"Five."

Theo made his choice.

Chapter 8

T heo's finger pressed the button. The satellite phone emitted a soft beep, confirming the transmission.

"Good choice," Carlos said, taking the phone back. "Get some sleep. Tomorrow will test us both."

As Carlos disappeared inside, Theo remained at the water's edge, watching moonlight dance across the delta. What he'd just done couldn't be undone. He'd crossed a line, becoming complicit in Carlos's schemes, yet something in him refused to accept this as his final path.

The following afternoon, Theo sorted supplies in the shed while Carlos worked outside. Golden light filtered through the mangroves, casting dappled shadows that shifted with the breeze. He'd spent the morning memorizing the coastline maps, plotting potential escape routes while pretending to study their planned course.

Theo stepped outside for air, the humidity pressing against his skin. Carlos's voice drifted from behind the structure. Instinctively, Theo moved toward the sound, stopping behind a cluster of mangrove roots.

"He's perfect for what we need," Carlos was saying. "Young, educated, looks innocent. Coast Guard won't look twice."

A deeper voice responded – a burly man with a scar across his jaw stood facing Carlos. "Marcus wants him delivered tonight. Says you've been playing games too long."

"Marcus works for me, not the other way around," Carlos snapped. "The price just went up. The kid's got diving skills we can use for the underwater drops."

The smuggler spat. "Fine. Ten more, but that's it. You're lucky the boss values your routes more than he dislikes your attitude."

"Twenty more. He's a biology student – knows the reefs better than any of our other divers. Tell Marcus I'll bring him tomorrow. Need time to prepare him."

Theo's breath caught in his throat. The betrayal hit like a physical blow, knocking the air from his lungs. The friendly fisherman, the shared meals, the stories of Carlos's grandfather – all fabrications designed to manipulate him.

Carlos wasn't just working with the smugglers. He was their leader, their "boss," orchestrating everything from the shadows. And now he was selling Theo to Marcus like cargo.

As the men continued negotiating his fate, Theo backed away silently, mind racing. The shed contained weapons, supplies, and a boat. Carlos had unwittingly provided everything Theo needed to escape – if he could act before nightfall.

Theo slipped back inside, heart pounding against his ribs. He had hours, perhaps minutes, before Carlos completed his transaction. Whatever happened next would determine whether he survived or became another body lost in the endless delta.

The delta held its breath under a three-quarter moon. Midnight had come and gone, leaving behind a stillness broken only by the occasional splash of hunting fish and the whisper of wind through sawgrass. Inside Carlos's shed, three men lay sprawled in various states of drunken slumber, empty bottles scattered around them like fallen soldiers.

Theo counted Carlos's breaths—slow, deep, rhythmic. The other two men snored in counterpoint, one with a whistling undertone that had been grating on Theo's nerves for the past hour as he feigned sleep. He'd watched them drink, matching toast for toast with water while they consumed the whiskey Carlos had proudly produced. A celebration, Carlos had called it. Their final night before the big job.

A bull alligator bellowed somewhere in the darkness, the sound rolling across the water like distant thunder. Theo seized the moment, sliding from his pallet with the silence of prey that knows its life depends on stealth.

His bare feet found the floorboards that wouldn't creak—he'd memorized them during daylight hours, testing each while pretending to pace in boredom. The knife from Carlos's collection slid into his waistband, its weight both reassuring and terrifying. He'd never used a weapon against another person. Tonight, he hoped that wouldn't change.

A water bottle. Fishing line coiled into his pocket. Nothing more. Anything else would slow him down, make noise, betray him. The men's weapons tempted him—the handguns would offer protection—but Theo knew the sound of a shot would bring every smuggler within miles. Better to disappear like morning mist.

Carlos shifted in his sleep, mumbling something in Spanish. Theo froze, muscles burning with the effort of perfect stillness. Five seconds. Ten. Carlos's breathing deepened again, and Theo released the breath he'd been holding.

The door latch lifted under his fingers with agonizing slowness. A night heron called, its harsh squawk masking the faint click as the door opened just wide enough for Theo's slim frame to slip through.

Outside, the air hung heavy with moisture and the green decay smell of the marsh. Moonlight transformed the landscape into silver and shadow, casting the familiar into something alien and threatening. Theo oriented himself using the North Star, just visible through a break in the cypress canopy. Northwest would take him toward the wildlife refuge and, eventually, to a ranger station.

He moved with deliberate care, placing each foot before shifting his weight, testing for submerged branches that might snap. Twenty yards from the shed, a twig cracked beneath his heel with a sound that seemed to Theo as loud as a gunshot.

He dropped instantly, becoming part of the landscape, heart hammering against his ribs. One heartbeat. Two. Three. The shed remained dark and silent.

A mosquito whined near his ear. An alligator slid into water somewhere to his right. The delta continued its nighttime symphony, indifferent to the human drama playing out within its domain.

Theo rose and pressed forward, deeper into the marsh, away from Carlos and his men. The mud sucked at his feet, threatening to hold him in place, but he pulled free with each step, moving steadily into denser vegetation.

By the time the eastern sky began to lighten, he had put two miles between himself and the shed. Not enough, but a start. Carlos would wake soon, discover his absence, and the hunt would begin. Theo knew he wasn't just running from Carlos anymore—he was running from Mendoza, the man who controlled these waters and the men who traveled them.

The delta stretched before him, beautiful and merciless in the growing light.

Dawn painted the eastern sky in watercolors of amber and rose as Theo paused to catch his breath. Hours of careful movement through the treacherous delta had left him exhausted, his muscles trembling with fatigue. Each step had been calculated—a delicate balance between speed and stealth. Carlos would be awake by now, his rage could be sensed even across the miles that separated them.

The light revealed what darkness had hidden: a natural depression in the landscape, cradled between the twisted roots of three ancient mangroves. Tall sawgrass formed a natural barrier around the perimeter, creating a pocket nearly invisible unless standing directly above it. Nature had crafted a fortress that even the most experienced delta hunters might pass without notice.

"Perfect," Theo whispered, his biologist's mind already cataloging the advantages. The depression sat just high enough to avoid the daily tidal floods, while the mangrove roots offered structural support. The surrounding *Spartina alterniflora* grew dense and tall, their serrated edges a natural deterrent to casual exploration.

He slid down into the hollow, feeling the firmness of the ground beneath his feet. Not too muddy, not too dry—an ideal microclimate. Overhead, the mangrove canopy provided partial shade without completely blocking sunlight. The depression measured roughly eight feet across, with a deeper section at one end where rainwater had carved a natural basin.

Theo worked methodically, his academic knowledge transforming into survival skills. He gathered fallen branches, testing each for strength and flexibility. The mangrove's aerial roots became the foundation for a sleeping platform sixteen inches above the ground—high enough to avoid any unexpected water rise during the night.

"Aunt Clara would approve," he murmured, weaving smaller branches between the support structure. His hands, once accustomed to delicate laboratory work, now moved with newfound purpose, stripping bark to create cordage from the inner fibers.

The sound of an airboat engine growled in the distance. Theo froze, then worked faster. The noise faded, moving away from his position, but its message was clear: the search had begun.

At the depression's edge, Theo cleared a minimal workspace, careful to disturb the natural arrangement of vegetation as little as possible. Any change to the ecosystem might signal his presence to observant eyes. He gathered three specific plants—*Bacopa monnieri* for its antimicrobial properties, *Salicornia* for its edible stems, and cattail roots for their starch content.

The rising sun brought heat and humidity. Sweat soaked through Theo's shirt as he completed the final touches on his sanctuary. He created a small drainage channel to direct rainwater away from his sleeping area and into the natural basin where he could collect it for drinking.

Exhaustion threatened to overwhelm him as he finally collapsed onto his newly constructed platform. His body demanded rest, but his mind raced with plans and calculations. This hidden pocket in the marsh represented more than shelter—it was his first deliberate stand against Carlos and his men.

The marsh awakened fully around him—egrets wading through shallow waters, mullet jumping with soft splashes, dragonflies darting between reeds. Life continuing its ancient rhythms, indifferent to human conflicts.

Theo's eyelids grew heavy as he gazed up through the mangrove branches at patches of blue sky. He was no longer just running, no longer merely a victim. In this hidden sanctuary, crafted through knowledge and determination, he had become something else—a survivor preparing to fight back.

Mid-morning sunlight filtered through the mangrove canopy, casting dappled shadows across Theo's hidden sanctuary. After a few hours of fitful sleep, he awoke with a clear purpose. His parched throat and empty stomach demanded attention, but addressing these needs carried risk. Any visible smoke would draw Carlos's men like sharks to blood.

Theo knelt in the driest corner of his depression, mentally calculating distances and angles. His fingers traced a circle in the sandy soil, roughly twelve inches in diameter. The knife Carlos had unknowingly provided became his primary tool as he began to dig.

"Twelve inches deep, sloped sides," he muttered, recalling the specifications from a wilderness survival book he'd studied years ago. "Then the air intake tunnel, angled upward."

The sandy delta soil yielded easily to his blade. Theo worked methodically, placing the excavated dirt on a piece of bark to avoid scattering evidence of his digging. Sweat beaded on his forehead as the morning heat intensified, but he maintained his focus.

Two feet away from the main hole, he started a second, smaller excavation. This would become the air intake tunnel, the key to the fire pit's efficiency. He dug at an angle, carefully connecting the two chambers beneath the surface. When his knife broke through the wall of the main pit, he felt a small rush of accomplishment.

"The Dakota fire hole," he whispered, running his hand along the smooth interior. "Hidden flame, minimal smoke."

Theo gathered the driest materials he could find—small twigs from the underside of fallen branches, papery mangrove seed pods, and fibrous inner bark. He arranged these in the main chamber, creating a careful structure that would catch quickly and burn efficiently.

Before lighting it, he paused to scan the horizon. No movement, no sound of engines. Only the occasional call of marsh birds and the gentle rustle of wind through sawgrass. He placed a handful of damp leaves nearby, ready to smother the flame if necessary.

The knife's blade struck against a small piece of quartz he'd found, creating sparks that caught on the fine tinder. A tiny flame emerged, hungry for oxygen. As it grew, Theo added slightly larger fuel, watching with satisfaction as the fire drew air through the intake tunnel, creating a powerful draft.

"Perfect," he breathed, observing how the flames burned sideways rather than upward, contained within the earth.

He positioned his water bottle, wrapped in wet clay from the marsh edge, at the pit's opening. The clay would prevent the plastic from melting while allowing the water to boil. Next came the *Salicornia* stems and cattail roots, placed on flat stones around the perimeter to cook.

What little smoke emerged dispersed through the mangrove branches, diffused by the morning breeze. Theo constantly checked the surroundings, tensing at every distant sound. But the Dakota fire hole performed exactly as intended—intense heat with minimal signature.

As the water began to bubble, Theo added the *Bacopa* leaves, creating a tea that would help fight infection in the cuts and scrapes that covered his hands and arms. The roots and stems sizzled on their stone plates, filling the air with an earthy aroma.

For the first time since fleeing Carlos's shed, Theo felt a measure of control. This wasn't just about immediate survival—it was about establishing a sustainable position. Each small victory, each problem solved, built his confidence and resources.

The fire burned hot and clean, leaving almost no ash. When finished, Theo would fill both chambers with soil, erasing all evidence of his ingenuity. Carlos might control the waterways and have men searching every inlet, but Theo had something perhaps more valuable—the knowledge to exist undetected in plain sight.

Late afternoon sun slanted through the mangrove branches, casting long shadows across the water's edge where Theo worked. His fingers, already scraped and sore, methodically stripped flexible green reeds he'd harvested from the shallows. The rhythm of the work—gathering, stripping, weaving—transported him across time and space.

"You've got to feel the give in it, son," his father's voice echoed in his mind, clear as the day he'd first heard it. "Too rigid and it'll snap when a fish hits it. Too loose and they'll swim right through."

Theo's hands paused as the memory washed over him. He was twelve again, sitting in their small johnboat on Copano Bay, watching his father's weathered hands demonstrate the proper weaving technique for a fish trap.

"Nature provides everything you need," his father had said, eyes crinkling at the corners as he smiled. "Just gotta know how to ask for it properly."

Theo selected a Y-shaped branch he'd cut earlier, testing its strength before driving it into the soft mud at the water's edge. The trap would funnel fish through a narrow opening, making escape impossible once they entered. His father had called it a "patience trap"—set it right, then let the fish do the work.

"Dad would be proud," Theo whispered, then swallowed hard against the sudden tightness in his throat.

Three years since they'd spoken. Three years of silence after the argument about Theo's decision to pursue marine biology instead of joining the family construction business. Words like "waste of potential" and "throwing away generations of tradition" still stung when he allowed himself to remember them.

Theo secured the frame of the trap with cordage twisted from inner bark, his movements automatic, embedded in muscle memory from countless childhood lessons. His father might have disapproved of his career path, but those early teachings were now keeping him alive.

Another memory surfaced—his father showing him how to identify edible plants along the shoreline.

"Sea purslane," Theo murmured, recognizing the succulent leaves nearby. He gathered a handful, adding them to the small pile of foraged food beside him. "High in vitamins and minerals. Tastes salty but good."

The trap took shape under his practiced hands. Theo wove the reeds tighter at the funnel entrance, creating the illusion of an easy passage that would prove impossible to navigate in reverse. His father had taught him that lesson on his fourteenth birthday, after Theo had caught nothing all day.

"Fish are like people," his father had explained, demonstrating the technique. "They'll always take what looks like the easy way in, never thinking about how they'll get back out."

The irony wasn't lost on Theo now. He'd swum into Carlos's world without considering the exit strategy.

As the sun dipped lower, Theo placed the finished trap in the shallow water, anchoring it securely. He sat back on his heels, surveying his work with critical eyes, just as his father would have done.

"Not bad, Theodore," he could almost hear his father say, using his full name as he always did when offering rare praise.

Theo wiped sweat from his brow, feeling the ache of separation more acutely than any physical pain. If—when—he made it out of this delta alive, perhaps it was time to bridge that gap. To acknowledge that while their paths diverged, the roots remained connected.

He adjusted the trap one final time, ensuring the funnel faced into the current.

"Thanks, Dad," he whispered to the gathering dusk.

Thunder rolled across the delta as rain pummeled the canopy above Theo's shelter. Water streamed down the carefully positioned palm fronds, creating a natural curtain that concealed his position while keeping him relatively dry. The tropical downpour had arrived with startling suddenness, transforming the quiet marsh into a symphony of splashing droplets and swaying vegetation.

Theo sat cross-legged on his elevated platform, grateful for the storm's cover. The rain washed away scents and tracks, erasing evidence of his presence from any pursuing nose or eye. Nature provided not just sustenance, but security—a lesson his father had taught him. But now, as darkness descended and lightning occasionally illuminated his small sanctuary, different memories surfaced.

Uncle Bud. Not a blood relative, but his father's best friend who had become family. The quiet man with the thousand-yard stare who rarely spoke of Vietnam, except on certain nights when the whiskey loosened something inside him.

"They called us ghosts," Uncle Bud had told him once, during a camping trip when Theo was sixteen. "Force Recon. We moved like shadows through jungle that wanted to kill us almost as much as the enemy did."

Lightning flashed, and Theo closed his eyes, recalling Uncle Bud's weathered face in the campfire light.

"Survival ain't about being the strongest or having the most firepower," Bud had said, tapping his temple with a calloused finger. "It's about this. Outsmarting. Outthinking. Becoming the environment instead of fighting it."

Theo opened his eyes, surveying his shelter with new perspective. Uncle Bud would approve of the concealment, but would criticize the single exit point. Tactical error.

"Always have at least three ways out," Bud's voice echoed in his memory. "Path of least resistance, path of most resistance, and the one nobody expects."

Tomorrow, Theo would create additional escape routes. Perhaps a false trail leading away from his actual path.

The rain intensified, drumming against the leaves. Theo pulled out the knife he'd taken from Carlos's shed, examining its edge in the dim light. Uncle Bud had never glorified killing—quite the opposite. He spoke of it as a last resort, a failure of strategy.

"Violence means you've run out of better options," he'd said. "But sometimes, you run out of options."

Theo hoped it wouldn't come to that.

He recalled more of Uncle Bud's practical wisdom: move at night when visibility favors those who know the terrain; use natural materials for camouflage rather than manufactured ones that stand out; study enemy patterns before making any move; never establish routines that create predictability.

Most importantly: "Know what you're fighting for. Not just what you're fighting against."

Theo was fighting against Carlos and his operation, yes. But what was he fighting for? Getting home safely. Exposing the truth about Marcus and the dive operation. Justice for the other divers who might have been harmed.

The storm began to ease, rain softening to a gentle patter. Darkness had fully enveloped the delta now, and with it came Theo's time to move. Uncle Bud had always emphasized the tactical advantage of darkness for the prepared mind.

"The night belongs to the patient," he'd said.

Theo gathered his few possessions, securing them in the makeshift pack he'd fashioned from palm leaves. The storm's passing left a preternatural quiet in its wake, broken only by water dripping from leaves and distant animal calls.

He was no longer just surviving. He was resisting. Planning. Becoming the ghost that Uncle Bud had been in another jungle half a world away and decades in the past.

"Thanks, Uncle Bud," Theo whispered to the darkness as he slipped from his shelter into the night.

Dawn bled across the delta in ribbons of pale gold, illuminating Theo's hands as they worked deftly with reeds and cordgrass. For the fourth consecutive morning, he rose before the sun, venturing out from his sanctuary to expand what had become both his lifeline and defense system.

The marsh responded to his presence differently now. Birds no longer startled at his approach. Fish swam closer to investigate his shadow. The land had begun to accept him as part of its ecosystem rather than an intruder—a transformation that filled Theo with quiet pride.

"Adaptation isn't just survival," he murmured to himself, echoing Professor Harmon's ecology lectures. "It's integration."

Three hundred yards southwest of his shelter, Theo waded knee-deep through brackish water, positioning another bottle trap. He'd scavenged the plastic container from debris washed up after the storm, cutting and inverting the top to create a funnel that would allow fish to enter but confuse their exit. Similar traps now dotted the waters surrounding his position, each carefully placed where currents naturally channeled small fish.

Further out, where a natural depression created a wider pool, Theo had spent two evenings constructing a small dam system of mud, sticks, and stones. The receding tide would trap fish in these pools, creating a reliable food source that required minimal energy to harvest.

Every trap served dual purposes. Beyond providing sustenance, each was positioned to create an early warning system—any disturbance would alert him to movement through his territory.

Carlos and his men would trigger these alarms long before reaching his sanctuary.

Despite the gnawing in his stomach and the persistent ache in his muscles, Theo worked methodically, fingers bleeding occasionally as he wove intricate funnel traps from reeds. The pain was insignificant compared to the satisfaction of watching his network expand.

By dusk on the fifth day, Theo stood at the edge of his camp, surveying his work with a biologist's analytical eye and a survivor's pride. Twenty-three traps formed concentric rings around his position. Some for food, others rigged with small pebbles that would rattle against shells if disturbed—primitive but effective alarms.

The delta was no longer just his hiding place. It had become his ally, his weapon, his fortress. For the first time since washing ashore, Theo felt something beyond mere determination.

He felt ready.

Morning light dappled through the canopy as Theo examined the angry red line streaking from the base of his thumb toward his wrist. The cut—earned three days ago while fashioning a particularly stubborn reed trap—had begun to throb with a heat that radiated beyond the wound itself. Infection. In the wetland environment, even minor injuries could quickly become life-threatening.

"Damn it," he muttered, flexing his fingers and wincing at the stiffness. The swelling had increased overnight, and tiny beads of yellowish fluid gathered at the edges of the laceration.

He needed medicine, and he needed it soon.

Theo ventured from his shelter toward a small clearing he'd discovered two days prior. The patch of higher ground caught sunlight for most of the day, creating a microclimate where different plants thrived compared to the shadowy marsh. As he approached, his trained eye scanned the vegetation, cataloging species with the precision that had earned him top marks in botanical identification.

Then he saw it—a cluster of plants with serrated leaves and small white flowers with yellow centers, growing in abundance along the clearing's edge.

"Bidens alba," he breathed, relief washing through him. Spanish Needles.

Aunt Clara's voice echoed in his memory as clearly as if she stood beside him. "Most folks call these pesky weeds, but that's just ignorance talking. The Seminoles knew better—they called it medicine."

Theo knelt beside the plants, carefully selecting mature specimens with the most developed flowers. He worked methodically, harvesting a substantial amount while leaving enough to ensure the patch would continue thriving. Each movement was deliberate, despite the throbbing in his hand.

"Always thank the plant," Clara had instructed during countless foraging expeditions. "Gratitude keeps you humble, and humble keeps you learning."

"Thank you," Theo whispered to the swaying flowers, feeling slightly foolish but honoring the tradition nonetheless.

Back at his shelter, Theo crushed the freshest leaves between two smooth stones, creating a green paste that released a slightly bitter aroma. He added a few drops of water to form a poultice, then bound it directly to the infected cut with a strip torn from his t-shirt.

The cooling sensation was immediate, though whether from the plant's properties or simply the moisture, he couldn't be certain. Science and folklore intertwined in his mind as he recalled Clara explaining the plant's antimicrobial properties while simultaneously reciting Professor Harmon's lecture on phytochemical compounds in common weeds.

With the remaining plant material, Theo created two preparations. The first, a concentrated tea brewed in his makeshift container, would serve as an internal complement to the external treatment. The second, a dried cache of leaves and flowers stored in a waterproof pouch fashioned from bark, would ensure he had medicine for days to come.

As he sipped the bitter infusion, Theo's gaze drifted across his sanctuary. Five days of careful construction had transformed this hidden depression from mere shelter to something approaching a home. His traps provided food, his fire pit offered warmth and protection, and now, with the addition of medicine, he had addressed another critical need.

The Spanish Needles represented more than just treatment for his wound. They symbolized his growing integration with this environment—not just surviving in it, but understanding it, working with it rather than against it.

By afternoon, the angry red streak had already begun to fade. Theo changed the poultice, noting with satisfaction that the swelling had visibly decreased. As he rebound the wound with fresh plant material, a half-smile crossed his face.

"Thanks, Aunt Clara," he murmured to the empty air. "Guess I was paying attention after all."

The sixth morning dawned with purpose. Theo spread his wetsuit across a flat rock at the edge of his sanctuary, surveying it with critical eyes. The black neoprene that had once served him well underwater now presented a fatal flaw—it stood out starkly against the muted browns and greens of the delta. Any movement would catch the eye, particularly to trained observers like Carlos and his men.

"Time to disappear," Theo murmured, gathering his materials with methodical precision.

He began with mud, selecting different consistencies from various locations around his camp. The dark, silty mud from the water's edge would provide the base, while the reddish clay from higher ground would add contrast. He mixed these in a broad palm frond, adding water until he achieved a paste-like consistency that would adhere to the neoprene without flaking off when dry.

As he worked the mixture into the wetsuit, memories of childhood games flickered through his mind. Hide and seek with his cousins in the woods behind Aunt Clara's house had once been about fun—now similar principles would determine whether he lived or died.

"Nature doesn't create straight lines," he reminded himself, applying the mud in irregular patterns that mimicked the dappled light filtering through the canopy.

From a distance, Carlos watched the clearing through binoculars, unaware that Theo was observing his movements from behind a screen of cattails. The smuggler's face betrayed frustration as he scanned the horizon, seeing nothing but endless marsh.

For the next phase, Theo crushed various plant materials, creating natural dyes. Cordgrass yielded a pale yellow-green, while the berries of a nearby palmetto produced a deep bluish-purple. Cattail roots, when mashed and mixed with water, created a rich brown paste. He tested each on small patches of the wetsuit, noting how they appeared in different lights.

"The human eye catches movement first," his Uncle Bud had explained during deer hunting trips. "Then it looks for shapes it recognizes. Trick both, and you're invisible."

Working with single-minded focus, Theo attached lengths of fishing line to strategic points on the wetsuit. To these, he affixed small branches, reeds, and clumps of Spanish moss, creating a three-dimensional effect that would break up his silhouette. The result resembled the ghillie suits used by military snipers, though crafted from entirely local materials.

By midday, sweat dripped from his brow as he held up his creation. The transformation was remarkable—what had been a sleek diving suit now appeared as an amalgamation of the wetland itself. He laid it in a patch of sunlight to dry, turning it occasionally to ensure even curing.

Across the delta, the airboats had fallen silent. The absence of noise proved more unsettling than their persistent drone had been. The hunters were changing tactics, perhaps preparing to move on foot through the marshes. Theo's window for reconnaissance was narrowing.

As afternoon shadows lengthened, he donned the modified wetsuit, feeling the stiff material conform to his body. The added weight of the vegetation created a peculiar sensation, as if the marsh itself had become a second skin. He moved to the small pool of still water near his shelter and studied his reflection.

A stranger looked back at him—or rather, no one looked back at all. Where Theo should have been, there appeared only a shifting collection of marsh elements, vaguely human-shaped but fundamentally altered.

He was no longer prey hiding from predators. With this transformation, Theo had become something else entirely—a counterforce, prepared to move through Carlos's territory undetected. The student of plant biology had evolved into a tactical opponent.

"Tonight," he whispered to his reflection, "we hunt."

Pre-dawn mist clung to the delta as Theo eased through the marsh, his camouflaged form barely disturbing the cattails. Each step was calculated—heel first, then rolling to toe, distributing his weight to minimize sound and movement. The eastern sky held just enough light to navigate by, but not enough to reveal his presence to watchful eyes.

After two hours of patient progress, he reached the elevated ridge overlooking the smugglers' camp. Settling into a depression between two fallen cypress trunks, Theo arranged fronds around his position and became utterly still. Below him, the camp stirred to life as darkness retreated.

The operation was far larger than Theo had imagined. What he had initially taken for a temporary outpost was in fact a sophisticated base with semi-permanent structures. Three wooden buildings formed a loose triangle around a central clearing, while six tents housed what appeared to be rotating crew members. A natural harbor had been expanded, now accommodating five boats of varying sizes—from nimble skiffs to a thirty-foot craft with powerful outboard motors.

Men moved with military precision, checking equipment and conferring in low voices. Theo counted seventeen smugglers, each armed and displaying the hypervigilance of men accustomed to danger. Their routines revealed a disciplined organization—guards rotated hourly, communications equipment was constantly monitored, and weapons remained within arm's reach at all times.

"Patrol leaving in five," a voice called out, prompting three men to gather their gear and head toward the smallest boat.

Theo noted the time—5:43 AM—and made a mental mark of the patrol's composition and direction. This was the third such departure he'd witnessed, each following different headings but maintaining identical protocols. The smugglers were systematically searching the delta, expanding outward in a grid pattern. His decision to move camp had been timely.

At 6:15, the atmosphere in the camp shifted. Men straightened their postures and conversations ceased as a figure emerged from the largest building.

Carlos.

Gone was any trace of the battered fisherman. He walked with the confidence of absolute authority, dressed in clean tactical gear and carrying a holstered sidearm. The other smugglers afforded him a wide berth, their body language communicating both respect and fear.

"Status report," Carlos commanded, his voice carrying clearly in the morning air.

A lieutenant approached with a tablet, gesturing to a digital map as he spoke. "Eastern quadrants clear. Northern search continuing. Southern teams report nothing since yesterday's false alarm near the old ranger station."

Carlos nodded, studying the map. "The Coast Guard?"

"Still focused on the western channel after that tip. Their patrol boats have been redirected exactly as planned."

Theo's stomach twisted. The "tip" had been his call from the satellite phone—the one Carlos had pressured him to make. He had indeed become an unwitting accomplice in their operation.

Carlos turned toward the harbor, pointing to the largest boat. "Prepare for tomorrow's shipment. I want double security on the transfer point. Our buyer is nervous after the Matagorda incident."

"And the student?" the lieutenant asked.

Carlos's expression hardened. "Find him. He's seen too much."

As the camp fully awakened, Theo remained motionless, absorbing every detail. The launch schedule, the guard rotations, the communication protocols—all valuable intelligence. But most critical was the confirmation of tomorrow's shipment and the undeniable truth about Carlos.

The man who had posed as his savior was indeed the mastermind behind it all. And now, with the full scope of the operation laid bare before him, Theo understood the magnitude of what he faced—not just a few smugglers, but an organized criminal enterprise with resources, discipline, and a leader who wanted him eliminated.

Dusk painted the delta in amber and purple as Theo maintained his vigil above the smugglers' camp. He'd remained motionless for nearly twelve hours, muscles cramping from the sustained stillness, but unwilling to surrender his vantage point. The camp's rhythm had revealed itself throughout the day—patrol rotations, communication schedules, supply deliveries—each detail meticulously recorded in his mental inventory.

As twilight deepened, floodlights snapped on around the perimeter, casting harsh white pools across the clearing. The camp's energy shifted. Men who had been lounging now stood alert, checking weapons and positioning themselves at strategic points around the harbor.

A radio crackled. "Incoming. Five minutes out."

Carlos emerged from the main building, surveying the preparations with a critical eye. "No mistakes tonight," he called out, his voice carrying across the water. "Our buyer pays premium for undamaged merchandise."

Merchandise. The word hung in the air, clinical and detached.

Theo's focus sharpened as a low thrumming sound approached from the east—not the high whine of patrol boats but the deeper pulse of a larger vessel. Minutes later, a weathered fishing trawler materialized from the darkness, its running lights dimmed. It eased into the harbor with practiced precision, the engine throttling down to a whisper.

Four armed men positioned themselves around the boat's stern as the captain cut the engines. A fifth man unlocked a heavy padlock on what appeared to be the hold. The hatch swung open.

What emerged wasn't cargo.

People. Human beings.

One by one, they climbed from the hold—men and women of varying ages, their clothes soiled and hanging loose on thin frames. Theo counted twenty-three individuals, moving with the stunned compliance of the utterly defeated. Two guards directed them into a line with practiced efficiency, while another passed through their ranks, removing what looked like crude plastic wristbands.

"Processing tags," a smuggler announced, dropping the collected bands into a bucket of what Theo recognized as acid. "All accounted for."

Carlos walked the line, inspecting each person with the detached interest of a rancher surveying livestock. He paused before a young woman who couldn't have been more than twenty, her eyes downcast.

"This one's worth double," Carlos remarked to his lieutenant. "Make sure she's separated for the premium buyer."

Bile rose in Theo's throat. The academic understanding of human trafficking transformed into visceral reality before his eyes. These weren't just smugglers moving contraband—they were trafficking human lives.

A covered truck backed toward the group, its rear doors swinging open to reveal a modified cargo area with bench seating. Armed guards herded the people inside, ignoring a muffled sob from somewhere in the group.

Theo's hands trembled against the earth. The stakes had shifted entirely. His predicament was no longer just about personal survival or exposing a drug operation. These were lives—people with families, dreams, futures—being sold like commodities.

The realization settled into his bones with cold certainty: he couldn't simply escape and report what he'd seen. By then, these people would vanish into a system designed to erase their existence. Whatever evidence he might eventually provide would come too late for them.

As the truck's doors slammed shut and the engine rumbled to life, Theo made a decision that transformed his mission entirely. This wasn't just about getting home anymore. It wasn't even about justice in some abstract sense.

It was about those twenty-three faces. About the young woman Carlos had marked for "premium" sale. About the fundamental wrongness of human beings in cages.

For the first time since washing ashore on the peninsula, Theo's path forward became absolutely clear. Whatever the risk, whatever the cost, he could not leave these people to their fate.

The darkest hour before dawn draped the delta in a suffocating blackness. Guards at the smugglers' camp slouched at their posts, victims of the human body's natural rhythm—that treacherous window when alertness ebbed to its lowest point regardless of training or discipline.

Theo moved like water through the shadows. Five nights of observation had revealed the pattern: twenty minutes past three, the eastern perimeter guard would duck behind the supply shed for a cigarette, creating a twelve-minute blind spot in their security.

Tonight, he would exploit it.

His camouflaged wetsuit melded with the darkness as he slipped past the first sentry post. The knowledge that twenty-three lives hung in the balance had transformed his fear into cold calculation. The weight of the homemade siphon—fashioned from scavenged tubing and a squeeze bulb salvaged from an abandoned fish tank—pressed against his thigh.

The fuel depot appeared ahead—four 55-gallon drums elevated on wooden pallets at the camp's edge. Close enough to the water for easy refueling operations, far enough from the main buildings to minimize fire risk. Smart placement, but isolated. Vulnerable.

Theo froze as a twig snapped somewhere to his left. He sank into a crouch, becoming part of the landscape, breathing shallow and controlled. A guard passed fifteen feet away, radio crackling with static, never glancing in Theo's direction. The man rounded the corner of a building and disappeared.

Sixty seconds later, Theo reached the drums.

"Basic chemistry," he whispered to himself, unscrewing the cap on the first barrel. The sharp tang of diesel fuel hit his nostrils. "Water and diesel don't mix."

From his pack, he extracted a flexible container filled with marsh water heavy with organic sediment—a deadly contaminant for marine engines. He inserted the siphon tube and began working the bulb, watching as the murky liquid disappeared into the fuel supply.

One barrel. Two. Three. Four.

The beauty of the sabotage lay in its subtlety. The heavier water would settle at the bottom of each drum, where the outlet pipes drew fuel. The engines wouldn't fail immediately—they'd run normally until the contaminated fuel reached the filters and injection systems, causing failures miles from shore.

No dramatic explosion. No immediate alarm. Just inevitable mechanical failure at the worst possible moment for the smugglers.

Theo secured the last barrel cap and wiped away any trace of his presence. As he prepared to retreat, a voice carried from the main building—Carlos, engaged in a heated phone conversation.

"I don't care what your concerns are. The merchandise moves tomorrow night. The buyers have already paid half."

Tomorrow night. The timeline had accelerated.

Theo slipped back into the marsh, leaving no sign of his intrusion. By the time he reached his hidden shelter, the eastern sky had begun to lighten. He stripped off his mud-caked wetsuit and collapsed onto his makeshift bed, muscles trembling with spent adrenaline.

He'd crossed a line tonight—from survival to resistance. From prey to predator. There would be no turning back.

"First step," he murmured to the brightening sky. The contaminated fuel would buy time—perhaps a day, perhaps only hours—but it was something. A beginning.

Tomorrow would bring consequences, both for his actions and inaction. The thought of those people loaded into trucks, of the young woman Carlos had marked for "premium" sale, hardened his resolve.

Sleep claimed him as birds began their morning chorus, nature indifferent to the human drama unfolding within its bounds. In his dreams, Theo saw the faces of the trafficked people, their eyes fixed on him with an unspoken question: What will you do next?

Chapter 9

The eastern sky brightened with the first whisper of daylight as Theo emerged from his shelter, moving with the quiet confidence of someone at home in the wilderness. Gone was the panicked student who had washed ashore weeks earlier. In his place stood a leaner, more deliberate figure—a man who read the landscape like text on a page.

Theo knelt at the water's edge, fingers probing the soft mud until they found the firm, rope-like rhizomes of cattail plants. He harvested them with practiced efficiency, sliding his knife beneath the surface and extracting the starchy roots that had become a staple of his diet. His movements disturbed nothing unnecessary, leaving most of the plant intact to continue growing.

"Thank you," he whispered to the plants, a ritual he'd developed that connected him to Aunt Clara's teachings about reciprocity with the natural world.

The rising sun cast long shadows across the delta as Theo moved to a patch of wild rice he'd discovered three days earlier. The grains weren't fully mature, but he collected what was ready, his fingers nimble from repetition. His mental map of food sources had expanded daily—wild grapes near the limestone outcropping, blackberries in the transition zone between marsh and woodland, even a stand of pawpaw trees beginning to bear their custard-like fruit.

Birds called overhead, announcing the day to one another. A great blue heron stalked the shallows thirty yards away, its patience a lesson Theo had internalized. They were colleagues now, fellow hunters in this watery realm.

Theo paused at a small clearing to transfer his morning's harvest to the woven bag at his hip. His body had adapted to this new existence—shedding unnecessary weight, developing calluses where they were needed, strengthening muscles used for climbing, wading, and carrying. Even his senses had sharpened, attuning to the subtle changes in wind direction and the warning calls of wildlife.

The theoretical knowledge from his biology studies had transformed into practical wisdom. He no longer simply identified plants—he understood their patterns, their relationships with the soil and water, their uses beyond mere sustenance.

As the heat of the day began to build, Theo returned to his camp with his bounty. The smugglers' compound lay miles to the south, a world away from this sanctuary he'd created. Here, in this pocket of wilderness, he had found more than just survival—he had discovered a forgotten connection to the natural world that his academic studies had only hinted at.

Theo spread his morning's harvest on a flat stone, sorting and preparing each item with reverence. Today's work was just beginning.

Mid-morning sun filtered through the canopy as Theo knelt at the northwestern approach to his camp. His fingers worked with practiced precision, bending a flexible sapling into a tension spring for a snare. The natural materials blended seamlessly with the surrounding vegetation—a deliberate choice that made his traps nearly invisible to the untrained eye.

Across the delta, Carlos and his men continued their search, but they hunted with the arrogance of those who believed themselves apex predators. They didn't understand that the marsh had accepted

Theo as one of its own, teaching him its secrets while concealing his presence.

"Pressure, not force," Theo murmured to himself, echoing his father's advice about setting triggers. He tested the tension on the sapling, ensuring it would release with just the right amount of pressure. The design was simple but effective—a small game trap that could provide food or, with slight modifications, serve as a perimeter alarm.

Twenty yards to the east, a similar trap waited, though this one Theo had modified with a trip wire connected to a collection of shells and dried seedpods suspended in a hollow reed. Any disturbance would create a distinctive rattle, audible only to someone listening for it. Not loud enough to give away his position, but sufficient warning of an approach.

The delta itself had become Theo's ally. He'd learned to read its patterns—which areas flooded during high tide, where solid ground could support weight, which passages remained navigable. This knowledge formed the foundation of his defensive strategy. Carlos's men would be forced to approach along predictable routes, each now lined with Theo's silent sentinels.

"Nature provides everything we need," Aunt Clara had often said. Theo now understood the depth of that wisdom as he fashioned fishhooks into trigger mechanisms and wove cordgrass into nearly invisible lines. His biology training helped him identify materials with the necessary properties—flexibility, strength, resilience—while his growing wilderness skills allowed him to transform those materials into practical tools.

By midday, Theo had established a complete perimeter. Eight snares for small game doubled as alarms. Three trip lines with shell-rattles guarded the most likely approach paths. A series of mud pits covered with light vegetation would capture footprints of any intruders, allowing him to track their movements even if they managed to avoid his other measures.

Standing back to survey his work, Theo felt a quiet pride. The defensive network was invisible unless you knew exactly what to look for—and even then, it required a trained eye to spot the subtle disturbances in the natural pattern. Carlos's men, accustomed to the brute force approach of firearms and intimidation, would likely miss these signs entirely.

Theo retrieved his water bottle and took a measured sip. The water tasted of the delta—slightly brackish but clean in its own way. He had come to appreciate its distinctive flavor, so different from the filtered water of his previous life.

From his vantage point, he could see three different escape routes he'd prepared—one leading deeper into the marsh, another toward higher ground, and a third that would take him to a hidden canoe he'd discovered and repaired. No matter which direction danger approached from, he had options.

A distant airboat engine growled somewhere beyond the eastern channel, then faded. Theo remained motionless, listening as the sound diminished. His boundaries would hold for now, but he harbored no illusions about the temporary nature of his sanctuary. Sooner or later, the lines he'd drawn would be tested.

He touched the knife at his belt—once Carlos's, now his—and continued his circuit of the perimeter, checking each trap and trigger with methodical care. The boundary between prey and predator had shifted, and Theo stood firmly on the side of the hunter.

Late morning sunlight danced on the surface of the secluded tidal pool, casting rippling patterns across its sandy bottom. Theo approached cautiously, scanning the surrounding area before setting down his handmade basket containing cattail fibers, dried moss, and several broad leaves carefully folded into packets.

This daily ritual had become as essential to his survival as food or shelter. The pool, nestled between two weather-worn limestone outcroppings, offered both privacy and relatively clean water—a luxury Theo no longer took for granted.

"Cleanliness isn't vanity out here," he murmured, recalling Professor Harmon's lecture on field hygiene. "It's survival."

Theo stripped off his camouflaged wetsuit, wincing as the neoprene peeled away from a raw spot on his shoulder. His body told the story of his time in the delta—a map of scratches, bruises, and calluses that hadn't existed three weeks ago. Each mark represented a lesson learned, often painfully.

The cool water embraced him as he waded in, sending a shiver up his spine. He'd timed his arrival precisely, when the incoming tide refreshed the pool but before it rose high enough to make the area visible from the main channel. Such calculations had become second nature.

First came the salt water rinse, moving methodically from face to feet. Then, using a handful of fine sand mixed with crushed yucca root—nature's soap—Theo scrubbed his skin with careful attention. The abrasive mixture removed grime and dead skin while the saponins in the yucca created a mild lather.

"The human body is remarkably resilient," Aunt Clara had once told him while treating a fishing hook embedded in his thumb. "But you have to give it the right conditions to heal."

Those words guided his actions now as he inspected each cut and scrape. A particularly angry-looking gash on his forearm received special attention—cleaned thoroughly, then packed with a poultice of chewed plantain leaves. He secured it with strips of clean bark fiber, his fingers working with practiced efficiency.

Theo moved to his feet next, where the constant exposure to marsh water had begun to cause problems. He dried them carefully with moss, applied a mixture of pine resin and cattail fluff to the cracked skin between his toes, then wrapped them in the broad leaves he'd collected.

"Prevention," he reminded himself. "Always easier than cure."

The wetsuit received similar treatment—rinsed thoroughly, scrubbed with sand, and laid out on sun-warmed stone to dry. He'd learned that maintaining his few possessions was as important as maintaining his body.

From somewhere in the distance came the faint sound of an airboat. Theo froze, listening intently, but the engine noise faded rather than approached. Still, the interruption served as a reminder of the constant danger.

While waiting for his skin to dry, Theo filtered water through a multi-layered system of sand, charcoal, and grass he'd constructed at the pool's edge. The resulting water wasn't pure by any scientific standard, but it was clean enough to drink without immediate consequences—another compromise between ideal and reality.

As he dressed in his now-dry wetsuit, Theo reflected on how these mundane tasks had taken on profound importance. In his previous life, hygiene had been automatic, thoughtless. Now it represented discipline, adaptation, and a refusal to surrender to circumstances.

The ritual complete, Theo gathered his supplies and erased all evidence of his presence. No footprints remained in the sand, no broken vegetation marked his path. He'd become a ghost in the delta—present but unseen, vulnerable yet persistent.

He touched the healing cut on his arm, feeling the plantain poultice beneath the wrapping. His body was both his greatest asset and his greatest liability in this struggle. Like the delta itself, it required constant attention, respect, and care to remain in balance.

Midday sun beat down on the small clearing, creating a pocket of warmth in the otherwise cool delta. Theo knelt at the edge, his eyes scanning the riot of green with the practiced assessment of a botanist. Where others might see weeds, he recognized allies.

"There you are," he whispered, spotting the telltale white flower heads of Bidens alba—Spanish Needles—growing in abundance along the clearing's southern edge. The plants stood tall and vibrant, their compound leaves reaching toward the zenith sun.

Theo approached reverently, remembering Professor Morales's lessons on medicinal ethnobotany. "Plants produce their highest concentration of essential oils when the sun is directly overhead," she had explained, tapping her watch at precisely noon. "Indigenous healers understood this timing was crucial for maximum potency."

He selected plants with care, avoiding those with yellowing leaves or insect damage. The healthiest specimens would contain the strongest antimicrobial compounds. His fingers worked methodically, harvesting just enough without depleting the stand—another lesson from Aunt Clara.

"Take what you need, not what you want," her voice echoed in his memory. "The plants are giving their lives for yours. Honor that sacrifice."

The Spanish Needles released their distinctive aroma as he crushed them between his palms. Theo breathed deeply, identifying the complex scent profile that confirmed he had the right species. Unlike Carlos and his men, who blundered through the marsh seeing only obstacles, Theo read the landscape like a familiar textbook.

He separated his harvest into two piles—one for a poultice, another for tea. The stems and tougher leaves went into his makeshift mortar, a depression worn into driftwood. Using a smooth river stone as a pestle, he ground them into a fibrous paste, adding drops of water to extract the medicinal oils.

"The compound you're after is thiophene," Professor Morales had said. "Remarkable antibacterial properties, particularly against Staphylococcus."

Theo applied the resulting paste to his most troublesome wounds, feeling the slight sting that indicated active compounds at work. The remainder he wrapped in leaves for later application.

For the tea, he selected the most tender leaves and flower heads, crushing them lightly before placing them in his bamboo water container. The sun-warmed water would draw out different compounds—anti-inflammatory agents that would work from within.

As he finished his preparations, a sense of quiet pride filled him. His education, once just theory and laboratory experiments, had transformed into practical knowledge that kept him alive. Where Carlos relied on weapons and brutality, Theo wielded understanding of the natural world—a different kind of power, but no less effective.

The Spanish Needles would fight infection, reduce inflammation, and help maintain his strength. In this unforgiving environment, nature itself had become his most reliable ally.

Early afternoon sun filtered through the canopy as Theo knelt beside his Dakota Fire Hole, a marvel of efficient design nestled between three cypress knees. The fire burned with remarkable intensity despite its small size, flames licking upward from the twelve-inch pit. Unlike a conventional campfire that would broadcast his location across the delta, this underground system remained nearly invisible.

"Feed the dragon slowly," Theo murmured, remembering his father's words as he carefully added finger-thin sticks to the flames.

The fire responded with increased heat rather than smoke, drawing oxygen through the sloping tunnel he'd dug at a precise angle. This created a natural draft, pulling air under the coals and producing a clean, hot burn. Above the pit, Theo had constructed a drying rack from green saplings, where strips of catfish and two skinned rabbits hung in neat rows.

He leaned forward, inspecting a strip of fish with critical eyes. The flesh had contracted, darkening at the edges as moisture evaporated. With practiced movements, he rotated each piece, ensuring even exposure to the heat while preventing any single portion from cooking rather than drying.

"Preservation, not consumption," he reminded himself, fighting the immediate hunger that gnawed at his stomach.

The Dakota Fire Hole represented more than just a cooking method—it embodied Theo's evolution from reactionary survivor to strategic planner. Three days ago, he'd caught more fish than he could immediately eat, forcing a decision: waste the surplus or find a way to extend its usefulness. The answer had come from deep childhood memories of a wilderness survival book that had fascinated him long before he understood its practical applications.

A wisp of smoke curled upward, and Theo immediately adjusted the airflow by clearing the intake tunnel with a stick. Smoke meant visibility. Visibility meant discovery. Discovery meant death—or worse, capture by Carlos and his men.

The rhythm of the work calmed him. Turn the meat. Check the fire. Listen for approaching danger. Repeat. Each action deliberate, each moment productive. Unlike his first panicked days in the delta, Theo now operated with purpose, his movements economical and precise.

Above the rack, he'd strung several cordgrass baskets containing wild rice and pawpaw fruits, using the heat to reduce their moisture content without cooking them. Nothing was wasted, nothing overlooked. The bounty of the marsh transformed into sustainable nutrition through ancient techniques refined by necessity.

"Three weeks of food security," he calculated, surveying his growing stockpile.

This wasn't just about tomorrow's meal—it was about creating options, building a foundation that would allow him to act rather than merely react. With preserved food, he could venture farther from camp, observe the smugglers' operations longer, or weather periods when hunting became impossible.

A red-winged blackbird called from nearby, its distinctive conk-la-ree breaking the silence. Theo froze, listening for any sound that didn't belong to the natural chorus of the marsh. Satisfied they remained alone, he returned to his work.

The smoke-preservation technique represented a pivotal realization: Carlos might control the waterways and command armed men, but Theo had become something altogether different—a ghost who moved between worlds, patient and prepared. While the smugglers crashed through the delta with their boats and guns, Theo had melded with it, drawing strength from its rhythms and resources.

He adjusted the final pieces on the drying rack and sat back on his heels, surveying his work with quiet satisfaction. The fire burned steadily below, nearly invisible but intensely effective—much like Theo himself.

The new moon cast no light over the delta as Theo approached the smugglers' camp. Midnight had come and gone, leaving only the distant chorus of frogs and the occasional splash of hunting fish to break the silence. His mud-darkened wetsuit blended perfectly with the shadows as he crouched at the perimeter, watching for signs of movement.

Three guard rotations. That's what he'd observed over four nights of surveillance. The first shift ended at midnight, followed by a fifteen-minute window when attention wavered as sleepy men replaced alert ones. The second shift guards were the weakest link—often fighting fatigue by 2 AM, their movements becoming predictable.

Tonight, Theo would exploit that pattern.

He pressed his body against the damp earth, counting his heartbeats to maintain calm. The camp sprawled before him—six tents, the main shed where Carlos slept, and the supply area near the eastern edge. Two guards patrolled the perimeter while another dozed in a chair near the radio equipment.

"Predictable," Theo whispered to himself, noting how the guards followed the same route they had for the past three nights.

When both guards converged at the north end, Theo moved. His feet found solid ground between patches of mud, leaving no tracks as he slipped toward the supply area. The smell of diesel and cigarettes grew stronger with each careful step.

A stack of plastic containers stood partially covered by a tarp. Theo eased between them, scanning for what he needed most. Unlike his first days in the marsh when panic drove his decisions, he now moved with purpose, mentally cataloging priorities against risks.

A small plastic toolbox sat unattended on a wooden crate. Theo eased it open, finding a treasure trove inside—a silver Zippo lighter, several packages of fishing hooks and line, and a small roll of duct tape. He pocketed these items silently, careful not to disturb the remaining contents.

Twenty feet away, a guard coughed and shifted position. Theo froze, becoming one with the shadows until the man turned away.

Next, he spotted a first aid kit hanging from a nail on the supply shed. Taking it would be noticed eventually, but the risk balanced against need. His infected cut had improved with plant medicine, but proper antiseptic would prevent future problems.

With three quick steps, Theo crossed to the shed, unhooked the kit, and retreated to the shadows. Inside, he found gauze, antibiotic ointment, and—most valuable of all—a small bottle of iodine tablets for water purification.

A sudden laugh from the dozing guard sent a jolt of adrenaline through Theo's system. The man was talking in his sleep, muttering Spanish phrases between chuckles. Theo used the noise as cover to move toward his final target—the food prep area.

There, in a plastic container, sat the object of his desire: salt. Not just any salt, but refined table salt—something impossible to find in the marsh and essential for preserving meat properly. Theo filled a small pouch with the white crystals, careful to take only a portion that might be attributed to spilling.

As he secured his treasures, Theo felt a shift within himself. He was no longer just surviving—he was fighting back. Each item taken weakened Carlos's operation in some small way while strengthening Theo's position.

A guard's footsteps approached the supply area. Theo melted into the underbrush at the perimeter, his breathing controlled despite the danger. The guard passed within three feet, never noticing the shadow that didn't belong.

Minutes later, Theo vanished into the marsh, carrying more than just supplies—he carried a new confidence. The hunted had become the hunter, the victim now a saboteur. As the camp disappeared behind him, Theo allowed himself a small smile. Tonight was just the beginning.

Pre-dawn light painted the eastern horizon in subtle gradations of blue as Theo moved through the delta with practiced silence. The marsh grass parted around him without sound, his camouflaged wetsuit breaking his silhouette into fragments that melted into the landscape. Three hours before sunrise marked the perfect time—when night guards grew sluggish and day guards had not yet stirred.

This morning, Theo wasn't hunting supplies. He was planting seeds of a different kind.

At the northwestern patrol point—a small rise where Carlos's men regularly stood watch—Theo knelt and carefully arranged seven smooth stones in a perfect circle. Inside, he placed a single Spanish Needle flower, its yellow petals vivid against the dark mud. Nothing in nature formed such precise geometry; the message was unmistakable: someone had been here, someone who wasn't afraid.

"Let them wonder," Theo whispered to the darkness.

Half a mile east, where the main patrol path narrowed between two cypress stands, Theo pressed his boot prints deeply into the soft earth, then deliberately walked backward in his own tracks before veering into the water. To anyone following, it would appear as though a man had simply vanished—or perhaps emerged from nowhere. The psychological impact would outweigh any tactical advantage.

The delta observed Theo's work with indifferent eyes. A night heron watched from a nearby branch as he meticulously placed three Spanish Needle plants in a triangle beside the path leading to the southern lookout. The plants weren't random—they were the same medicinal herbs he'd used to heal his infection. A subtle reminder that he wasn't just surviving; he was thriving.

In the smugglers' world, fear came from direct threats—guns, knives, explicit warnings. But Theo understood a different kind of fear: the creeping dread of the unknown. Every stone arrangement, every footprint that defied explanation, every carefully placed plant spoke a message: I see you, but you cannot see me.

Near the eastern perimeter, Theo found the crude lean-to where the morning guard took shelter during rain. He slipped inside and left a small bundle of dried Spanish Needles tied with marsh grass on the makeshift seat. The guard would find it when he sought refuge—a gift from a ghost.

Dawn approached as Theo completed his circuit, moving toward the safety of his hidden camp. He paused at the water's edge, studying the first golden rays touching the cypress tops. In the distance, a smuggler's voice called out—the morning shift change beginning.

Soon they would find his messages. Soon the whispers would start.

Theo smiled, remembering Professor Harmon's ecology lectures about predator-prey relationships. "Sometimes," the professor had said, "the most effective hunting strategy isn't the direct attack, but creating an environment where the prey never feels safe."

Carlos and his men had guns, boats, and numbers. Theo had knowledge, patience, and now, psychological leverage. They would waste energy looking over their shoulders, jumping at shadows, questioning each other's vigilance. Meanwhile, Theo would continue his careful observation, identifying weaknesses, building strength.

As he slipped back into the protective embrace of the marsh, Theo felt a quiet confidence settle in his chest. Physical survival he had mastered in these past days. Now he was fighting a different battle—one for mental dominance.

The Spanish Needles in his pocket brushed against his hand, reminding him of Aunt Clara's wisdom: "Plants have power beyond healing the body—they can speak to the soul."

Today, they would speak of fear.

Mid-morning sun beat down on the delta, turning the marshland into a shimmering cauldron of heat and humidity. From his vantage point in the hollow of a massive cypress, Theo watched four of Carlos's men slog through the marsh, their faces slick with sweat and twisted in frustration. The psychological warfare he'd begun at dawn was bearing fruit faster than he'd anticipated.

"I'm telling you, someone's out here messing with us," growled a stocky man with a neck tattoo, slapping at mosquitoes that swarmed his exposed skin. "Those rocks didn't arrange themselves."

"Shut up and keep looking," snapped the leader—a lean, hard-faced man Theo recognized as Carlos's lieutenant. "Carlos wants this ghost found by sundown."

Theo allowed himself a small smile. They'd found his messages, all right. And now they were dancing to his tune.

Twenty yards ahead of the search party lay a patch of deceptively solid-looking ground that Theo knew concealed knee-deep mud. Yesterday, he'd carefully placed three broken reeds pointing directly toward it—a sign that would appear to the untrained eye as someone's hasty passage.

The leader spotted the bent reeds and gestured sharply. "This way. Fresh trail."

Theo watched as all four men charged forward, then sank suddenly to their thighs in viscous black mud. Their curses echoed across the water as they struggled to extract themselves, weapons held awkwardly above their heads.

"Goddamn swamp!" The tattooed man hurled his cap into the water. "We're chasing ghosts while that college kid is probably halfway to Corpus by now!"

But the leader wasn't convinced. "Carlos says he's still here. And Carlos is never wrong."

The delta itself seemed to conspire with Theo. A cloud of mosquitoes descended on the search party, drawn by their exertion and exposed skin. The men's slapping and cursing intensified as they finally extracted themselves from the mud pit.

Theo slipped down from his perch and moved silently through the underbrush, circling behind them. He'd prepared another false trail leading to a nest of fire ants he'd discovered yesterday—large enough to be visible but easy to miss if you were focused on human tracks.

The marsh had become Theo's ally, its secrets revealed to him through patient observation. What these men saw as a hostile environment, he now recognized as a complex ecosystem with rhythms and patterns that could be read like a book. The knowledge Professor Morales had insisted he memorize—which plants grew in brackish versus freshwater, which insects indicated what conditions—now translated into tactical advantage.

"Check the high ground," ordered the lieutenant, pointing toward a hammock where palmetto grew thick. "No one stays in water this long."

Theo watched them trudge toward the hammock—directly past his ant nest marker. Right on cue, the tattooed man stepped into the nest, and chaos erupted as angry ants swarmed up his legs.

The man's howls echoed across the marsh as he tore off his pants, dancing in his underwear while his companions alternated between concern and barely suppressed laughter.

"This is insane," gasped one of the men, helping brush ants from his companion. "It's like the swamp itself is fighting us."

The lieutenant scanned the surroundings, his eyes narrowed. For a moment, his gaze passed directly over Theo's position, separated by only fifty yards of seemingly impenetrable saw grass.

"He's watching us," the lieutenant said quietly. "I can feel it."

Theo remained perfectly still, one with the marsh grass. The hunter and the hunted, separated by knowledge rather than distance.

As the search party regrouped and moved on, Theo slipped away to prepare his next move. The delta had taught him patience—and today, patience was his greatest weapon.

Late afternoon sunlight slanted across the delta, turning the marsh grass golden and casting long shadows across the water. Theo crouched at the edge of a wide section of marshland, carefully collecting cattail shoots. The air hummed with life—dragonflies darted above the water's surface, frogs called from hidden pockets, and all around him, birds waded through the shallows, pecking at tiny fish and invertebrates.

A great blue heron stood motionless twenty feet away, seemingly unbothered by Theo's presence. Two weeks ago, the bird would have taken flight at his approach. Now, it barely acknowledged him. The realization sent a quiet thrill through Theo's body—he had become part of this place, accepted by its inhabitants as something other than a threat.

Professor Harmon's words from his wetland ecology course echoed in his mind: "Birds are the sentinels of any ecosystem. Learn to read their behavior, and you'll never be surprised."

Theo paused his harvesting, wiping sweat from his brow. The rhythmic feeding of the birds around him had become a language he could now interpret. Their movements formed patterns—predictable, meaningful—that told stories about the marsh's condition.

A distant flutter caught his attention. Half a mile away, a cloud of white ibises suddenly took flight, their wings flashing against the blue sky. Theo froze, watching intently. Nothing natural would disturb so many birds at once.

The disturbance moved, creating a ripple effect through the wildlife. A flock of terns rose next, followed by a group of egrets.

The pattern tracked west to east—something was moving through the marsh, something the birds recognized as danger.

Humans. Carlos's men.

Theo abandoned his gathering and slipped behind a cluster of mangroves, his eyes tracking the moving disturbance. He couldn't see the smugglers, but the birds told him everything he needed to know. Their flight patterns revealed not just the patrol's location but their direction and speed.

A pair of ospreys circled anxiously above their nest, their agitation growing as the unseen threat approached their territory. Theo calculated the patrol's path—they would pass within fifty yards of his current position.

He melted deeper into the vegetation, his mud-camouflaged wetsuit blending with the shadows. The marsh grass barely moved as he passed, his footfalls silent on the soft ground. Two weeks ago, he would have crashed through this terrain like a wounded bull. Now he moved like water.

A kingfisher darted from its perch with an alarmed rattle. Theo immediately dropped flat against the ground, becoming one with the mud and roots. Through a screen of cordgrass, he spotted movement—the flash of a machete cutting through vegetation, followed by men's voices.

"—waste of time. We should be preparing for tomorrow's shipment."

"Carlos wants him found. That's all that matters."

The voices passed without the speakers ever coming into view. Theo remained motionless, counting his breaths until a marsh wren resumed its chattering nearby—the all-clear signal he'd learned to trust.

The delta itself had become his ally, its creatures his sentinels and shields. While Carlos's men fought against the environment, Theo had learned to listen to it, move with it, become part of its ancient rhythm. Every rustling leaf and startled bird carried information for those who understood the language.

As the sun dipped lower, Theo rose and continued his gathering, following the birds back to their feeding grounds. They resumed their activities as if nothing had happened, accepting his presence once again. In their eyes, he was no longer an intruder like the smugglers—he had become just another creature of the marsh, moving through the landscape with the same purpose and belonging.

The transformation was complete. The delta had claimed him as its own.

Midday heat shimmered across the delta as Theo crouched in the shelter of a dense thicket of black mangroves. He'd been tracking game paths when the sound of voices carried across the water—human voices, not the usual whispers of marsh grass or calls of herons.

He froze, then carefully parted the foliage. Fifty yards away, a small fishing skiff sat awkwardly tilted in the shallow water, its outboard motor raised. A young woman with dark hair pulled into a practical braid knelt beside the engine, tools scattered around her on the deck. A man stood in the bow, scanning the horizon with the tense vigilance of someone accustomed to looking over his shoulder.

"How much longer, Elena?" the man asked, his voice tight.

The woman—Elena—wiped sweat from her forehead with the back of her wrist. "I can't perform miracles, Mateo. The shear pin is broken, and I'm missing the right wrench to remove the prop."

"We need to be moving. If Mendoza's men find us here..." Mateo didn't finish the sentence.

Theo's pulse quickened. These weren't Carlos's people. They were afraid of them.

Elena attacked the engine with renewed determination. "I know what's at stake. Just keep watch."

Theo observed them for nearly twenty minutes. They weren't moving with the practiced efficiency of smugglers. The woman clearly knew engines, but she was working with limited tools. The man alternated between helping her and nervously scanning their surroundings. Most telling was their conversation—fragments about "getting the information to the right people" and "making things right."

Theo weighed his options. After two weeks alone in the marsh, human contact represented both opportunity and danger. But something about their predicament resonated with him. They were trapped, just as he had been.

He made his decision.

"The trash in these channels will break any shear pin at some point," Theo called out, emerging slowly from the mangroves with his hands visible. "But the metal tube in the ball point pen I see in your pocket will work if you're desperate."

Both figures whirled toward him. Mateo's hand moved to his waistband before stopping.

"Who are you?" Elena demanded, gripping a wrench like a weapon.

"My name's Theo. I'm..." he hesitated, "...hiding from Carlos Mendoza. Same as you, it sounds like."

Their suspicion was understandable. Mateo stepped slightly in front of Elena.

"You're alone out here?" Mateo asked, skepticism heavy in his voice.

Theo nodded. "Been surviving in the marsh for a while now. I was on a dive boat. Mendoza's operation. It went bad."

Recognition flickered in Elena's eyes. "The marine biology student. They've been looking for you."

A tense silence stretched between them. Then Elena lowered her wrench slightly.

Mateo and Elena exchanged a look that contained an entire conversation.

"I'm Elena Vega," she finally said. "This is Mateo Diaz. My father's a fisherman in Port Lavaca. Mateo was... well..."

"I worked for Mendoza," Mateo said flatly. "Until I saw what he was really doing. Human trafficking. I got out, but now I'm helping Elena gather evidence against his operation."

Theo waded toward their boat, still maintaining a cautious distance. "That fuel line needs more than cordgrass. I've been watching Carlos's camp. I know their patrol schedules, their routes."

Elena studied him, her practical assessment almost tangible. "And we have a boat. Or will, once it's fixed. Plus connections to people who can actually do something about Mendoza."

"I also have supplies," Mateo added. "Food that isn't marsh rabbits and cattail roots."

The proposition hung in the air between them—an alliance born of necessity.

"I've been sabotaging their operation," Theo said. "Small things. Contaminating fuel. Moving supplies. But I can't stop what's coming tomorrow night. Not alone."

Elena wiped her hands on a rag and extended one toward him. "Then maybe we don't have to do it alone."

Theo hesitated only briefly before taking her hand. After weeks of solitude and survival, the simple human contact felt foreign yet desperately needed. "Three ghosts instead of one. I like those odds better."

As Theo waded back to shore to gather the plants he needed, he felt something he hadn't experienced since washing up on the peninsula—hope that extended beyond mere survival. In Elena's mechanical ingenuity and Mateo's inside knowledge, he'd found not just allies, but the first pieces of a way home.

The golden hour stretched across the delta, bathing everything in amber light as Theo moved through his daily ritual. What had begun as desperate measures for survival had evolved into something approaching art—a methodical system of traps, snares, and warning devices that formed a protective web around his sanctuary.

Theo knelt beside a deadfall trap constructed from driftwood and stones, carefully resetting the trigger mechanism. The trap had yielded nothing today, but its purpose extended beyond catching game—it was part of a larger network, a circuit of security that Theo maintained with religious dedication.

"Trap seven, clear," he murmured to himself, making the mental note as he had each day for the past week.

His fingers, once soft from academic life, had hardened into calloused tools that worked with practiced precision. The transformation extended beyond his hands—his entire being had adapted to this new existence. His movements were economical, his senses attuned to the subtlest shifts in his environment.

Fifty yards east, Theo checked a snare set along a small game trail. A juvenile raccoon had triggered it but managed to escape, leaving behind only tufts of fur. Theo adjusted the wire loop, lowering it slightly to better match the height of the rabbits that frequented this path.

"Trap eleven, reset," he noted mentally, adding it to his internal map.

As he moved through the marsh, the circuit became a meditation. Each trap represented a point of control in a world that had spiraled beyond his grasp. The university student who had arrived on that dive boat weeks ago would hardly recognize the lean, focused survivor who now navigated the delta with the confidence of a native.

The light shifted as the sun sank lower, casting longer shadows across the landscape. Theo quickened his pace slightly. Two more traps to check before darkness fell.

Trap eighteen had yielded success—a small marsh rabbit hung limp in the snare. Theo whispered thanks to the creature as he removed it, securing it to his belt with practiced hands. Tonight's meal, tomorrow's strength.

"Final trap," he reminded himself, moving toward the northwestern perimeter of his territory—the border that faced Carlos's compound.

This last trap was different from the others—not meant for game but for warning. A simple tripwire connected to a cluster of dried reeds that would rustle loudly if disturbed. Theo approached it cautiously, always alert near the boundaries of his sanctuary.

He froze, noticing immediately that something was wrong. The wire hung loose, the trigger mechanism sprung. Kneeling, Theo examined the ground, finding footprints that didn't belong to any marsh creature. Human prints, partially obscured as if their owner had attempted to cover their tracks.

His eyes narrowed as he spotted something caught in the wire—a small scrap of black fabric with a distinctive red thread running through it. Theo recognized it immediately from his observations of the camp. This wasn't from any random trespasser—this belonged to one of Carlos's elite guards, the ones who wore tactical gear with red-stitched reinforcements.

Theo held the fabric between his fingers, his mind racing. This wasn't a random patrol that had stumbled upon his trap. This was deliberate—someone had penetrated deeper into his territory than ever before, approaching within half a mile of his shelter.

The sanctuary had been compromised.

Theo scanned the surrounding marsh, suddenly aware of how the lengthening shadows could conceal watchers. The golden hour that had seemed so beautiful minutes ago now felt exposing, threatening. He pocketed the fabric scrap and reset the trap with swift, silent movements.

As he straightened, Theo made a decision. He could no longer remain purely defensive. Carlos was tightening the net, and tomorrow's shipment would bring more innocent lives into danger. The time for hiding was coming to an end.

The marsh rabbit hung heavy at his belt as Theo melted into the gathering darkness, his mind already formulating a new plan—one that would take him from hunted to hunter.

Behind him, the delta settled into evening stillness, unaware that the delicate balance it had maintained was about to shatter.

Chapter 10

D awn painted the eastern sky in muted oranges and pinks as
Theo settled into his observation post—a dense thicket of
mangroves overlooking the smugglers' compound. His camouflaged
form blended seamlessly with the vegetation, a ghost watching the
living.

Below, the compound stirred to life. Men emerged from tents
and temporary structures, their movements lacking the crisp
efficiency that had marked them just a week earlier. Theo noted their
sluggish pace, the wary glances cast toward the surrounding marsh,
the hands that never strayed far from weapons.

Marcus Delgado stood at the center of the clearing, his formerly
composed demeanor fractured by agitation. He paced as his
lieutenants gathered—Vince with his perpetual scowl, Rodriguez
with dark circles beneath his eyes, and Tanner whose hand trembled
slightly as he clutched a clipboard.

"Seven days," Marcus hissed, his voice carrying clearly to Theo's
position. "Seven days of missed schedules, equipment failures, and
men jumping at shadows."

The assembled crew shifted uncomfortably. Several sported
bandages from Theo's traps, while others exhibited the hollow-eyed
look of those who hadn't properly slept in days.

"The Miami shipment was delayed by twelve hours," Vince
reported, his voice flat. "Buyers are getting nervous."

Marcus slammed his fist against a supply crate. "And why was it delayed? Because two boats had contaminated fuel, and because the night crew was too busy chasing ghosts to maintain the schedule!"

Rodriguez stepped forward. "The men are saying—"

"I don't give a damn what the men are saying!" Marcus's voice cracked with strain. "Superstitious garbage about marsh spirits and curses. We're losing thousands every day because of incompetence."

Theo allowed himself a small smile beneath his mud-streaked face. The Spanish Needles he'd been leaving—tokens of his presence—had worked better than he'd hoped. The men had created their own ghost stories to explain the inexplicable sabotage.

"Three men want to quit," Tanner said, consulting his clipboard. "Perez says someone left those flowers in his locked footlocker. Inside his locked room."

Murmurs rippled through the gathered smugglers. Theo hadn't managed that particular feat, but he wasn't about to correct their assumption. Fear bred more fear.

"Anyone who leaves doesn't get paid," Marcus snapped. "And might find themselves explaining things to our associates." The threat hung in the air, heavy and explicit.

A skinny man with a bandaged arm spoke up. "The traps are everywhere now. Rico stepped in one yesterday that nearly took his foot off."

"Then watch where you're stepping!" Marcus roared. "We control this territory. We've operated here for three years without a problem until that college kid disappeared."

Theo felt a surge of satisfaction. They still didn't know if he was alive or dead, still couldn't determine if their problems stemmed from one man or many.

"Double the patrols," Marcus ordered. "And I want the perimeter sensors checked hourly. The next shipment cannot be delayed. Our buyers won't tolerate another failure."

As the meeting broke up, Theo observed the disorganization that followed. Men argued over patrol assignments, equipment malfunctioned, and tempers flared. Where once they had moved with military precision, now they stumbled over each other like amateurs.

The first cracks had appeared in Marcus's operation, spreading through the foundation of his criminal enterprise. Theo watched as Marcus retreated to his quarters, shoulders tight with tension, face etched with the strain of maintaining control.

Seven days of psychological warfare had accomplished what Theo had hoped—the slow, inexorable erosion of confidence and cohesion. The smugglers were beginning to fear the marsh itself, seeing threats in every shadow and hearing pursuers in every rustle of vegetation.

As the compound descended into bickering and recrimination, Theo slipped away, already planning the next phase of his campaign. The cracks were forming—now it was time to shatter them completely.

The smugglers' harbor lay still under the moonless sky, water lapping gently against hulls of patrol boats. At precisely 1:55 AM, three figures materialized from the darkness, moving with practiced stealth toward the docks. The night wrapped around them like a protective cloak, their silhouettes barely distinguishable from the shadows.

Theo led the way, his wetsuit now fully camouflaged with mud and plant matter. Behind him moved Elena, her slight frame belying the strength in her hands that could dismantle an engine and reassemble it blindfolded. Her father's fishing boat had been seized by Carlos three years ago, forcing her family into poverty. Tonight was her reckoning.

Mateo brought up the rear, his eyes constantly scanning for threats. Once Carlos's trusted lieutenant, he had witnessed one too many atrocities before fleeing the operation. The scar across his cheek—Carlos's parting gift—served as a constant reminder of his former life.

"Guard change begins in four minutes," Theo whispered, checking his watch. "We'll have exactly fifteen minutes before the new rotation settles in."

Elena nodded, patting the waterproof toolkit strapped to her thigh. "I'll handle the ignition systems. Three minutes per boat."

"I'll manage the hulls," Mateo said, producing a hand drill with a bit no thicker than a needle. "Just above the waterline, where they won't notice until they're already moving."

Theo gripped their shoulders. "I've got the fuel. Remember—we work clean, we leave nothing behind, and we're ghosts by 2:15."

They watched as the guard at the dock's edge checked his watch and yawned before ambling toward the compound for the shift change. The moment he disappeared from view, they moved.

Each took their assigned vessel, working with the efficiency of those who understood that survival depended on speed and silence. Theo crawled into the first patrol boat, a sleek craft with twin outboards. He located the fuel line and carefully introduced a mixture of marsh water and fine sediment that would pass through filters initially but gradually clog fuel injectors and corrode engine components.

On the second boat, Elena's fingers danced across wiring harnesses, creating subtle modifications to the ignition system. The boat would start normally, run for approximately ten minutes, then die without warning—a fault nearly impossible to diagnose in field conditions.

Mateo worked on the third vessel, drilling microscopic holes just above the waterline. The perforations would remain sealed while stationary but would allow water ingress once the boat reached cruising speed, creating a slow, persistent leak that would eventually overwhelm the bilge pumps.

The harbor remained eerily quiet, with only the occasional splash of fish breaking the silence. In the distance, voices signaled the new guards preparing to take their positions.

"Two minutes," Theo breathed.

They completed their sabotage with practiced precision, each manipulation designed to create maximum disruption with minimum evidence. These weren't random acts of vandalism but calculated strikes against the smugglers' mobility—their ability to patrol, transport goods, and respond to threats.

As footsteps approached the dock, the three shadows slipped into the water, leaving barely a ripple. They swam beneath the surface, using the darkness for cover, emerging only when they reached the protective shelter of the mangroves fifty yards downshore.

"Clean job," Elena whispered, water streaming from her hair.

Mateo nodded. "By tomorrow afternoon, they'll have no operational vessels. They'll be blind and immobile."

Theo gazed back at the harbor, where the new guard had resumed his post, unaware that the critical infrastructure under his watch had been compromised. "This isn't just about damaging boats," he said quietly. "It's about making them feel vulnerable. Every failure compounds their fear."

The three melted back into the night, leaving no trace of their presence except for the invisible sabotage that would reveal itself at the most inopportune moment for Carlos and his operation.

The marsh welcomed them back into its protective embrace, the delta becoming not just their hiding place but their ally in the asymmetric warfare they waged against forces that had once seemed invincible.

Rain hammered against the metal roof of the generator shed, a blessing that drowned out any sound Theo might make. The tropical downpour had descended upon the delta with biblical fury, transforming the compound into a maze of puddles and reducing visibility to mere yards. Lightning periodically illuminated the scene in stark white flashes, followed by thunder that rattled through bone and metal alike.

Theo crouched beneath a stand of palmetto, water streaming down his camouflaged wetsuit. He pressed a finger to his ear, activating the waterproof radio Elena had salvaged from an abandoned Coast Guard cache.

"Position check," he whispered.

"North ridge clear," Mateo's voice crackled through the earpiece. "You have four minutes before the patrol reaches the eastern perimeter."

"South marsh secure," Elena confirmed. "No movement near the barracks."

Theo took a deep breath, mentally reviewing the compound layout he'd sketched from memory after days of observation. The generator shed stood thirty yards from his position—a corrugated metal structure housing the diesel generator that powered the entire operation's communications, security systems, and lighting.

"Moving now," he murmured, and slipped from his hiding place.

The mud sucked at his boots as he crossed the open ground in a half-crouch. Each flash of lightning forced him to freeze, becoming part of the landscape until darkness returned. The rain plastered his hair to his forehead, water streaming into his eyes as he counted his steps.

Twenty yards. Fifteen. Ten.

The generator's rumble grew louder, a mechanical heartbeat pumping electricity through the veins of the compound. Theo reached the shed's rear wall and pressed himself against it, feeling the vibration through his shoulder blades.

"Eastern patrol turning south," Mateo warned. "Two minutes."

Theo slid along the wall to the padlocked door. From his pocket, he produced a tension wrench and pick—tools he'd fashioned from spare parts in Elena's toolkit. Professor Harmon's criminology elective, which Theo had taken on a whim last semester, suddenly proved its worth as he manipulated the lock with practiced precision.

The padlock clicked open.

Inside, the generator's roar was deafening, a massive diesel unit that had clearly been stolen from an industrial site. Theo closed the door behind him and pulled a small flashlight from his belt. The beam revealed a complex array of wiring, fuel lines, and control panels.

"One minute," Elena's voice warned.

Theo worked methodically, locating the control panel and carefully removing its cover. Inside lay a circuit board with a cooling fan. He extracted a small vial from his pocket—saltwater mixed with fine sediment from the marsh—and carefully dripped it onto the circuit board's cooling vents.

The beauty of the sabotage lay in its subtlety. When the generator heated up under load, the water would evaporate, leaving behind salt crystals and sediment that would gradually corrode connections and clog cooling channels. The unit would continue running, but efficiency would decrease until eventual failure—appearing as a mechanical breakdown rather than deliberate sabotage.

"Patrol approaching the shed," Mateo hissed. "Get out now."

Theo replaced the panel, closed the vial, and moved to the door. He listened for footsteps outside, hearing nothing but rain. With careful movements, he slipped out, replaced the padlock, and melted into the shadows just as a beam of light swept across the area.

Two guards passed within feet of him, hunched against the downpour, their attention focused on reaching shelter rather than security. Theo remained motionless until they disappeared around the corner.

"Clear," he whispered. "Heading to extraction point."

As Theo retreated through the storm, he knew the compound would wake tomorrow to failing systems, deteriorating communications, and increasing isolation. The smugglers would blame the weather, equipment age, or bad luck—never suspecting that the marsh itself had infiltrated their technology, corroding it from within just as Theo's resistance corroded their operation.

Back at their hidden camp, Elena and Mateo would be waiting with dry clothes and hot tea. But for now, Theo embraced the rain, letting it wash away any trace of his presence as he disappeared into the delta that had become both his sanctuary and his weapon.

The smugglers' camp buzzed with activity as the afternoon sun beat down on the corrugated metal roofs. From their vantage point in the mangroves, Theo and Carmen observed the increased tempo of preparations. A shipment was coming—the largest one yet, according to Elena's intelligence.

"They're bringing in twenty more people tomorrow night," Theo whispered, passing the binoculars to Carmen. "We need to reduce their operational capacity before then."

Carmen nodded, her weathered hands steady as she adjusted the focus. At fifty-three, she was the oldest member of their resistance cell, a local herbalist who had joined after Carlos's men threatened her village for protection money. Her knowledge of the delta's flora was unmatched, even by Theo's academic understanding.

"The distraction will begin in ten minutes," Theo continued. "We'll have maybe five minutes to access their provisions."

Carmen lowered the binoculars and patted the canvas bag at her side. "This will work. Not enough to kill—just enough to make them wish they were dead for a day or two."

Inside her bag lay carefully measured portions of local plants: wild senna pods, water hemlock root in minute quantities, and crushed pokeweed berries. Combined, they created a potent purgative that would spread through the camp like wildfire.

Across the compound, Mateo was preparing to create their diversion—a small controlled fire in the brush near the fuel depot that would draw every available guard to prevent an explosion.

Theo checked his watch. "Two minutes."

Carmen touched his arm. "You're troubled by this."

It wasn't a question. Theo had been uncharacteristically quiet during the planning phase, his usual tactical precision clouded by something deeper.

"We're poisoning them," he said finally. "It crosses a line."

"Yes," Carmen agreed simply. "It does."

In the distance, the first wisps of smoke began to rise from the brush. Guards shouted, and men began running toward the emerging threat.

"It's time," Theo said, pushing aside his moral quandary. "Let's move."

They slipped from the mangroves, crossing the open ground in a low crouch. The supply shed stood unguarded now, its padlock hastily secured in the guards' rush to respond to the fire.

Theo made quick work of the lock while Carmen kept watch. Inside, the provisions were neatly organized—clearly the work of someone with military experience. Large water barrels lined one wall, while shelves of canned goods and dry staples occupied another.

Carmen worked methodically, adding her herbal mixture to the water barrels and sprinkling a fine powder over the open containers of rice, beans, and flour. She paid special attention to the coffee grounds—knowing the bitter taste would mask any subtle changes.

"They'll start feeling the effects by midnight," she whispered. "Full impact by morning."

Theo nodded, keeping his eyes on the door. The sounds of shouting continued from the fuel depot, but they wouldn't have much longer.

As Carmen finished her work, Theo caught her arm. "Will anyone die from this?"

Her eyes met his, steady and unflinching. "No. But they will suffer. Every man in this camp has caused suffering. Do you think Carlos loses sleep over the people he's trafficked? The lives he's destroyed?"

Theo had no answer. He thought of the terrified faces of the people he'd seen unloaded from the trawler, the young woman Carlos had marked for "premium sale." His resolve hardened.

"Let's go," he said.

They slipped out of the shed, resealed the lock, and vanished back into the mangroves just as the first guards returned from the false alarm at the fuel depot.

That night, as they rejoined Elena and Mateo at their hidden camp, Theo stared into the small cooking fire. Tomorrow, Carlos's operation would be crippled by illness—unable to process the new arrivals, creating a window for potential rescue or escape.

The line had been crossed. Theo knew there would be others ahead, each one blurring the distinction between resistance fighter and something darker. He wondered what his father would think of him now, or Aunt Clara, or his professors back at the university. Would they recognize the man he was becoming?

The delta had changed him. Carlos had changed him. And there was no going back.

The smugglers' compound lay quiet under a half-moon, the perimeter lights casting harsh shadows across the clearing. Inside the barracks, men tossed fitfully on their cots, some still clutching their stomachs from Carmen's herbal assault. At the northeastern watchtower, Vince fought to keep his eyes open, his face drawn and pale.

A mile away, hidden in a dense thicket of palmettos, Theo checked his watch: 12:42 AM.

"Everyone knows their positions?" he asked, his voice barely above a whisper.

Four teenagers nodded in the darkness—Miguel, Lucia, Javier, and Tomas—all from the nearby fishing village that had suffered under Carlos's protection racket. None were older than seventeen, but their eyes carried the hardened look of those who had seen too much, too soon.

"Remember," Theo continued, "no direct contact. No heroics. If you're spotted, disappear immediately." He tapped his crude hand-drawn map. "We rotate positions every forty minutes. Miguel starts northeast, Lucia northwest, Javier southwest, Tomas southeast."

Miguel grinned, hefting a small sack of metal scraps. "They won't know what hit them."

"That's the point," Theo replied. "They shouldn't see anything at all—just hear things, glimpse movements, chase shadows."

Lucia, the youngest at fifteen but with the stealth of a natural hunter, pulled a carved wooden whistle from her pocket. "My grandfather used this to call coyotes. It'll carry for half a mile on a night like this."

Theo nodded approvingly. "Perfect. Remember your timing—seventeen minutes past each hour, forty-two minutes past, and three minutes before. Never establish a pattern they can predict."

The teenagers dispersed into the darkness, each heading toward their assigned positions. Theo remained behind, watching the compound through binoculars. Tonight would be the first of many sleepless nights for Carlos's men.

At 12:57 AM, a metallic clatter erupted from the northeast corner of the compound. Through his binoculars, Theo watched two guards bolt from their posts, weapons raised. Miguel had timed it perfectly—a handful of scrap metal tossed against the chain-link fence, then immediate withdrawal.

The guards swept their flashlights across empty terrain, finding nothing.

They had barely returned to their posts when a coyote's mournful howl rose from the northwest perimeter. Lucia's whistle work was flawless—the sound seemed to drift from everywhere and nowhere. More guards emerged, scanning the darkness.

By 1:42 AM, Javier had created his distraction—a series of small stones thrown at intervals against the metal roof of the supply shed. The irregular tempo prevented the guards from triangulating the source.

Inside the compound, lights flickered on in the barracks. Men stumbled out, cursing the interruption of their already troubled sleep.

At 2:17 AM, Tomas dragged a branch slowly through the underbrush, creating the unmistakable sound of something large moving parallel to the fence line. Guards fired three shots into empty darkness.

The pattern continued through the night—seventeen minutes past, forty-two minutes past, three minutes before. Each disturbance calculated to allow the guards just enough time to return to their posts or drift back to sleep before the next disruption.

By 3:30 AM, the compound was in a state of constant alert. Sleep-deprived men stumbled through patrols, jumping at shadows. Arguments broke out between guards over imagined movements in the brush.

At 4:05 AM, Theo gathered his team at the rendezvous point, each teenager flush with the success of their mission.

"We did it," Lucia whispered, eyes bright with adrenaline.

"Tonight was just the beginning," Theo replied, leading them back toward their camp. "Tomorrow night, we change positions, change timing, change tactics. They'll never adapt because there's no pattern to adapt to."

Behind them, the compound remained illuminated, guards pacing nervously along the perimeter. No one had been harmed, no shots fired at the teenagers, yet the damage was profound. The psychological toll had begun—Carlos's operation was fracturing from within.

As dawn approached, Theo knew that in war, battles were won long before the first shot was fired. Tonight, they had planted the seeds of defeat in the minds of their enemies.

The mid-morning sun filtered through the canopy as Theo crouched beside Esteban, a weathered hunter in his fifties whose calloused hands worked with practiced precision. On Theo's other side, Rodrigo, Esteban's nephew, unspooled fishing line with quiet efficiency.

"The trick," Esteban murmured, "is not to think like you want to kill them. That makes you careless." He stretched nearly invisible fishing line across the path at eye level, anchoring it between two saplings. "You want them hurting, thinking, and most importantly—talking to each other about what happened."

Theo nodded, absorbing the lesson as he secured his own line a few yards further along the patrol route. Three carefully placed fish hooks dangled at face height, their barbs gleaming dully in the dappled light.

"The hooks won't blind them," Rodrigo explained, noticing Theo's momentary hesitation. "But they'll catch cheeks, ears, maybe scalps. Nothing that won't heal, but nothing they'll forget either."

The three men had been working since dawn, moving methodically along the five main patrol routes Carlos's men used to sweep the surrounding jungle. Their approach was systematic—each path receiving different types of painful surprises.

"The first night, they'll think it's bad luck," Esteban said, repositioning a thorn bush so its branches extended across a narrow section of trail. "The second night, they'll be afraid. By the third night, they'll refuse to patrol altogether."

Rodrigo grinned as he dug a shallow pit in the middle of the path, lining it with dried palmetto fronds to disguise its presence. Into this depression, he scattered dozens of sand spurs and cockleburs—natural caltrops that would embed themselves in boots and ankles.

"My grandfather fought this way against the government soldiers," Rodrigo said. "Never meeting them directly, just making every step they took on his land painful until they decided it wasn't worth it."

By midday, they had prepared the northern approach with twenty-seven different hazards—tripwires connected to whip-like branches, hidden patches of poison ivy strategically transplanted overnight, and paths subtly rerouted toward wasp nests.

Theo wiped sweat from his brow as they paused to drink from their canteens. "Will this be enough?"

Esteban shook his head. "It's never about enough. It's about consistency. Tomorrow we move everything—new locations, new traps. They adapt, we adapt faster."

The eastern patrol route received special attention. Here, they scattered tiny thorns from the devil's walking stick tree—nearly invisible but capable of causing intense, burning pain when embedded in skin.

"This is where they'll expect trouble after tonight," Rodrigo explained as they worked. "So we give them exactly what they expect, but worse than they imagine."

As afternoon stretched toward evening, they finished with the southern approach, creating a gauntlet of discomfort and surprise. None of their traps would kill or permanently maim—that wasn't the objective. Each was designed to inflict just enough pain to create hesitation, just enough fear to breed doubt.

"Tonight," Esteban said as they gathered their remaining supplies, "the jungle itself becomes their enemy."

Theo surveyed their work with grim satisfaction. The traps were virtually invisible, blending seamlessly with the natural environment. Even knowing where they were, he had to strain to spot them.

"When does a man become truly defeated?" Esteban asked, shouldering his pack.

Theo considered the question. "When he can no longer fight?"

"No." The older man shook his head. "When he becomes afraid to take the next step. That's when you've truly won."

As they melted back into the jungle, Theo understood. By sunrise tomorrow, Carlos's men would be questioning every shadow, every rustling leaf. The physical pain would heal quickly—the psychological wounds would fester.

Dusk settled over the delta, transforming solid forms into shifting shadows. Theo crouched at the edge of the northern ridge, watching the smugglers' compound through borrowed binoculars. Carlos's men moved with new caution, their earlier confidence replaced by wary glances toward the darkening tree line.

"Everyone in position?" Theo whispered into the walkie-talkie Carmen had stolen three days earlier.

Four clicks answered him—Miguel to the east, Lucia south, Javier west, and Esteban's nephew Rodrigo circling to complete their phantom perimeter. Each carried identical supplies: flashlights wrapped in colored cellophane, small mirrors, lengths of rope with metal scraps attached, and handmade reed whistles.

"Remember," Theo said, "fifteen-minute intervals, never from the same spot twice."

The smugglers had doubled their guards after the traps claimed six victims that afternoon. One man still limped from Rodrigo's sand spur pit, while another's face bore angry scratches from Esteban's eye-level fishing line. Their fear was palpable even from this distance.

"Begin," Theo whispered.

A flash of green light appeared briefly at the eastern perimeter, then vanished. Thirty seconds later, metal clinked against metal from the south—Lucia dragging her noisemaker through the underbrush. Before the guards could investigate, a bird call pierced the twilight from the west—Javier's signal, too perfect to be natural.

Through his binoculars, Theo watched confusion spread across the compound. Guards pointed in different directions, unsure which threat to address first. A red light blinked three times from the northwestern approach, then disappeared.

"They're splitting up," Theo murmured with satisfaction. Two guards headed east, another pair south, while a fifth man radioed frantically for instructions.

For the next hour, the phantom resistance maintained its illusion. Lights appeared and vanished at irregular intervals. Strange sounds—whispers, metallic scraping, and rustling vegetation—emanated from different points around the perimeter. Twice, Theo caught glimpses of Carlos himself, emerging from his cabin to assess the situation, face tight with anger.

By full darkness, the smugglers had exhausted themselves chasing shadows. Their defensive perimeter had stretched thin, with pairs of men stationed at wide intervals around the compound—exactly as Theo had hoped.

"Phase two," he whispered into the walkie-talkie.

As the guards settled into their new positions, the resistance members began moving between stations, creating the impression of a much larger force converging from multiple directions. The compound descended into chaos as Carlos's men fired wildly into the darkness, wasting ammunition on phantoms.

Theo smiled grimly. By dawn, the smugglers would be convinced they faced an army, not five determined individuals with nothing but cleverness and desperation on their side.

Morning fog clung to the delta's maze of waterways as Theo studied the hand-drawn map spread across a fallen cypress log. Five local fishermen—Esteban, Miguel, Rodrigo, Paulo, and old man Vargas—huddled around him, their weathered faces intent. These men had navigated these channels since childhood, their knowledge of the terrain more valuable than any satellite imagery.

"Carlos uses these three main routes," Esteban traced thick fingers along pencil lines. "The northern channel for bringing in supplies, the eastern passage for moving people, and this southern route when Coast Guard patrols get too close."

Theo nodded, committing each path to memory. "We don't need to block them completely. Just make them unpredictable."

"Like a game of roadblock roulette," Paulo grinned, revealing a gap where his front tooth should be.

Over the next five days, they executed their plan with methodical precision. The resistance split into teams, each targeting different segments of the smugglers' transportation network. They worked in shifting patterns—never establishing routines that Carlos's men might anticipate.

On the first day, Theo and Esteban felled a young mangrove across the northern supply route, positioning it to appear as natural storm damage. They left just enough clearance for a boat to squeeze through—but only after twenty minutes of maneuvering.

"Not an impassable barrier," Theo explained as they concealed their saw marks with mud. "Just enough to slow them down, make them vulnerable."

Meanwhile, Miguel and Rodrigo repositioned the channel markers along the eastern passage, shifting them just enough to guide boats toward a sandbar rather than away from it. When smugglers' vessels ran aground that afternoon, the resistance was already moving to their next target.

Old man Vargas proved particularly ingenious. Using his lifetime of knowledge, he identified tidal pools where submerged logs could be placed to damage propellers during low tide—obstacles that would disappear entirely during high water.

"The delta breathes," Vargas told Theo as they worked. "We make its breath become our weapon."

By the third day, Carlos's operation showed visible signs of strain. Boat engines growled at all hours as they searched for clear passages. Twice, Theo observed supply vessels return to the compound with their cargo still aboard, unable to navigate the constantly shifting obstacles.

Paulo reported overhearing radio chatter about fuel shortages as boats burned through their reserves navigating the longer, more circuitous routes they were forced to take.

"We're not fighting the men," Theo explained during their fourth-day planning session. "We're fighting their system."

The resistance never struck the same route twice in succession. They created false channels that led nowhere, displaced navigational markers, and scattered broken branches to mimic storm damage where none existed. Nature itself became their ally—the resistance merely rearranged what was already there, making the familiar suddenly treacherous.

On the fifth morning, Theo watched through binoculars as a smuggler's boat attempted three different approaches to the compound before finding a clear path. The captain's frustration was evident even from a distance as he gestured angrily at his navigator.

"See that?" Esteban whispered beside him. "They doubt themselves now. Not just the path, but their own knowledge."

Theo nodded. "That's more valuable than any physical barrier we could build."

As they slipped away to plan the day's disruptions, Theo felt a grim satisfaction. Carlos's operation depended on predictability and control—both now systematically undermined by people who understood the land better than any outsider ever could.

Dusk settled over the delta as Theo and Lucia crouched in their makeshift blind, a carefully constructed nest of mangrove branches and palmetto fronds overlooking the smugglers' communications center. The small wooden structure sat thirty yards from the main compound, housing the satellite equipment and radio systems that formed the nerve center of Carlos's operation.

"There," Lucia whispered, adjusting her binoculars. "That's Emilio on the evening shift."

Theo studied the lean man hunched over the radio console. "Is he the one you said was sloppy with the encryption protocols?"

"The very same." Lucia's smile carried the confidence of someone who had spent years mastering her craft. Before joining the resistance, she had worked for a telecommunications company in Corpus Christi, her technical knowledge proving invaluable against Carlos's operation.

They watched as Emilio stretched and stepped outside for a cigarette, leaving the communications room momentarily unattended.

"Amateurs," Lucia muttered, reaching for the modified handheld radio they'd salvaged from an abandoned Coast Guard outpost. She adjusted several dials, her fingers moving with practiced precision. "Ready to cause some chaos?"

Theo nodded, feeling a flutter of anticipation. Their sabotage had evolved beyond physical disruption. Information was the true currency of Carlos's empire—who was coming, what was being transported, when exchanges would occur. Disrupting that flow would create fractures throughout the entire operation.

The first transmission came at 7:42 PM—a scheduled check-in from one of the perimeter outposts. Lucia intercepted it cleanly, altering the coded message before relaying it to the main compound.

"What did you change?" Theo asked.

"Their all-clear signal to a request for immediate backup." She grinned. "Northern perimeter is about to get very confused."

Within minutes, two guards sprinted from the main building toward the northern checkpoint, weapons drawn. Through his binoculars, Theo watched the subsequent argument between the confused outpost guards and their reinforcements, each insisting the other had made a mistake.

As darkness deepened, the frequency of transmissions increased. A shipment was arriving tomorrow, and coordination messages flew back and forth across the network. Lucia intercepted each one, sometimes delaying delivery, other times subtly altering coordinates or timing.

"The beauty is in the subtlety," she explained, adjusting her headset. "Change too much, they'll realize they're being jammed. Change just enough..."

"And they'll suspect each other," Theo finished.

By midnight, the effects rippled through the compound. A supply boat arrived at the wrong location. A security patrol showed up three hours early for a shift change. Twice, Theo observed Carlos himself storming between buildings, gesturing angrily at his subordinates.

"This message is from their eastern outpost," Lucia said, her expression suddenly serious as she listened to an encrypted transmission. "They've spotted a Coast Guard cutter moving along the outer channel."

Theo felt his pulse quicken. "Is it really there?"

"Doesn't matter." Lucia's fingers flew across her equipment, jamming the transmission completely. "What matters is that Carlos won't know about it until it's much closer."

The compound erupted into activity an hour later when the Coast Guard vessel's spotlight swept across the eastern shoreline. Theo watched through his binoculars as men scrambled to conceal evidence, their movements frantic and uncoordinated without proper warning.

"We're not just fighting them physically anymore," Theo observed as they packed up their equipment before dawn. "We're getting inside their decision cycle."

Lucia nodded, her eyes reflecting the determination that united their growing resistance. "Information is power. And we've just shown them they don't control it anymore."

As they slipped away through the marsh, Theo realized how far they had come from simple acts of sabotage. They were dismantling Carlos's operation from within—turning his own systems against him like a virus gradually consuming its host.

A slate-gray dawn broke over the delta as Theo settled into his observation point among the tangle of mangrove roots. The smugglers' compound lay before him, its central courtyard visible through gaps in the perimeter fence. For three hours, he remained motionless, his mud-camouflaged wetsuit rendering him nearly invisible against the marsh vegetation.

Activity inside the compound had reached a fever pitch. The previous night's Coast Guard incursion had cost Carlos's operation dearly—two boats abandoned, a shipment of contraband dumped overboard, and three men narrowly escaping capture. The accumulated stress of the resistance's campaign was beginning to show.

At precisely 7:30 AM, Marcus Delgado emerged from the main building, his face contorted with barely contained rage. Gone was the affable diving instructor who had once charmed tourists at Fisherman's Wharf. In his place stood a man transformed by power and paranoia, his eyes darting across the compound as he barked orders at the men assembling before him.

"Everyone in the courtyard! Now!" His voice carried across the compound, drawing men from their posts and quarters.

Theo shifted slightly, adjusting his position to better observe the unfolding scene. Twenty-three men gathered in the courtyard, forming a rough semicircle around Marcus. Among them stood

Vince, the heavyset enforcer who had been with Marcus from the beginning, and Lieutenant Ramirez, who oversaw security operations.

"Three weeks," Marcus began, pacing before his assembled crew. "Three weeks of failures, mishaps, and incompetence." He paused, scanning the faces before him. "Someone wants to explain to me why our operation is falling apart?"

Silence greeted his question. Men stared at the ground, avoiding eye contact.

"No one?" Marcus's voice dropped dangerously low. "Ramirez. You're my head of security. Explain to me why we've been compromised."

Lieutenant Ramirez stepped forward, a man in his forties with the hardened look of someone who had survived previous purges. "We're dealing with locals who know the terrain, sir. They're using—"

The crack of the pistol echoed across the compound. Ramirez crumpled to the ground, a red stain blossoming across his chest. The men in the courtyard flinched but held their positions.

"Excuses," Marcus spat, the gun still smoking in his hand. "I don't accept excuses."

Theo fought to control his breathing, the sudden violence confirming what he had suspected: Marcus was unraveling.

"Vince," Marcus turned to his longtime associate. "You're in charge of security now. Find these saboteurs. Find them today."

Vince nodded stiffly, his expression carefully neutral, but Theo caught the flicker of fear in the man's eyes.

"The rest of you," Marcus continued, holstering his weapon, "double the patrols. Anyone caught sleeping on watch joins Ramirez. Anyone who fails to report suspicious activity joins Ramirez. Anyone who talks about leaving..." he gestured toward the body on the ground, "joins Ramirez."

As the men dispersed, Theo noticed something significant—the way they moved away from Marcus rather than toward him. Fear might ensure compliance, but it eroded loyalty. Several men exchanged glances that spoke volumes, their allegiance visibly wavering.

Most telling was Vince's reaction. The enforcer knelt beside Ramirez's body, his face a mask of controlled emotion. When he looked up at Marcus's retreating back, something had changed in his expression—the unquestioning loyalty replaced by calculation.

Theo remained motionless until the courtyard emptied, processing what he had witnessed. Marcus had just eliminated one of his most experienced men and alienated others, including his closest lieutenant. The organizational structure was fracturing under pressure.

As he slipped away from his hiding spot, Theo understood that their campaign had entered a new phase. Marcus's brutality had opened fissures within his own organization—potential weaknesses the resistance could exploit. The tyrant's greatest vulnerability wasn't his operation but his own deteriorating control.

Dusk descended over the delta as the generators sputtered, coughed, and finally died. The compound plunged into darkness, followed by shouts of confusion from the guards. Theo smiled grimly from his position in the thick brush thirty yards from the northern perimeter fence. The saltwater solution he had introduced into the fuel system days earlier had finally done its work.

"Right on schedule," he whispered to himself, checking his watch. 8:47 PM.

Inside the compound, flashlight beams cut erratic paths through the darkness as men scrambled to restore power. Orders shouted in Spanish and English competed with the sounds of equipment being dragged across gravel. The confusion created the perfect cover for what Theo needed to do.

He slipped forward, moving with the measured patience of a heron stalking fish. Three weeks in the delta had transformed his movements, teaching him to place each foot with deliberate care, to test weight before committing, to blend with the rhythm of the wetlands. The mud-darkened wetsuit broke up his silhouette as he approached the fence line.

Beyond the chain-link barrier stood a long, windowless structure—the barracks where Carlos kept his human cargo. Intelligence gathered from Elena and the villagers suggested it held between twenty and thirty people awaiting transport north. Men, women, and children destined for labor camps, prostitution rings, and worse.

Theo reached the fence, pressing himself flat against the ground as a guard passed five yards away, cursing the darkness. When the beam of light moved on, Theo extracted a pair of wire cutters from his belt. Three strategic snips created an opening just large enough to squeeze through.

The compound's attention focused on the generator building at the southern end, leaving the northern sector relatively unguarded. Still, Theo counted four men patrolling the immediate area around the barracks, their movements agitated by the darkness.

He darted between shadows, reaching the building's eastern wall. Pressing his back against the corrugated metal, he inched toward a small ventilation grate near ground level. Kneeling, he peered inside.

The interior was dimly lit by a single battery-powered lantern that cast long shadows across a space crowded with people. Theo counted eleven women sitting or lying on thin mats along the wall nearest him. Beyond them, separated by a makeshift partition, he glimpsed at least a dozen men. In a corner, three children huddled together, the oldest no more than ten, keeping watch over the younger two as they slept.

Their conditions were appalling. Water was rationed in plastic jugs. A single bucket served as a toilet. The stench of unwashed bodies and fear permeated the air. Yet what struck Theo most was the silence—the unnatural quiet of people who had learned that drawing attention meant punishment.

A young woman with hollow cheeks noticed Theo's eyes at the grate. For a moment, terror flashed across her face before understanding dawned. She gave an almost imperceptible nod before turning away, careful not to alert the others to his presence.

Moving along the wall, Theo found a padlocked door reinforced with steel bars—the only entrance. Two guards stood nearby, their attention divided between the barracks and the commotion at the generator building.

He completed his circuit of the building, noting the thickness of the walls, the absence of windows, and the precise positions of guards. In his mind, he mapped escape routes, calculating distances to the fence, to the boats, to the relative safety of the mangroves beyond.

The temporary blackout wouldn't last much longer. Theo retreated the way he had come, slipping through the cut fence and back into the protective embrace of the marsh. The faces of the captives—especially the children—burned in his memory, transforming his mission from mere survival to something more profound.

This wasn't just about escaping Carlos or exposing Marcus anymore. Those people needed him. Needed the network of resistance he had helped build.

As he disappeared into the night, Theo knew that whatever plan they developed would have to account for thirty-two lives—thirty-two people who couldn't swim through marshes or hide in mangrove thickets. Their rescue would require more than sabotage and distraction.

It would require a miracle.

The afternoon sun beat down on the smugglers' compound as Theo lay motionless in the tall cordgrass, observing the command center through binoculars. Two weeks of relentless psychological warfare had transformed the once-orderly operation into a powder keg of suspicion and fear. The door to the main building stood wide open, allowing voices to carry across the clearing.

Inside, Marcus Delgado paced like a caged animal, his composure shattered. Maps and papers littered the floor around the central table where five men stood in various states of agitation. Through the doorway, Theo could see the veins bulging in Marcus's neck as he slammed his fist down.

"I don't give a damn what your men think!" Marcus shouted at Vince, who had taken a half-step back. "They're not being paid to think. They're being paid to follow orders!"

"Three boats sabotaged, fuel contaminated, communications jammed," Vince countered, his voice strained but defiant. "We lost contact with the northern checkpoint yesterday. That's the fourth post to go silent. My men think we're dealing with a military operation."

"It's the damn villagers," Marcus spat. "A handful of fishermen and that college kid."

A third man, wiry with a salt-and-pepper beard, shook his head. "No way. There's at least twenty, maybe thirty operators out there. Professional. Military-trained."

Theo suppressed a smile. Their resistance numbered exactly fourteen—nine villagers, four escaped captives, and himself. Yet the perception of a larger force had taken root exactly as planned.

"We should postpone the shipment," suggested a fourth man, his voice barely audible from Theo's position. "Until we secure—"

"Postpone?" Marcus grabbed the man by his collar. "Do you have any idea what happens if we miss this delivery? Do you?"

Outside the command center, three smugglers loaded personal belongings into a jeep. They moved with hurried efficiency, glancing frequently toward the woods. These weren't the first to desert—Theo had counted seven departures over the past three days.

"We lost another four men this morning," Vince said, prying Marcus's hand from his colleague's shirt. "They took supplies, ammunition, and one of the working boats."

"Cowards," Marcus hissed. "When I find them—"

"You won't find them," the bearded man interrupted. "And that's the point. Whatever's out there—whoever's out there—they're winning. We're down to eighteen men from thirty-two. The locals won't come near us. The Coast Guard intercepted our last two shipments."

"So what are you suggesting?" Marcus's voice dropped dangerously low.

"We cut our losses," Vince said flatly. "Salvage what we can and move the operation."

Marcus drew his pistol in one fluid motion, pressing it against Vince's forehead. "Is that your professional assessment? That we run?"

The room fell silent. Through his binoculars, Theo could see the tremor in Marcus's hand—not fear, but uncontrolled rage. The other lieutenants backed away, creating a circle around the confrontation.

"I built this," Marcus whispered, though his words carried in the silence. "Everything we have. And you want to abandon it because of some ghosts in the marsh?"

Vince didn't blink. "Those ghosts have cost us half a million in product and equipment. They've turned your men against you. They're watching us right now."

As if on cue, a distant whistle echoed from the western treeline—one of Lucia's signals, though Theo hadn't planned it. Marcus whirled toward the sound, firing three wild shots into the forest.

"See?" Vince said, using the distraction to step away from the gun. "They're toying with us."

Two more men slipped out the back door of the command center, heading for the eastern perimeter. No one moved to stop them.

Theo lowered his binoculars, satisfaction warming his chest. The breaking point had arrived. The organization was fracturing before his eyes—men abandoning posts, leaders turning on each other, paranoia replacing discipline.

This was the moment he had methodically engineered. The window they needed.

Tomorrow, they would move to free the captives.

Chapter 11

The full moon hung suspended in the inky sky, casting silver light across the delta's landscape. Theo's breath came in measured intervals as he crouched in the dense cordgrass at the northern edge of the smugglers' camp. His mud-camouflaged wetsuit blended perfectly with the surrounding vegetation, rendering him nearly invisible in the moonlight.

Through gaps in the vegetation, he tracked the movements of the guards. What a difference from the confident men who had patrolled these grounds just two weeks ago. These guards moved with hunched shoulders, their rifles clutched too tightly against their chests. Every few steps, they cast nervous glances over their shoulders, as though expecting phantoms to materialize from the darkness.

"Anything?" one guard called out, his voice barely above a whisper.

"Nothing," came the reply, equally hushed. "Just like the last three hours."

"Ramirez and Alvarez were supposed to be back by now."

"They're not coming back. Nobody comes back."

The men fell silent, continuing their patrol with visible unease. Their flashlight beams jerked erratically across the compound, more likely to betray their positions than illuminate any threat.

Theo checked his watch: 11:47 PM. In thirteen minutes, the midnight rotation would create a ninety-second window when the northeastern corner of the compound would stand unguarded. The timing couldn't be better.

Marcus Delgado hadn't been seen since his confrontation with Vince that afternoon. His absence had only deepened the unrest among the remaining men. Without their leader's ruthless presence, discipline had further deteriorated. Three more guards had disappeared during the evening meal, taking weapons and supplies with them.

Theo's gaze drifted to the barracks—a long, low building with barred windows where the captives were held. A single guard stood at the entrance, shifting his weight from foot to foot, eyes darting toward every sound from the surrounding marsh.

From his position, Theo could make out the entire compound. What had once been an efficient operation now resembled a sinking ship. Equipment lay abandoned, communications remained sporadic, and the remaining men clustered together rather than maintaining proper perimeter positions.

The transformation within himself seemed equally profound. The seasick biology student who had stumbled off that dive boat now felt like a stranger. In his place stood a tactician who had systematically dismantled a criminal enterprise, using the very environment they had sought to exploit against them.

Theo touched the knife at his belt, then checked the wire cutters in his pack. Everything was ready. Elena and Mateo waited at the rendezvous point with the boat, while Rodrigo and the others prepared diversions along the eastern perimeter. Each piece of the plan had been meticulously arranged.

A sound from the barracks caught his attention—a child's muffled cry quickly silenced. The sound hardened his resolve. Those people had suffered long enough.

He checked his watch again: 11:54 PM. Six minutes until the guard rotation. Theo settled deeper into the cordgrass, his muscles coiled with anticipation. The weeks of psychological warfare had led to this moment. The smugglers' operation had reached its breaking point, creating the perfect opportunity for the rescue attempt.

As midnight approached, Theo drew a slow, centering breath. The marsh had taught him patience, and now that patience would bear fruit. The liberation was about to begin.

Midnight came, and with it, Theo's moment to act. He slipped from his hiding place in the cordgrass, a shadow among shadows. The mud-camouflaged wetsuit that had once felt alien against his skin now served as his second nature, breaking up his silhouette against the moonlit delta.

Theo moved with deliberate precision across the marshy ground. Each footfall represented a calculation—testing the surface before committing his weight, rolling from heel to toe to distribute pressure evenly. The techniques Esteban had taught him now manifested as instinct rather than conscious thought.

Fifty yards from the compound's northeastern corner, Theo froze. Two guards conversed in hushed tones, their cigarettes glowing like fireflies in the darkness. Neither man looked directly at the marshland where Theo stood motionless, yet discovery remained just one careless movement away.

"I'm telling you, man, we should grab what we can and go," one guard whispered. "Marcus has lost it."

"And go where? You think he won't find us?"

The men's fear hung in the air, nearly palpable. When they finally moved on, continuing their patrol, Theo released the breath he'd been holding and advanced toward the perimeter fence.

A splash to his right—perhaps a night heron or jumping fish—drew a nervous burst of gunfire from somewhere in the compound. Theo dropped instantly, pressing his body into the mud as shouting erupted. He remained perfectly still, heart hammering against his ribs while his mind stayed clear and focused.

The commotion subsided after several minutes. False alarm. The guards were shooting at shadows—exactly as Theo and his allies had conditioned them to do over the past week.

He resumed his approach, now crawling on elbows and knees through ankle-deep water. The fence loomed ahead, its chain links reflecting dull silver in the moonlight. Theo reached for the wire cutters in his pack, his fingers finding them without needing to look.

As he prepared to cut through the fence, Theo realized how completely he had transformed. The plants surrounding him were no longer specimens to be cataloged but allies providing concealment. The mud wasn't something to wash away but essential camouflage. The darkness wasn't something to fear but his greatest advantage.

Professor Harmon would never recognize the student who had once meticulously labeled plant specimens in the university greenhouse. Aunt Clara, however, would recognize this version of her nephew—the one who had finally embraced her teachings about the natural world not as academic curiosities but as essential knowledge for survival.

Three days earlier, Esteban had shown Theo how to set the traps. The old fisherman's weathered hands had worked with practiced efficiency, demonstrating how to suspend the nearly invisible fishing line at precisely the right height.

"Not to kill," Esteban had emphasized, his voice barely above a whisper. "To distract, to confuse. The hook catches, they forget everything else. Pain becomes their world."

Now, crouched in the shadows twenty yards inside the perimeter fence, Theo carefully tied the last of seven traps. Each consisted of monofilament fishing line stretched across the narrow footpaths used by the sentries. At face height hung small, sharp hooks—the kind used for catching speckled trout in the shallows of the bay. Not large enough to cause permanent damage, but more than sufficient to create excruciating, disorienting pain.

From his position, Theo could see three guards patrolling the outer compound. The nearest one, a stocky man with a neck tattoo Theo recognized from previous observations, moved with the mechanical rhythm of someone fighting exhaustion. His patrol route would bring him directly into the path of Theo's first trap in approximately forty seconds.

Theo remained motionless, watching the sentry's approach. The guard's flashlight beam swept lazily across the ground, never rising high enough to reveal the thin line suspended at eye level. Twenty feet away. Ten feet. Five.

The guard's sudden cry pierced the night as the hook caught his right cheek. His hands flew to his face, dropping both flashlight and weapon as he stumbled sideways, disoriented by the unexpected pain. Blood trickled between his fingers as he tried to understand what had happened.

Theo didn't move. Not yet.

The guard's muffled curses continued as he fumbled in the darkness, trying to remove the hook without tearing his flesh further. His attention completely consumed by pain and confusion, he staggered away from his post, heading toward the barracks.

Only then did Theo advance, slipping past the abandoned post like a shadow. One down, two more to neutralize before reaching the main compound.

The second guard fell victim to a similar trap five minutes later. This time, the hook caught in the man's ear. His reaction—dropping to his knees, radio clattering to the ground—created precisely the window Theo needed to move closer to the captives' quarters.

The third guard proved more observant, pausing before the trap and tilting his head as if sensing something amiss. For a breathless moment, Theo thought his plan would fail. Then the guard's radio crackled to life with a request for status. As he reached to respond, his attention diverted, he stepped forward—directly into the path of the hook.

This time, Theo didn't wait to watch the aftermath. He moved swiftly through the gap in the security perimeter, his path to the compound now clear. Behind him, confusion spread as the first guard reached the barracks, his face bloodied, babbling about invisible attackers in the darkness.

No shots had been fired. No alarms raised. Just enough chaos to create the opportunity Theo needed.

The moral calculation had been simple for Theo. These men weren't innocent, but neither did he wish to become a killer. Incapacitation served his purpose without crossing a line he couldn't uncross. As he approached the darkened building where the captives were held, Theo felt a grim satisfaction. The guards would recover from their injuries. The same couldn't be said for what Marcus had done—and planned to do—to his victims.

Theo pressed his body against the rough wood of the supply crates, feeling splinters dig into his palms. Twenty feet ahead, the captives huddled around a small fire that cast long, dancing shadows across the compound's central clearing. The flickering orange light illuminated their faces in brief, haunting glimpses—twelve souls whose freedom now rested in his hands.

An older man with silver-streaked hair cradled a boy no older than ten against his chest, both their faces gaunt from days of insufficient food. Beside them, a woman in a torn blouse stared vacantly into the flames, her eyes reflecting nothing but resignation.

Three teenage girls huddled together for warmth, whispering occasionally, while a middle-aged couple sat back-to-back, supporting each other in their exhaustion. The remaining captives—two young men and three women of varying ages—maintained the thousand-yard stare of those who had abandoned hope.

"They're bringing in another boat tomorrow," one guard said, shifting his weight and adjusting the rifle that hung carelessly from his shoulder. His voice carried clearly through the night air. "Bigger haul than this one, according to Vince."

The second guard snorted, flicking a cigarette butt into the darkness. "If there even is a tomorrow. Way things are going, we'll be lucky if the whole operation doesn't collapse before sunrise."

Their conversation drifted to complaints about Marcus's leadership, their attention wavering from their charges. Neither noticed the shadows shifting unnaturally behind the nearest stack of crates.

Theo studied the guards' positions, calculating. The first guard stood with his back partially turned, focused on his conversation. The second faced the captives but gazed absently over their heads, lost in thought. Both men had grown complacent, convinced their prisoners were too broken to attempt escape.

A log in the fire collapsed, sending a shower of sparks skyward. In that moment of distraction, Theo slipped from behind the crates, using the elongated shadows as cover. He moved in perfect synchronization with the flickering light, advancing when shadows stretched and freezing when they receded.

Three quick movements brought him to the edge of the captive group. The silver-haired man noticed him first, his eyes widening slightly before his expression carefully reset. A subtle shake of Theo's head prevented the man from reacting further.

Theo eased himself into a sitting position at the periphery of the group, his mud-camouflaged wetsuit blending with the darkness beyond the firelight. To the inattentive guards, he appeared as just another huddled figure among many.

"Don't look directly at me," Theo whispered, his voice barely audible above the crackling fire. "I'm here to help you escape."

The woman in the torn blouse stiffened but kept her gaze fixed on the flames.

"When I create a distraction, move toward the eastern fence," Theo continued, his lips barely moving. "There's a cut section. Friends are waiting beyond with boats."

The silver-haired man gave an almost imperceptible nod while drawing the boy closer.

"Twenty minutes," Theo breathed. "Be ready."

One of the teenage girls began to quietly weep, though whether from fear or sudden hope, Theo couldn't tell. The sound drew a guard's attention.

"Shut it," he barked, taking two steps toward the group.

Theo remained motionless, feeling the guard's gaze sweep over the captives. For three heartbeats, he feared discovery. Then the guard turned away, resuming his conversation.

What had been abstract—a moral imperative to free nameless victims—had become devastatingly personal. These weren't faceless statistics but people with lives that had been violently interrupted. The resignation in their eyes struck Theo more deeply than any physical wound could have.

He melted back into the shadows, his resolve hardened. Twenty minutes to set the final pieces in place. Twenty minutes until everything changed.

The guards turned away, distracted by a noise from the perimeter—likely another of Theo's traps claiming a victim. In that precious moment, Theo seized a stick from the edge of the fire pit and dropped to one knee. His fingers moved with practiced precision, etching lines into the dirt just beyond the firelight's reach.

First came the rectangular outline of the compound, then quick marks indicating the barracks, the main building, and the eastern fence where he'd created the opening. His stick moved faster, sketching the surrounding marsh with its distinctive channels and the three possible routes that led to safety.

The silver-haired man noticed first. His weathered face remained impassive, but his eyes tracked every movement of the stick. He shifted slightly, his shoulder nudging the woman beside him. She glanced down, understanding immediately, and pressed her foot against the teenage girl's ankle.

Like a silent current, awareness spread through the group. One by one, they absorbed the crude map without a single telling glance or word. The middle-aged couple leaned forward as if warming their hands, their eyes memorizing the escape routes. The young men studied the diagram from the corners of their eyes, their expressions unchanged.

Theo added three wavy lines for the water channels, then marked the spots where Elena, Mateo, and the others waited with boats. He drew arrows indicating primary and secondary escape paths, then a third route marked with a question mark—the emergency option if everything went wrong.

The silver-haired man's eyes met Theo's for a fraction of a second. In that brief connection, Theo saw understanding, determination, and something he hadn't expected: trust. The man gave an almost imperceptible nod before looking away.

"Hey! What are you looking at?" One guard's voice cut through the quiet.

Theo's foot swept across the dirt, erasing the map in one smooth motion as he melted back into the shadows. The guard approached, suspicious, but found only captives huddled around a dying fire.

"Nothing," the silver-haired man muttered, poking at the embers. "Just wondering if we'll get more wood for the night."

The guard spat on the ground and walked away. But something had changed among the captives. Where before there had been resignation, now a current of energy passed between them—subtle but unmistakable. They had a plan. They had direction. And most importantly, they had hope.

Theo pressed against the supply crates, watching the captives through narrow gaps between wooden slats. The guards paced at the perimeter, their attention momentarily diverted by the commotion his traps had caused. He needed a primary contact among the captives—someone who could silently coordinate the others.

His gaze settled on a woman cradling a sleeping child against her chest. Unlike the others whose postures conveyed defeat, something in her eyes remained alert, watchful. She sat slightly apart, positioned where she could observe both the guards and her fellow captives.

Theo waited until she glanced in his direction, then deliberately caught her eye. Her body remained perfectly still, but her gaze locked onto his with fierce intensity.

He tapped his wrist where a watch would be, then raised five fingers. *Five minutes.*

She blinked once, slowly.

He pointed to himself, then to the eastern fence where he'd cut an opening, and made a running motion with two fingers.

The woman's arms tightened almost imperceptibly around her child. Her chin dipped in the slightest nod.

Theo gestured to include all the captives, then repeated the running motion toward the escape route.

The woman's eyes narrowed in understanding. She shifted her weight, adjusting the child in her arms. The movement seemed natural, but it allowed her to lean toward the silver-haired man.

No words passed between them. She simply repositioned her hand so that five fingers splayed against the child's back where only he could see them. The man's shoulders straightened almost imperceptibly.

One of the guards spat into the fire, causing it to hiss. "Quit your fidgeting," he barked at no one in particular.

The captives remained outwardly still, their faces masks of resignation. But beneath that facade, a current of energy pulsed through the group.

The silver-haired man stretched his arms above his head—a casual movement that disguised how his fingers flashed five to the teenage boy beside him. The boy scratched his neck, accidentally bumping the woman next to him while holding his hand in a way that showed all five fingers.

Theo watched in amazement as the message rippled through the group. A cough here, a shift there—each movement conveying the signal while appearing natural to the guards. Within a minute, every captive had received the message.

The woman with the child began subtle preparations. She tightened the makeshift sling holding her child, securing it to prevent it from slipping during their escape. The others made equally discreet adjustments—tying shoelaces, securing loose clothing, shifting positions to face the eastern fence.

Three minutes left.

A guard approached, and all movement ceased instantly. He surveyed the group with bored contempt before continuing his patrol.

Two minutes.

The woman caught Theo's eye again. She raised her eyebrows slightly—a question. *Are you sure?*

Theo nodded once, firmly.

One minute.

The captives maintained their facade of broken spirits while coiled energy built within them. Their breathing had synchronized, bodies leaning almost imperceptibly toward the eastern fence. Hands moved to children's shoulders. Parents positioned themselves to shield the youngest.

Thirty seconds.

Theo readied himself, muscles tense, breathing measured. The woman adjusted her grip on her child one final time, her eyes never leaving the spot where Theo hid.

The time had come.

The stones felt cool and solid in Theo's palm as he weighed them one final time. He'd selected them carefully from the marsh—each one smooth enough to throw, heavy enough to make noise. The fuel depot stood thirty yards away, metal drums arranged in neat rows. Perfect for creating chaos.

Theo drew his arm back and released. The stones arced through the darkness, clattering against the metal drums with a sound like gunfire.

"What the hell was that?" A guard spun toward the noise, rifle raised.

"Check it out!" another shouted, already moving toward the depot.

Three guards converged on the fuel drums, their flashlight beams cutting through the darkness. In their haste, they left the captives momentarily unwatched.

Theo emerged from his hiding place, locking eyes with the woman with the child. He nodded once.

She rose in a single fluid motion, the sleeping child secure against her chest. The silver-haired man followed, then the teenage boy, then the others—twelve souls moving as one entity, rising from around the fire without a word.

They flowed across the compound like a shadow, following the path Theo had drawn in the dirt. The woman led them with unwavering certainty, her steps quick but measured, her body angled to shield her child.

A guard shouted from the fuel depot. Another responded from the western perimeter.

The captives moved faster, maintaining their formation. The strongest positioned themselves on the edges of the group, creating a human shield around the children and elderly. No one panicked. No one broke formation. They moved with the quiet determination of people who understood this might be their only chance.

Fifty yards to the fence.

A flashlight beam swept the compound, missing the group by inches as they pressed against a storage shed. The woman held up her hand, and everyone froze. When the light passed, they continued.

Thirty yards.

A child stumbled. Before he could fall, two sets of hands steadied him, lifted him, carried him forward without breaking stride.

Twenty yards.

The silver-haired man spotted the cut in the fence before the others. He tapped the woman's shoulder, redirecting her slightly. She adjusted their course without hesitation.

Ten yards.

Theo materialized from the shadows at the fence line, gesturing urgently toward the opening. The woman reached him first, eyes fierce with determination.

"Through here," Theo whispered, pulling back the section of chain-link he'd cut earlier. "Stay low. The marsh is fifty yards ahead."

The woman ducked through, child clutched tight against her. The others followed in the same order they'd risen from the fire—a choreographed procession of silent movement.

A shout erupted from behind them. "The prisoners! Check the prisoners!"

"Move," Theo urged, counting heads as the captives slipped through the fence. Ten. Eleven. Twelve. All accounted for.

He took up the rear position, scanning for pursuit as they crossed the exposed ground between the compound and the marsh. The captives moved with surprising speed despite their exhaustion, following the woman who seemed to absorb Theo's directions instinctively.

Flashlight beams crisscrossed the compound behind them. Guards shouted contradictory orders, their discipline fracturing under pressure.

The marsh loomed ahead, a wall of darkness promising concealment. The woman reached it first, disappearing into the vegetation with her child. The others followed, bodies bending low beneath the cordgrass, feet finding purchase in the soft earth.

Theo was the last to enter the marsh. He paused at the edge, watching the chaos unfold in the compound. For a moment, standing between two worlds—the brutality of the smugglers and the wild sanctuary of the delta—he felt a surge of fierce satisfaction.

Then he turned and melted into the cordgrass, following the captives into the darkness where Elena and Mateo waited to guide them deeper into the delta's protection.

"They're gone! All of them!" The shout echoed across the compound, carrying through the night air to where Theo led the escapees deeper into the marsh.

Flashlight beams sliced through the darkness behind them, bouncing wildly as guards scrambled to organize a search. The woman with the child glanced back, her face illuminated momentarily by the distant lights.

"Keep moving," Theo whispered. "We have a lead, but they know these waterways too."

The marsh stretched before them like a living labyrinth—a complex network of channels, islands, and vegetation that changed with each tide. To the smugglers, it was hostile territory. To Theo, it had become home.

He led them along a narrow ridge of solid ground, invisible to anyone who hadn't spent weeks mapping the terrain. The silver-haired man followed directly behind him, then the woman with her child, with the others forming a silent chain through the darkness.

"Step only where I step," Theo instructed, pointing to a seemingly innocuous patch of ground ahead. "That looks solid but it's quicksand. We go around here."

The group adjusted their path without question. Behind them, engines roared to life—airboats preparing to search the waterways.

A young boy of perhaps seven stumbled, his foot sliding into the water with a splash that seemed deafening in their heightened state. His mother pulled him back instantly, eyes wide with fear.

Theo held up his hand, and the entire group froze.

"It's okay," he mouthed silently, nodding reassurance to the frightened child.

They pressed on, Theo leading them through a stand of cypress trees. He navigated by touch and memory, using the distinctive shapes of cypress knees as markers. Third knee from the left, turn north. Cluster of five, head east.

The distant sound of an airboat grew louder. Flashlight beams swept across the water half a mile back.

"Down," Theo whispered urgently.

The group dropped as one, pressing themselves into the mud and vegetation. A small girl whimpered as insects found her exposed skin, but her father cupped his hand gently over her mouth. Her eyes were wide above his fingers, but she nodded understanding.

The airboat's engine growled closer, its mounted spotlight sweeping across the marsh in wide arcs. Theo and the escapees lay motionless, barely breathing as the light passed within twenty feet of their position, illuminating the Spanish moss hanging from cypress branches above them.

"See anything?" a voice called.

"Nothing but swamp," another replied. "They couldn't have gotten this far anyway."

The spotlight lingered for an excruciating moment, then swept onward. The airboat's engine faded as it continued down a parallel channel.

Theo waited until the sound diminished before signaling the group to rise. The silver-haired man helped an elderly woman to her feet, brushing mud from her clothes with gentle hands.

"How much farther?" the woman with the child whispered.

"Another mile," Theo replied. "There's a high spot where friends are waiting with supplies. We'll rest there before continuing."

They moved on, skirting the territory of a bull alligator Theo had observed for weeks. The massive reptile controlled this section of marsh, and Theo had learned to identify the subtle signs of its presence—broken reeds, slide marks on the banks, the particular stillness of water in its favorite hunting spots.

A twig snapped somewhere to their left. The group tensed, but Theo recognized the sound pattern—too light for human footsteps.

"Marsh rabbit," he whispered. "We're okay."

The silver-haired man nodded, impressed. The woman adjusted her sleeping child, who somehow remained peaceful despite the chaos surrounding them.

The voices of pursuers rose and fell like the tide, sometimes alarmingly close, sometimes distant. Each time, Theo found places to hide—beneath overhanging banks, behind dense vegetation, once even standing perfectly still among cattails as a boat passed within yards of them.

The marsh protected its own. And somehow, Theo had become one with it.

The escapees huddled together on the small island of solid ground that Theo had prepared days earlier. Elena and Mateo distributed water and blankets while the silver-haired man organized the group, whispering reassurances. The woman with the child looked up as Theo approached.

"You're leaving again," she stated, reading his intent before he spoke.

Theo nodded. "They'll keep hunting unless I end it."

The woman studied his face, noting the transformation that had occurred since their first silent exchange at the compound. "You're not the same person who came to the Gulf, are you?"

"No," Theo answered simply. "I'm not."

He turned to Elena. "Give me thirty minutes. If I'm not back by then—"

"We'll be gone," she promised. "But you'll be back."

Theo slipped away from the group, his movements fluid and purposeful. The marsh welcomed him, each sound and scent familiar now. He navigated without hesitation, following paths invisible to anyone who hadn't lived as he had these past weeks.

The smugglers' compound glowed in the distance, generators humming as guards shouted orders. Chaos reigned—exactly as Theo had planned. The escape had drawn most of the men into the marsh on a futile search, leaving the camp vulnerable.

At the edge of the clearing, Theo paused beside a hollow cypress stump. He reached inside and retrieved a waterproof bag he'd hidden three days earlier. Inside lay his final insurance: waterproof matches and a bottle of diesel fuel siphoned from the smugglers' own supply.

The irony wasn't lost on him. Marcus's resources would be his undoing.

Theo moved like a shadow along the perimeter. Two guards remained at the boat dock, but their attention focused outward, searching for returning search parties. They never thought to watch their backs.

The first boat ignited with a soft whoosh. Theo had already moved to the second when the guards noticed the flames. Their shouts carried across the compound as Theo set the third and fourth boats ablaze.

Fire climbed the sides of the vessels, consuming weathered wood and fiberglass. Black smoke billowed into the night sky. The guards ran toward the inferno, forgetting all else in their panic.

Theo circled behind them, making his way to the communications shed. He poured fuel along its base, struck a match, and watched as flames licked up the wooden walls. Inside, radio equipment crackled and popped as circuits melted.

The fuel depot was his final target—a cluster of barrels behind the main building. Theo worked methodically, creating a trail of fuel between them. He struck his last match, touched it to the liquid, and stepped back as fire raced along the path he'd created.

The first explosion rocked the compound. Then another. Guards scattered like startled birds as ammunition stored nearby began to cook off, sending bullets whizzing through the air.

Theo melted into the marsh as the night turned to day behind him. The fire painted his back with orange light as he ran, following the same invisible path that had brought him here. Behind him, Marcus's empire collapsed in flames.

He paused once, looking back at the inferno. The smugglers wouldn't pursue tonight. Their boats were ashes, their communications silenced, their organization in ruins. By morning, the Coast Guard would investigate the explosions, and whatever remained of Marcus's operation would scatter to the wind.

Theo turned away from the fire and continued through the marsh. The delta had taught him patience, resourcefulness, and when necessary, destruction. He was no longer the seasick student who'd arrived on a dive boat. He had become something else—shaped by necessity and forged in survival.

The flames behind him illuminated his path forward, toward the people waiting for his return. Toward a new version of himself he was only beginning to understand.

Theo rejoined the group, his clothes singed and face streaked with soot. The escapees huddled together on the small island, eyes wide with a mixture of hope and fear. Elena pressed a water bottle into his hands while Mateo kept watch, scanning the darkness for pursuers.

"We need to move," Theo said after taking a long drink. "This position is too exposed."

The silver-haired man nodded in agreement. "Where?"

"Higher ground," Theo replied, pointing northwest. "There's a limestone ridge that overlooks the whole delta. We'll be able to see anyone coming."

The woman with the child adjusted her grip on the sleeping toddler. "How far?"

"Half a mile. Difficult terrain, but we can make it."

They moved as a single unit through the marsh, Theo leading while Elena and Mateo guarded the rear. The escapees followed in silence, their faces set with determination. The distant glow of the burning compound cast long shadows across the wetlands, illuminating their path in an eerie orange light.

The ridge rose gradually from the delta, a rare elevation in the otherwise flat landscape. Limestone outcroppings provided natural steps as they climbed, helping one another over the steeper sections. By the time they reached the summit, the first hints of dawn colored the eastern sky.

"Rest here," Theo instructed, gesturing to a depression in the rock that would hide them from casual observation. "We should be safe until—"

His words died as a glint of metal caught his eye. Far below, where the delta waters opened into the Gulf, a sleek black vessel approached the burning compound. Unlike the weathered boats of local fishermen or the utilitarian craft of the Coast Guard, this one moved with purpose and precision.

"Get down," he hissed.

The group flattened themselves against the limestone as Theo crawled to the edge for a better view. The boat cut through the water without running lights, its hull so dark it seemed to absorb rather than reflect the flames from the shore.

As it neared the dock—or what remained of it—figures emerged on deck. Even at this distance, their movements betrayed military training. They disembarked in formation, assault rifles held at the ready, sweeping the area with practiced efficiency.

"Cartel," whispered the silver-haired man, who had crawled up beside Theo. His voice trembled. "Not local men. These are enforcers from the mainland."

A small sound made Theo turn. Behind them, several of the escapees had recognized the newcomers as well. A woman pressed her fist against her mouth to stifle a sob while others shrank back against the rock, terror evident in their eyes.

"You know them?" Theo asked.

The silver-haired man nodded grimly. "They are the ones who truly run things. Your Marcus—he was just a middleman."

Theo watched as the cartel members moved through the burning camp, their gestures sharp with anger as they surveyed the destruction. One man, taller than the rest, stood apart, speaking into a satellite phone.

"We've disrupted one link in their chain," the silver-haired man continued. "Now they will send more men. Better equipped. More ruthless."

The realization hit Theo like a physical blow. What he'd believed was a decisive victory was merely the beginning of something far more dangerous. The fire he'd set hadn't ended their ordeal—it had escalated it, drawing the attention of those higher in the criminal hierarchy.

"What have I done?" Theo whispered.

The woman with the child placed a hand on his shoulder. "You saved us," she said simply. "But now we must save ourselves again."

Below them, the cartel enforcers fanned out, beginning a methodical search of the surrounding area.

Dawn broke over the delta in shades of crimson and gold, but the beauty was lost on the group huddled on the limestone ridge. They lay prone against the cool rock, barely breathing as they watched the scene unfold below.

The cartel enforcers moved with military precision through the smoldering remains of the camp. Four men in tactical gear dragged struggling smugglers from hiding places, forcing them to kneel in a row near the dock. Their weapons, once carried with such swagger, lay in a pile at the feet of the tall man with the satellite phone.

"They're not treating them like allies," Elena whispered.

Theo nodded grimly. "They're treating them like problems."

A black SUV appeared on the narrow access road, its tires crushing debris as it rolled to a stop. The driver emerged first, scanning the area before opening the rear door. A man in an expensive charcoal suit stepped out, adjusting his cuffs with practiced nonchalance. Even from a distance, his authority was palpable.

"El Patrón," the silver-haired man breathed, his voice barely audible. "I never thought I would see him in person."

The suited man surveyed the destruction with cold detachment, then signaled to his men. They disappeared into the remaining structures, emerging moments later dragging a bloodied figure between them.

"Marcus," Theo said, recognizing the former dive instructor despite his battered condition.

They watched as Marcus was thrown at the suited man's feet. A conversation followed, Marcus gesturing wildly, his voice carrying across the water in desperate fragments. The suited man listened impassively, then checked his watch as if bored by the entire exchange.

When Marcus finished speaking, the suited man made a dismissive gesture with his hand. No anger, no shouting—just the casual flick of fingers that sealed Marcus's fate.

One of the enforcers stepped forward, drew a pistol with a suppressor attached, and fired a single shot into the back of Marcus's head. He collapsed face-first onto the muddy ground. The execution was clinical, efficient—a business transaction completed.

The woman with the child clutched her toddler closer, her lips near Theo's ear. "They're cleaning house," she whispered, her voice trembling.

One by one, the kneeling smugglers met the same fate. No questions, no chances for explanation. Each body was dragged to a waiting boat, wrapped in chains, and weighted with concrete blocks before being dumped into the deep channel.

"Jesus," Mateo murmured, turning away.

"No," the silver-haired man corrected. "Not Jesus. This is the devil's work."

The suited man supervised the operation with detached efficiency, occasionally speaking into a phone. More men arrived, bringing gasoline cans. They doused the remaining structures and set them ablaze, erasing all evidence of the operation.

"They can't afford loose ends," Theo realized aloud. "Or witnesses."

The woman nodded. "Few ever see this and survive to speak of it."

For an hour, they watched in horrified silence as the cartel methodically eliminated all traces of the smuggling operation. Bodies, equipment, buildings—all evidence vanished into fire or water.

"We have to move," Theo finally said. "If they find us..."

He left the sentence unfinished. They all understood the stakes now. They possessed knowledge that made them targets—knowledge of faces, methods, and the very existence of this operation.

The suited man made one final call before returning to his SUV. As the vehicle pulled away, the cartel enforcers spread out, beginning a grid search of the surrounding area.

"They're hunting for survivors," Elena whispered.

Theo met the eyes of each person in their group. "And we're what they're looking for."

The pale light of dawn stretched across the delta, washing the landscape in shades of pearl and silver. Theo led the group back toward the camp in silence, each step measured and cautious. They moved like ghosts through the marsh, following the narrow paths only Theo could see.

When they reached the edge of the clearing, Theo raised his hand, signaling them to wait while he surveyed the area. The compound lay before them, a skeleton of its former self. Where guards had patrolled and captives had huddled in fear, only emptiness remained.

"They're gone," he said finally.

The group emerged from the marsh, stepping into the clearing with the hesitant movements of prey venturing into an open field. The cartel's cleanup had been thorough. Bodies had vanished, vehicles disappeared. Only scattered debris, dark bloodstains on the earth, and the acrid smell of burned plastic remained as evidence of what had transpired.

The silver-haired man crossed himself. "I never thought I would walk here freely."

Elena moved through the space, examining the charred remains of the communications shed. "They didn't want anyone knowing they were here."

Mateo pointed toward the water. "The boats are gone too. Everything."

The captives drifted through the compound, their expressions a complex mixture of disbelief and caution. A middle-aged woman touched the fence that had contained her, running her fingers along the wire as if to convince herself it no longer held power over her. A teenage boy kicked at the ashes of what had been the guards' quarters, his face hard with memories.

Theo walked to the edge of the dock, staring out at the water. The rising sun cast long reflections across its surface, deceptively peaceful. He felt hollow, emptied of the rage and determination that had driven him these past days. They had won, but victory tasted strange on his tongue.

"You're thinking about what comes next."

The woman with the child stood beside him, her toddler balanced on her hip. The little boy's eyes were wide, taking in the open sky as if seeing it for the first time.

"I am," Theo admitted.

"So am I." She shifted the child to her other hip. "My name is Isabella. This is Diego."

Theo nodded, the simple exchange of names somehow profound after everything they'd endured.

"What happens now?" Isabella asked, giving voice to the question hanging over all of them.

Theo looked back at the group. Some were sitting in exhaustion, others exploring the boundaries of their newfound freedom. All were waiting, looking to him with expectations he wasn't sure he could fulfill.

"I don't know," he answered honestly. "We're alive. We're free. But we're still in the middle of nowhere, with no transportation, limited supplies, and people who might come looking for us."

Isabella nodded, unsurprised by his answer. "And we've seen things we shouldn't have seen."

"Yes."

Diego reached out a small hand toward the water, babbling something only he understood.

"The nearest town is twenty miles northwest," Theo said. "But getting there means crossing open marshland, with no guarantee of safety."

"And if we make it?" Isabella asked. "What then? Do we tell someone what happened here? Who would believe us? Who would protect us?"

Theo had no answer. They had escaped one prison only to find themselves trapped in a larger, more complex one—the prison of knowledge, of having witnessed things powerful men would kill to keep secret.

The sun climbed higher, burning away the morning mist. Their shadows stretched behind them, elongated and fragile against the weathered wood of the dock.

"We take it one step at a time," Theo said finally. "First, we survive. Then we decide what truth we can afford to tell."

Chapter 12

The limestone ridge rose like a sentinel above the delta, offering what Theo needed most: perspective. He'd chosen this spot carefully—a natural depression behind a cluster of scrub oak and palmetto, invisible from below yet providing clear sightlines to the abandoned camp through gaps in the foliage.

From this vantage point, the smugglers' compound looked deceptively peaceful. No movement disturbed the eerie stillness that had settled over the place. The charred remains of the communications shed stood as a blackened skeleton against the landscape. Blood had darkened to rust-colored stains on the packed earth.

"You don't have to do this alone," Elena had argued when he'd explained his plan. "We can take shifts."

But Theo had been firm. "You need to keep everyone together. Find water, gather food. I need to know they're not coming back."

Now, as the first day's afternoon heat pressed down on him, Theo maintained his vigil. He'd fashioned a crude scope from a broken pair of binoculars he'd found in the compound, removing the cracked lens and creating a makeshift spyglass. Every twenty minutes, he methodically scanned the perimeter, the dock area, the approach channels, and the sky.

His emergency pack sat beside him—water bottle, protein bars, compass, knife, and the satellite phone he'd taken from Carlos's supplies. The phone remained off to conserve its battery, to be used only in the direst emergency.

"Two hours watching, one hour resting," he whispered to himself, establishing the rhythm that would carry him through this vigil.

As dusk approached, mosquitoes swarmed around him. Theo applied mud to his exposed skin, the coolness a momentary relief from the heat. The marsh came alive with night sounds—frogs calling, insects buzzing, the occasional splash of something entering the water.

The first night passed without incident. Stars wheeled overhead, indifferent to the human drama below. Theo fought sleep, pinching himself and chewing on bitter leaves to stay alert. When exhaustion threatened to overwhelm him, he allowed himself precisely twenty-minute naps, using a small pile of pebbles to mark time, moving one from left to right after each interval of watchfulness.

Dawn brought no boats, no men, no threat. Just birds reclaiming their territory, their calls echoing across the water.

By the second day, hunger gnawed at Theo's stomach. He rationed his supplies carefully, taking small sips of water, eating half a protein bar in tiny bites. The sun beat down mercilessly, but he remained motionless, his body becoming part of the landscape.

Isabella visited once, bringing fresh water and wild berries.

"The others are getting restless," she told him. "They want to leave, find help."

"Not yet," Theo said, his voice hoarse from disuse. "We need to be certain."

She nodded, understanding the stakes. "Diego asked about you."

Something in Theo's chest tightened at the mention of the child. "Tell him I'm keeping watch. Like the herons do."

The second night descended, cooler than the first. Theo's muscles ached from immobility, but his mind remained sharp, cataloging every sound, every shadow. The half-moon cast silver light across the delta, transforming it into an alien landscape.

By the dawn of the third day, Theo had reached his conclusion. Forty-eight hours had passed without a single sign of human presence. The cartel had finished their business here—they had no reason to return to a compromised location.

Theo gathered his supplies and took one final, comprehensive scan of the horizon. The emptiness before him confirmed what he already knew: this chapter had ended. The smugglers were gone.

It was time to lead his people home.

Dawn painted the eastern sky in watercolor strokes of amber and rose as Theo descended from his limestone perch. His body protested after forty-eight hours of near immobility, joints cracking and muscles seizing. He paused at the base of the ridge, stretched his limbs methodically, and drank the last of his water.

The delta awakened around him—ibises probing the shallows, fish breaking the surface in silver flashes, dragonflies skimming across the water. Nature reclaiming its rhythm, indifferent to the human dramas that had unfolded here.

Theo moved with purpose now, no longer the panicked student who had washed ashore weeks ago. Each step calculated, each sense attuned to his surroundings. He circled wide around the compound, approaching from downwind. The wetsuit that had once felt alien against his skin now moved like a second skin, the mud-camouflage patterns refreshed daily until they became part of his ritual.

He paused at the tree line, studying the compound through his makeshift spyglass. Nothing moved except a turkey vulture perched atop the burned communications shed.

"Systematic," Theo whispered to himself. "Quadrant by quadrant."

He began at the eastern perimeter, noting the deep gouges in the mud where boats had been hastily launched. Fresh marks, no more than three days old. The dock pilings stood bare, stripped of ropes and cleats—everything of value taken.

Moving clockwise, Theo examined the barracks where the captives had been held. The door hung open, revealing empty space within. He stepped inside, crouching to examine the floor. Boot prints overlapped each other in chaotic patterns, telling the story of a rapid evacuation. In one corner, a child's crude drawing scratched into the wall caught his eye—a boat with stick figures. Theo touched it briefly, then continued his survey.

The main building yielded more evidence of hasty departure. File cabinets stood open and empty, their contents likely burned in the smoldering pile outside. Theo sifted carefully through the ashes with a stick, finding melted plastic and the charred remains of what might have been passports or identification papers.

"Covering their tracks," he murmured.

Behind the building, fresh earth marked shallow graves—the cartel's executions. Theo counted six distinct mounds. He stood silently for a moment, not out of respect for the dead but acknowledging the finality of what had happened here.

The communications shed was nothing but a blackened skeleton. The generator building stood empty, its valuable equipment removed. In the weapons cache, only empty crates remained.

At the western edge of the compound, Theo found what he was looking for—vehicle tracks leading inland, toward the county road miles away. Four distinct tire patterns, heavy vehicles, probably SUVs. They had loaded everything of value and departed by land.

The beach access point told the final part of the story. The sleek black vessel that had brought El Patrón was gone, but its landing point remained visible—a deeper cut in the shoreline where its bow had rested. No new marks indicated return.

Theo stood at the water's edge, watching the tide erase the last traces of human presence. The morning sun now cleared the horizon, illuminating the entire delta. Birds called. Fish jumped. The world continued.

He turned back toward the limestone ridge where Elena, Isabella, and the others waited. For the first time in days, Theo allowed his shoulders to relax. His methodical reconnaissance confirmed what his instincts had already told him—the danger had passed.

It was time to go home.

Mid-morning sun filtered through the cypress canopy as Theo retraced familiar paths through his survival territory. The delta seemed different now—no longer a prison but a place of transformation. Birds called to one another across the water, unaware of the human drama that had played out beneath their wings.

His first cache lay nestled in the hollow of a lightning-struck oak. Theo knelt, reaching deep into the scorched cavity. His fingers found the waterproof bag he'd fashioned from a piece of tarp, secured with cordgrass twine. Inside, his earliest notes remained intact—hasty sketches of the smugglers' compound, patrol schedules, and guard rotations. The paper had yellowed at the edges, but the pencil marks remained clear.

"First intelligence," Theo murmured, tucking the papers into his pack.

A quarter-mile west, beneath a distinctive limestone outcropping, Theo recovered a small tin containing the satellite phone's SIM card he'd managed to extract before discarding the device. On its plastic surface, he'd etched coordinates and frequencies with the tip of his knife. Evidence that might connect Marcus to the larger operation.

The third cache proved less fortunate. Water had seeped into the PVC pipe he'd buried near the marsh's edge, turning his careful documentation of overheard conversations into a sodden mess. Theo spread the pages on a sun-warmed rock, but the ink had run, rendering most illegible.

"Damn it," he whispered, salvaging only three pages where his writing remained decipherable. Names, dates, and destinations—fragments that might still prove useful.

Near the freshwater seep that had sustained him, Theo dug up a small jar containing personal treasures: his university ID, a smooth river stone from Aunt Clara, and a faded photograph of his father standing on a fishing boat. The glass had cracked, allowing moisture to seep in. The photo's edges curled, his father's face partially obscured by water damage.

Theo touched the image gently. "Sorry, Dad."

He transferred the items to a dry pouch, the photograph leaving a damp outline on his fingers.

At the base of a sprawling mangrove, Theo recovered his most valuable cache—a waterproof field notebook containing detailed accounts of the trafficking operation. Here he'd documented everything: descriptions of boats, cargo manifests glimpsed from hiding places, conversations between Marcus and his associates. The evidence that would bring them to justice.

Fire ants had colonized his sixth cache, forcing Theo to abandon the small compass and multi-tool he'd hidden there. The insects swarmed over his hand as he quickly resealed the container, leaving it to the colony.

His final cache lay beneath the shelter he'd first constructed. Theo knelt, digging through soft earth until his fingers touched metal. The tin box contained seeds he'd collected—sea oats, spartina, and wild rice—intended for replanting if his stay extended through winter. A promise to give back to the land that had sheltered him.

Theo stood in the clearing, his pack now filled with the physical record of his ordeal. Some items lost, others preserved—much like the parts of himself transformed by these weeks in the wilderness. The student who had arrived seasick on a dive boat no longer existed. In his place stood someone harder, more capable, intimately connected to this landscape of salt and mud and survival.

He surveyed his territory one last time. The rising tide would soon erase his footprints, but the knowledge he carried would endure.

"Time to go," Theo said to the watching marsh.

He turned toward the limestone ridge where the others waited, the evidence of crimes and corruption secure against his back, each step carrying him closer to justice.

Late morning sunlight filtered through the mangrove canopy, casting dappled patterns across Theo's primary shelter. The structure stood as a testament to his survival—a once-hasty assembly of driftwood and palm fronds that had evolved into an intricate haven against storms and pursuers alike.

Theo stood before it, pack heavy on his shoulders, experiencing the strange hollowness that accompanies departure from a place that has become home. In the distance, Isabella and the others waited on the limestone ridge, but this moment belonged to Theo and the marsh that had both threatened and saved him.

"Last rites," he murmured, setting his pack down.

With methodical care, Theo began dismantling the shelter. Each piece of driftwood was returned to where the tide might claim it. The cordgrass he'd woven into walls was scattered to decompose naturally. The elevated sleeping platform—his first true achievement—was the last to go, its components separated and laid flat against the earth.

As he worked, birds called from the canopy above. A raccoon watched curiously from behind a cypress knee, perhaps already planning to investigate once the human departed. The marsh would reclaim this space within days, erasing all evidence of his presence.

Theo moved to the small garden he'd cultivated near the freshwater seep. Wild rice stood tall alongside cattails and arrowhead. He knelt in the soft mud, harvesting several cattail shoots and a handful of sea purslane with his knife. Each cut was precise, taking only what he needed for a final meal, leaving roots intact to regrow.

"Thank you," he whispered, the words feeling both foolish and profoundly necessary.

Near the fire pit, Theo prepared the plants with the same ritual that had sustained him for weeks. He washed each one in collected rainwater, separating the edible portions with practiced movements. His hands, once soft from university life, now bore calluses that spoke of labor and survival.

The Dakota fire hole—one of his proudest accomplishments—burned hot and nearly smokeless as he cooked his final marsh meal. Eating slowly, Theo tasted not just the plants but the knowledge they represented. Each bite contained lessons from Aunt Clara, from his father, from Professor Morales, all woven together with what the marsh itself had taught him.

When finished, Theo extinguished the fire with careful attention, stirring the embers with a stick until they cooled, then covering them with soil. He filled the hole completely, patting the earth flat.

Standing in the clearing that had been his sanctuary, Theo turned slowly, taking in the view from all directions. The marsh extended in every direction—a labyrinth of channels and islands that had transformed from terrifying wilderness to intricate ecosystem in his perception. He knew its rhythms now: which birds announced morning, how the light changed with approaching storms, where tidal waters would rise and fall.

"I never expected to belong here," Theo said to the watching marsh.

The wilderness offered no response beyond the constant symphony of insects and distant water. Yet Theo felt a connection that transcended words—a belonging born of necessity but evolved into something deeper.

He shouldered his pack, the weight of his recovered caches reminding him of responsibilities beyond this place. Justice awaited. Home awaited. But something of him would remain here, just as something of the marsh would travel with him.

Theo took a final breath of the brackish air, rich with decay and growth and possibility, then turned away from his dismantled shelter. He left no footprints as he departed, careful to step on firm ground and disturb nothing in his passage.

The student who had stumbled seasick from a dive boat was gone. In his place walked a man who had learned to read the language of the wild, who had found strength in solitude, and who carried both evidence and enlightenment away from the marsh that had made him.

Early afternoon sun beat down on the rocky shoreline, harsh and unforgiving compared to the filtered light of the mangrove canopy. Theo moved steadily along the coast, his mud-camouflaged wetsuit now dry and cracking in places, his skin beneath tanned dark where exposed. The limestone ridge had given way to increasingly rocky terrain as he'd left the heart of the marsh behind.

Three miles from his former territory, Theo spotted it—the unmistakable silhouette of a small fishing boat bobbing just offshore. His pulse quickened, the first human contact beyond his group of survivors in weeks suddenly imminent. He stopped, instinctively dropping into a crouch before catching himself.

"Not prey anymore," he whispered, forcing himself to stand upright.

The boat's lone occupant, an elderly man with skin like tanned leather and a shock of white hair beneath a faded cap, worked methodically with a cast net. His movements spoke of decades on the water—efficient, practiced, without wasted effort. He hadn't yet noticed Theo on the shoreline.

Theo raised his arm to wave, then hesitated. What would this fisherman see? A wild man emerged from the marsh, covered in dried mud, carrying a makeshift pack? He swallowed hard and called out.

"Hello! On the boat!"

The old man's head snapped up, his hands freezing mid-task. He squinted toward shore, then reached quickly for something beneath his seat. When his hand reappeared, it held a revolver, not aimed directly at Theo but ready.

"Stay where you are," the fisherman called, voice carrying clearly across the water. "What's your business?"

"I'm not—" Theo's voice cracked from disuse. He cleared his throat. "I'm not a threat. I've been stranded. Weeks in the marsh."

The fisherman studied him, suspicion evident even at a distance. He adjusted something on the boat's small console, then slowly maneuvered toward shore, keeping a cautious distance.

"University student," Theo added, the words feeling strange in his mouth. "Dive boat. There was trouble."

As the boat drew closer, the old man's expression shifted from wariness to concern. His eyes traveled over Theo's weathered appearance, the improvised gear, the gauntness of his frame.

"Lord Almighty, son. You look half-wild." He tucked the revolver away and guided the boat to a natural jetty of rocks. "Name's Harold Buchanan. Most call me Buck."

"Theo Mercer."

Buck secured his boat and stepped carefully onto the rocks, keeping a respectful distance. "When'd you last have clean water? Food?"

"This morning. Found a freshwater seep weeks ago."

Buck nodded, retrieving a steel thermos and a wrapped package from his boat. He set them on a flat rock between them.

"Water's cold. Sandwich is grouper I caught yesterday."

Theo approached slowly, aware of how his movements had changed—more deliberate, lower to the ground. He uncapped the thermos, the scent of clean, unchlorinated water filling his nostrils. The first sip was a shock to his system—so pure compared to the filtered marsh water he'd grown accustomed to.

"Thank you," he managed.

Buck watched him with a mixture of fascination and concern. "You said there was trouble? Others with you?"

"Yes. Twelve others. They're waiting back at a limestone ridge." Theo unwrapped the sandwich, the smell of seasoned fish overwhelming. "It's complicated. There were smugglers. Human trafficking."

Buck's weathered face hardened. He reached for a radio clipped to his belt.

"Coast Guard station monitors this channel," he said. "You ready to tell your story, son?"

Theo looked out over the water, then back toward the marsh that had been his world. The evidence in his pack, the survivors waiting for his return, the justice still to be sought—all of it depended on this moment of transition.

"Yes," he said. "I'm ready."

The Coast Guard cutter's engines hummed beneath Theo as it cut through the Gulf waters. Two officers had arrived within an hour of Buck's radio call, their crisp uniforms and official manner marking Theo's first step back toward civilization. They'd wrapped him in a silver thermal blanket despite the heat, protocol for rescued individuals.

"ETA twenty minutes to Port Aransas," the communications officer announced. "Medical team standing by."

Theo nodded, struggling to process the rapid transition. Just hours ago, he'd been dismantling his shelter; now fluorescent lights and radio chatter surrounded him. His senses, honed for survival in the marsh, recoiled at the unfamiliar stimuli.

The ambulance ride from the dock to the regional hospital passed in a blur of sirens and questions. Paramedics checked his vitals, started an IV for hydration, and radioed ahead his condition. Theo answered mechanically, his mind still partially in the delta.

The hospital doors slid open automatically, unleashing a sensory assault. The antiseptic smell hit him first—sharp, chemical, nothing like the organic scents of the marsh. Fluorescent lights buzzed overhead, their brightness painful after weeks of natural illumination. Voices echoed off hard surfaces, creating a cacophony that made Theo wince.

"BP is 100 over 60, heart rate elevated at 92," a paramedic reported as they wheeled him into an examination room. "Patient shows signs of moderate dehydration, multiple lacerations with evidence of self-treatment, and approximately fifteen percent weight loss."

Doctors and nurses moved around him with practiced efficiency, their gloved hands prodding, measuring, and assessing. A physician with silver-rimmed glasses examined the healing cut on his arm.

"You treated this yourself?" she asked, voice clinical but not unkind.

"Spanish Needles," Theo replied. "Bidens alba. Anti-inflammatory and antibacterial properties."

She raised an eyebrow, impressed. "Well, it prevented a serious infection. Though I'd still like to clean it properly and run some blood work."

The examination continued—weight, temperature, blood pressure, blood draws, cultures from his wounds. Each touch, each question pulled Theo further from the marsh and back into a world of medical charts and clinical terminology.

"Where are the others?" Theo asked suddenly, sitting upright. "The people I was with—"

"Being tended to at another facility," a nurse answered, gently pressing him back onto the examination table. "Coast Guard is coordinating everything."

As the medical team dispersed to process samples and orders, a nurse with warm brown eyes and gray-streaked hair remained. She adjusted his IV and noticed his discomfort.

"First time in a hospital?" she asked, her name badge reading "Gloria."

"No, but it feels..." Theo struggled to articulate the sensory overload.

"Like too much," Gloria finished for him. "I've worked with rescue cases before. Your senses are overwhelmed."

She dimmed the overhead lights and closed the door partway, muffling the corridor noise.

"Better?"

Theo nodded gratefully.

"I'll bring you some real food—not that cafeteria nonsense," she promised. "And some clothes that don't smell like a laboratory."

When Gloria returned, she carried a tray with simple food—a sandwich, apple slices, and water—along with folded clothing.

"My son's about your size," she explained. "These might help you feel more human again."

Theo's throat tightened unexpectedly. "Thank you."

As evening settled outside the window, Theo sat on the edge of the hospital bed in borrowed clothes, the clinical assessment complete: moderate dehydration, minor infections successfully self-treated, fifteen pounds lost, elevated liver enzymes from his improvised diet, mild anemia.

Gloria appeared in the doorway. "Doctor says you're staying overnight for observation and hydration."

Theo nodded, watching the IV drip that was replenishing what the marsh had taken from him. His body was being reclaimed by medicine, just as his mind would soon need to process all that had happened.

"One day at a time," Gloria said softly, seeming to read his thoughts. "That's how we come back."

Morning light filtered through the hospital conference room's blinds, casting striped shadows across the table where Theo sat. Three cups of coffee in, his hands had finally stopped shaking. The room, hastily converted into an interview space, contained a peculiar mix of hospital and law enforcement—medical diagrams on the walls, recording equipment on the table, and the lingering scent of antiseptic mingling with coffee.

Agent Daniels of the DEA placed a digital recorder between them. Beside him sat Officer Martinez from local police and Lieutenant Commander Wilson from the Coast Guard, their expressions professionally neutral but eyes sharp with interest.

"Let's continue where we left off yesterday," Daniels said, his voice carrying the fatigue of someone who'd been processing information all night. "You mentioned Carlos revealed himself as Mendoza. Can you elaborate on the exact nature of the operation?"

Theo reached for the waterproof notebook he'd carried throughout his ordeal. The pages were crammed with observations—dates, times, coordinates, descriptions—written in increasingly steady handwriting that tracked his evolution from terrified student to methodical survivor.

"Human trafficking primarily, with drug shipments as a secondary revenue stream," Theo explained, flipping to a diagram he'd sketched of the compound. "The captives were housed here, while the shipments came through these channels based on the tidal patterns."

Wilson leaned forward. "And you determined these routes how exactly?"

"I observed their boat schedules against the tide charts I memorized for my dive trip," Theo replied. "The deep-draft vessels could only navigate certain channels during high tide, which created predictable windows for their operations."

Martinez exchanged glances with Daniels. The skepticism was subtle but unmistakable.

"You're saying you tracked complex smuggling operations while simultaneously surviving in a coastal marsh with no supplies?" Martinez asked, pen hovering above her notepad.

"I had my wetsuit, a multi-tool, and botanical knowledge," Theo answered simply. "The marsh provided the rest."

He described the plants he'd used for food and medicine, how he'd constructed shelters and set traps, filtered water and created defensive perimeters. With each detail, the officers' expressions shifted from doubt to cautious belief.

"And this Spanish Needles plant—you're claiming it prevented infection?" Wilson asked, examining photos of Theo's healing wounds.

"Bidens alba contains polyacetylenes and flavonoids with antimicrobial properties," Theo explained. "My aunt taught me to identify it years ago. The hospital lab actually confirmed its effectiveness on my cultures yesterday."

Daniels studied a map where Theo had marked the smugglers' patrol routes and blind spots. "These observations are remarkably precise for someone in survival mode."

"I'm a biologist," Theo said. "Observation is what I do."

He slid across a SIM card in an evidence bag. "This contains photos and audio I managed to capture. The phone died, but I preserved the card."

The investigators' demeanor shifted noticeably. What had begun as routine questioning of a possibly traumatized victim had evolved into debriefing a valuable witness.

By the afternoon of the second day, exhaustion had settled into Theo's bones. His voice grew hoarse as he described the final raid to free the captives and the cartel's subsequent cleanup operation.

"They executed Marcus and his men," Theo said quietly. "Burned everything. If we hadn't hidden in the marsh..."

The room fell silent. The three investigators exchanged glances, their earlier skepticism replaced by somber understanding.

"Mr. Mercer," Daniels finally said, stopping the recorder, "what you've provided will likely dismantle operations across three states. The U.S. Attorney will want to speak with you directly."

As they gathered their materials, Wilson paused. "For what it's worth, your survival techniques... they're being added to our training protocols. Not many people could have done what you did."

Theo nodded, too tired for pride. The marsh had taught him that survival wasn't about heroics—it was about paying attention to what the world was telling you, one careful observation at a time.

The hospital cafeteria hummed with afternoon activity—visitors seeking comfort in coffee, staff grabbing quick meals between shifts. In a corner booth away from the bustle, Theo sat across from Detective Sarah Linden, a woman in her forties with prematurely gray hair and eyes that had witnessed too many tragedies.

"I appreciate you meeting me here instead of another conference room," Linden said, sliding a cup of tea toward Theo. "Thought you might need a change of scenery."

Theo wrapped his hands around the warm cup, noticing how the bandages on his palms contrasted with the white ceramic. His body felt foreign after days of medical attention—clean, treated, but somehow less his own than when he'd been covered in marsh mud.

"I need to tell you about the other divers," Linden continued, her tone gentle but direct. "Most were rescued three days after the incident when a fishing vessel spotted their emergency raft."

Theo's head snapped up. "They survived? Danny? Martina and Klaus?"

"Danny Reeves was among them, yes. He's already been released from medical care." She consulted her notes. "The German couple, Klaus and Martina Weber, were also recovered. They've returned to Hamburg but have provided statements."

Relief washed through Theo, followed immediately by a cold wave of realization. "You said most."

Linden nodded, her expression softening. "Two divers remain unaccounted for. Lisa Chen and Mark Holloway."

The names struck Theo like physical blows. He remembered Lisa's quiet competence checking her equipment, Mark's enthusiasm about marine photography.

"According to the others, when Marcus abandoned the dive boat, there was chaos. They managed to deploy the life raft, but in the confusion..." She paused. "The Coast Guard conducted an extensive search."

Theo stared into his tea. "I could have gone back for them."

"Back to the boat? In your condition?"

"I knew something was wrong with Marcus from the beginning. If I'd spoken up sooner—"

"Theo," Linden interrupted gently, "you were seasick, alone on an abandoned vessel, and then fighting for survival in a coastal marsh against armed traffickers. The fact that you're sitting here is remarkable."

But Theo's mind was already calculating alternative scenarios—if he'd stayed on the boat instead of diving into the Gulf, if he'd tried to radio for help before fleeing, if he'd somehow managed to track the life raft instead of swimming to shore.

"The dive company is under investigation," Linden continued. "Serious negligence charges, potentially criminal. Turns out Marcus Delgado's background check was falsified. The owner cut corners on safety protocols."

"And Lisa and Mark pay the price," Theo said bitterly.

"As did you," Linden reminded him. "Different outcomes, same victims."

Theo pushed his tea away. "Does it get easier? This feeling?"

Linden considered the question with the weight it deserved. "Survivor's guilt is complicated. It assumes you had control over circumstances that were beyond your control."

"I made choices."

"Choices to survive. That's not the same as choosing for others not to."

A cafeteria worker dropped a tray nearby, the clatter making Theo flinch. His nerves remained raw, his senses still calibrated to the marsh's subtle warnings.

"The human trafficking victims you helped rescue—they're safe because of you," Linden said. "That doesn't balance the scales. Nothing does. But it matters."

Theo nodded, unable to fully accept her words but recognizing their intent.

"When you're ready," Linden said, sliding her card across the table, "the families of Lisa and Mark would like to hear your story. Not for closure—there's no such thing—but to understand the last days of their loved ones' lives."

Theo took the card, its weight disproportionate to its size.

"You don't have to decide now," Linden added. "Some stories need time."

Outside the cafeteria windows, afternoon sunlight painted the hospital grounds in gold. Somewhere beyond the parking lot, the coast waited—the same waters that had nearly claimed him, had claimed others, and yet still called to him with an undeniable pull.

Evening shadows stretched across Theo's hospital room, casting the growing collection of get-well cards and potted plants in a gentle half-light. A spider plant from Professor Harmon's greenhouse sat beside a flowering cactus from his lab partners. His aunt Clara had sent a terrarium of coastal succulents—life contained but thriving.

Agent Daniels knocked once before entering, his suit as crisp as it had been during their morning debriefing. The agent carried a manila folder and the weight of news on his shoulders.

"Thought you might want an update," Daniels said, settling into the visitor's chair. "We got him."

Theo adjusted himself against the pillows. "Marcus?"

"Marcus Delgado was apprehended at Brownsville International, attempting to board a flight to Cancún under an alias." Daniels opened the folder, revealing a booking photo of Marcus—unshaven, hollow-eyed, defeated. "He had sixty thousand in cash and three different passports."

The sight of Marcus's face triggered a cascade of memories: his enthusiastic dive briefing, his confident commands on the boat, his cold efficiency directing smugglers in the marsh. The contrast was dizzying.

"He was working with them the whole time," Theo said, not a question but a confirmation.

"For at least three years," Daniels nodded. "The dive operation was perfect cover. Regular, predictable trips to remote locations, legitimate reason to be in coastal waters. He'd drop divers at the reef while making contact with smugglers."

"And we were just props," Theo said, a bitter taste rising in his throat. "Window dressing for his real business."

"Your statement confirmed what we suspected—that he deliberately selected that dive site to coordinate with the trafficking operation. What he didn't anticipate was you witnessing the exchange."

Across the room, a nurse adjusted something on Theo's IV monitor, then quietly withdrew, respecting the gravity of their conversation.

"I trusted him," Theo said quietly. "We all did. He knew so much about marine ecosystems, seemed to care about conservation."

"The best covers aren't completely false," Daniels replied. "Makes them more convincing."

Outside, hospital lights flickered on against the approaching night. Theo felt an uncomfortable tangle of emotions—satisfaction at Marcus's capture twisted together with a profound sense of betrayal. The man who had guided them into the Gulf's waters had led Theo into danger, had abandoned him, had left others to die.

"What happens to him now?" Theo asked.

"Multiple federal charges. Human trafficking, drug smuggling, fraud, criminal conspiracy, abandonment resulting in death." Daniels closed the folder. "He won't see freedom again."

Theo nodded, finding the justice appropriate but hollow. No punishment could restore what had been lost—the lives, the trust, the innocence of a simple diving trip.

"Your testimony will help ensure that," Daniels added. "When you're ready."

Morning light spilled through the hospital blinds, casting warm stripes across Theo's bed. The antiseptic smell that had dominated his room for two days now mingled with something far more welcome—the rich aroma of slow-cooked brisket, collard greens, and cornbread.

Aunt Clara bustled around the small space, transforming the sterile environment with her presence. She'd arrived an hour earlier, arms laden with colorful Tupperware containers and a weathered canvas bag filled with sprigs of fresh herbs.

"You're still too skinny," she declared, arranging the food on the rollaway table. Her hands, gnarled from decades of working the land, moved with practiced efficiency. "But we'll fix that."

Theo watched her with a lump in his throat. Clara looked exactly as she always had—silver hair pulled into a practical braid, faded denim shirt with rolled sleeves, the turquoise bracelet she'd worn for as long as he could remember. The familiarity was overwhelming after weeks of strangeness.

"I used Spanish Needles," Theo said quietly. "For the infection. Just like you showed me."

Clara paused, her eyes meeting his. "Did you remember to thank the plant?"

"Every time."

She nodded, satisfied, and continued arranging their meal. "The old ways work. They always have."

As they ate, Theo found himself sharing details he'd withheld from the authorities—how he'd spoken to the plants while harvesting them, the way he'd built his shelter following the patterns she'd taught him during childhood summers, how her voice had guided him through the darkest moments.

"I kept hearing you say, 'The land provides if you know how to ask,'" he admitted.

"And it did," Clara replied simply.

She didn't diminish his experience with platitudes about bravery or luck. Instead, she listened, occasionally nodding when he described a particular plant use or survival technique.

"The knowledge was always in you," she said finally, her weathered hand covering his. "I just helped plant the seeds."

In that moment, Theo understood that the line between his past and present wasn't broken. Clara had given him more than wilderness skills—she'd given him a way of seeing the world that had kept him alive when everything familiar had been stripped away.

"Thank you," he whispered, the words inadequate for the gift she'd given him.

Clara smiled, the corners of her eyes crinkling. "That's what family does. We pass down what keeps us alive."

"Remarkable adaptation," Dr. Winters murmured, making notes on her tablet as she examined the calluses on Theo's palms. Afternoon sunlight streamed through the examination room window, illuminating dust motes that danced between them.

Four days after his rescue, Theo stood shirtless before the full-length mirror mounted on the back of the door. The man who stared back at him was both familiar and foreign. His frame had always been lean, but now corded muscle wrapped his torso and arms—not the sculpted physique of a gym enthusiast, but the functional strength of someone who had wrestled with nature and survived.

"Your body composition has shifted significantly," Dr. Winters continued, her clinical tone belied by genuine fascination. "You've lost approximately twelve percent body fat, but maintained muscle mass despite caloric restriction. That's unusual."

Theo traced a finger along a half-healed cut on his forearm. The marsh had marked him with dozens of such souvenirs—some from sharp reeds, others from close encounters with the mangroves. Each told a story only he could read.

"Can you still see the halos around lights at night?" Dr. Winters asked.

Theo nodded. "And I can distinguish more shades of green than before."

"Your eyes have adapted to low-light conditions. The rods in your retina have become more sensitive." She stepped back, studying him with professional curiosity. "And your olfactory sensitivity tests are off the charts. You identified seventeen out of twenty scents at concentrations most people can't detect."

The hospital smells that had overwhelmed him upon arrival—antiseptic, floor cleaner, the lingering traces of cafeteria food—had organized themselves into a readable map in his mind.

Even now, he could detect the coffee on Dr. Winters' breath, the faint lavender of her shampoo, the sterile latex of her gloves.

"The human body is remarkably plastic," she said, handing him his shirt. "But I've rarely seen adaptations this pronounced in such a short period."

Theo pulled the shirt over his head. The cotton felt impossibly soft against skin that had grown accustomed to neoprene and mud.

"It wasn't just my body that changed," he said quietly.

Dr. Winters waited, giving him space to continue.

"I see connections now that were invisible before. How water moves through a landscape. Which plants grow together and why. The way animals respond to changes in barometric pressure." Theo met her eyes. "It's like I was looking at the world through a keyhole before, and now the door is open."

The doctor set down her tablet. "That's not unusual for survival situations. The brain forms new neural pathways under extreme stress."

"It's more than that." Theo turned back to the mirror, studying his reflection. "I'm not seeing more things—I'm seeing the same things differently."

In the glass, he caught sight of a small spider building its web in the corner of the window. Four days ago, he might have brushed it away without thought. Now, he observed its methodical work with appreciation, understanding its role in the hospital ecosystem.

"The marsh didn't just change my body," Theo said. "It changed how I understand what it means to be alive."

Dr. Winters nodded slowly. "Well, Mr. Mercer, medically speaking, you're clear for discharge tomorrow. Your adaptations may diminish over time as you reacclimate to normal life, or they may persist."

Theo touched the healing scar on his palm—a reminder of the first snare he'd set. "Some changes can't be undone," he said. "And I'm not sure I'd want them to be."

The afternoon sun cast long shadows across Highway 35 as Clara's weathered pickup rumbled southward. Theo sat in the passenger seat, his hospital discharge papers tucked into the backpack between his feet. Neither had spoken much since leaving Port Aransas—Clara focusing on the road, Theo lost in the landscape flowing past his window.

As they approached the causeway into Rockport, the familiar silhouette of his hometown emerged against the golden horizon. But the Rockport before him now was not the Rockport he had left behind.

"The tide's coming in fast," Theo observed, watching the water push into the salt marsh. "Storm somewhere offshore."

Clara glanced at the cloudless sky. "Forecast says clear through the weekend."

"Water doesn't lie," Theo replied simply, noting the behavior of gulls along the shoreline—their frantic feeding suggesting changing pressure systems.

The truck crossed onto the causeway, and Theo's eyes tracked the vegetation along the roadside. Salicornia glistened in the evening light, its succulent stems perfect for harvesting. Sea purslane clustered nearby, and further back, yaupon holly with berries just beginning to ripen.

"Never realized how much food grows right along the road," he said.

Clara smiled knowingly. "Been trying to tell you that since you were knee-high."

The familiar streets of Rockport unfolded before them—the harbor, the maritime museum, the old oak trees lining Austin Street. Yet each familiar sight revealed new dimensions: the subtle tilt of a weather vane, the particular shade of green on storm-weathered copper, the way certain buildings channeled the coastal wind.

Neighbors waved as Clara's truck pulled into the driveway of the modest house where Theo had grown up. Mrs. Abernathy from next door hurried over, her relief evident as she embraced him.

"We've been praying for you, young man," she said, her eyes moist.

After polite conversation and promises of casseroles, Clara led Theo inside. The house smelled of lemon polish and the faint ghost of his father's pipe tobacco that never quite left the walls.

That night, after a quiet dinner, Theo stood in his bedroom doorway. The space was untouched since his departure—posters of marine ecosystems, bookshelf crammed with field guides, his childhood bed with the blue quilt.

He tried the bed, lying flat on his back, but the softness felt suffocating. After an hour of restless turning, Theo gathered the quilt and a pillow, spreading them on the floor beneath the open window. The salt-laden breeze carried the symphony of the coast—waves against the shore, night birds calling, the distant clank of rigging against masts in the harbor.

As sleep finally claimed him, Theo's hand rested palm-down on the wooden floor, fingers splayed as if reading the pulse of the earth beneath his childhood home.

Chapter 13

Morning light filtered through the blinds of Dean Williams's office, casting striped shadows across the polished oak desk between them. Theo shifted in the leather chair, its cushioned comfort still foreign after weeks of survival in the marsh. The walls were adorned with framed diplomas and nature photographs—an attempt to soften the formality of the space with images of the natural world he had so recently inhabited in a much more intimate way.

Dean Williams adjusted her reading glasses and closed Theo's file with deliberate care. Her gray-streaked hair was pulled back in a neat bun, and she wore the kind expression of someone delivering what she believed was good news.

"So that's where we stand, Mr. Mercer. The university is implementing a mandatory recovery period—one full semester. Your professors have unanimously agreed to grant incompletes rather than failures for your current coursework."

Theo's fingers traced the edge of the chair's armrest, feeling the smooth wood grain. "I appreciate that, but I'm ready to return now. My notes from before—"

"This isn't negotiable, Theo," Dean Williams interrupted gently. "What you experienced goes beyond typical hardship. The psychology department was quite clear about the adjustment period trauma survivors require."

Across campus, Professor Harmon was lecturing on coastal ecosystems to a class where Theo's seat remained empty. In the biology lab, his research partner Lisa was carefully tending the experiments they had started together, honoring a promise to keep them viable until his return.

"Your spot in the marine biology program is secure," the Dean continued. "Your scholarship will remain intact. We're not punishing you—we're giving you space to heal."

Theo felt an uncomfortable mixture of gratitude and resistance. The same institution that had taught him to push through challenges was now forcing him to stop. The paradox wasn't lost on him.

"What am I supposed to do for four months?" he asked, his voice revealing more vulnerability than he intended.

Dean Williams smiled. "Whatever you need to do. Some students travel. Others seek therapy. You might find working with your aunt's foraging could be therapeutic."

Outside the administrative building, students hurried to classes, laughing and complaining about assignments. Their concerns seemed simultaneously trivial and enviable to Theo. None of them had faced death in a delta marsh or dismantled a human trafficking operation.

"Your professors were quite impressed with your application of botanical knowledge in the field," Dean Williams added. "Professor Morales suggested you might consider documenting your experience when you're ready."

Theo nodded, understanding that while his academic life had been paused, his education had never stopped—it had simply moved beyond classroom walls into the harshest laboratory imaginable.

Afternoon sunlight filtered through the gauzy curtains of Dr. Mercer's office, casting soft shadows across the pale blue walls. Theo sat rigid on the edge of a plush armchair, his fingers drumming against his knee in a rhythm that betrayed his discomfort. This was his third session, and he still felt like an intruder in this carefully constructed space of healing.

Dr. Mercer, no relation despite the shared surname, observed him from her seat across the small coffee table. Her silver-streaked hair framed a face marked by laugh lines that suggested a life fully lived. She wore a cardigan the color of sea foam and possessed a stillness that somehow never felt forced.

"The nightmares," she said, picking up where they had left off last session. "You mentioned they're becoming more frequent?"

Theo's gaze drifted to the potted peace lily in the corner. "Three times this week."

"Can you describe one of them for me?"

"Same as before." He shrugged, aiming for nonchalance. "Just bits and pieces."

Dr. Mercer waited, her silence an invitation that hung in the air between them. Outside the window, a cardinal landed on the bird feeder in her small garden, a flash of vivid red against the greenery.

"It starts with the water," Theo finally said, his voice low. "I'm back in the delta, but it's different. The water's rising fast, and I can hear the airboats coming."

His fingers stopped their tapping, curling instead into a loose fist.

"I'm trying to lead everyone to safety, but the mud keeps pulling us down. Then the shooting starts."

The cardinal took flight, startled by something unseen.

"I see their faces. The people who didn't make it." Theo's voice cracked unexpectedly. "Isabella's little boy is crying, and I can't—I can't reach him. Then Marcus is there, laughing, saying I should have stayed on the boat where I belonged."

Dr. Mercer leaned forward slightly. "What happens next?"

"I wake up." Theo swallowed hard. "Sometimes I'm screaming. My aunt says she can hear me from down the hall."

"These people who didn't make it in your dream—did they die in reality?"

Theo looked up, meeting her eyes for the first time that session. "Two of them. We were pinned down on the beach. They tried to run for the trees when the cartel opened fire."

His voice broke again, and this time he couldn't pull it back together. "I should have stopped them. I knew better. I knew the marsh, the sight lines. If I'd just—"

"Theo," Dr. Mercer said gently, "how many people did you help escape?"

"Twelve. But—"

"And you were how old again?"

"Twenty-two," he whispered.

"Twenty-two years old, with no military training, no experience in combat situations, thrust into a leadership role during a crisis most people will never face in their lifetime." Her tone remained level, neither accusatory nor pitying. "What you're experiencing is called survivor's guilt. It's your mind's way of trying to maintain the illusion of control in an uncontrollable situation."

Theo stared at his hands. They looked clean now, the cuts and calluses healing, but he could still feel the marsh mud under his fingernails sometimes.

"If you blame yourself," she continued, "then the world makes sense. The alternative—accepting that sometimes terrible things happen regardless of our actions—that's much harder."

A tear slipped down Theo's cheek, followed by another. He didn't bother wiping them away.

"I see their faces every night," he admitted. "Not just in dreams."

Dr. Mercer nodded, the compassion in her eyes balanced by professional calm. "That's where we'll start then. With the faces. Not to forget them—but to understand what they're trying to tell you."

"One more set, Theo. You've got this."

Marcus Alvarez, physical therapist at the university medical center, stood with arms crossed, his bright blue polo shirt emblazoned with the facility logo. His perpetual enthusiasm contrasted sharply with Theo's grimace of pain.

"Said that three sets ago," Theo muttered, gripping the resistance band tighter. Sweat beaded along his hairline as he pulled the band outward, working the damaged muscles in his shoulder.

"That's because I know you can handle it." Marcus checked his clipboard. "Your numbers are improving every week."

The rehabilitation facility hummed with morning activity. An elderly woman worked with a walker nearby, while a college athlete tested his repaired knee on a stationary bike. Physical pain and determination filled the air in equal measure.

Theo completed the repetition, his arm trembling with exertion. Six weeks after his rescue, his body remained a battlefield of healing wounds and atrophied muscle.

"There it is." Marcus nodded approvingly. "Now hold for five seconds."

Theo's teeth clenched as he maintained the position. The scar tissue pulled tight across his shoulder blade where he'd torn through muscle while climbing out of the marsh that final night. His body remembered every moment of survival, carried it in flesh and bone.

"Time." Marcus offered a towel. "You're making remarkable progress, considering where you started."

Theo wiped his face. "Still can't lift half of what I could before."

"That'll come." Marcus made notes in Theo's chart. "Your body endured extreme conditions. Starvation, dehydration, physical trauma. Recovery isn't linear."

In the changing room afterward, Theo stood before the full-length mirror, cataloging the changes in his body. The new scar on his shoulder formed a jagged pink line against his skin. His ribs still protruded despite six weeks of regular meals. The muscle definition in his arms had begun returning, but differently—leaner, more functional than aesthetic.

His hands told the clearest story. The calluses he'd developed from making traps and climbing through mangroves refused to fade. His palms bore a topography of hardened skin that no amount of lotion seemed to soften.

"The body remembers," Dr. Winters had told him during his discharge evaluation. "Long after your mind processes the trauma, your muscles and skin will carry the experience."

Theo pulled his shirt back on, wincing slightly. His fingers traced the outline of his shoulder through the fabric.

"Ready for your next appointment?" Marcus appeared in the doorway, clipboard in hand and enthusiasm undimmed.

Theo nodded, shouldering his gym bag. His body might remember the pain, but it also remembered how to survive. And right now, that was enough.

The sedan slowed to a crawl as Theo's father approached their driveway. A woman with a camera and a man clutching a notebook stood near the mailbox, scanning the street with predatory vigilance.

"Not again," Theo's father muttered, knuckles whitening on the steering wheel.

Theo sank lower in the passenger seat, the physical therapy's afterglow instantly evaporating. Two months after his rescue, the media vultures still circled, hungry for scraps of his story.

"I'll handle this," his father said, pulling into the driveway with deliberate speed that forced the reporters to step back.

The woman raised her camera anyway. Theo turned his face away, a reflex now as natural as breathing. Through the window, he caught fragments of his father's firm dismissal—"already declined," "respect our privacy," "contact our lawyer"—while Theo remained frozen in the car, trapped by unwanted attention.

Inside the house, sanctuary had become siege. Blinds remained drawn. The answering machine blinked with seventeen messages.

"Your mother unplugged the phone earlier," his father explained, tossing his keys onto the counter. "They called six times before noon."

Theo nodded, throat tight. His father hesitated, then retrieved a folded newspaper from beneath a stack of mail.

"Might as well see what they're saying now."

The Port Aransas Gazette featured a half-page spread with the headline: "DELTA SURVIVOR: THE HARROWING JOURNEY OF ROCKPORT STUDENT." A blurry photo showed Theo being escorted from the Coast Guard vessel, thermal blanket clutched around his shoulders.

Theo's eyes skimmed the article, anger building with each paragraph. The writer described him as "battling alligators daily" and "living off nothing but raw fish." They quoted a "fellow student" claiming Theo had military training. The article speculated about "possible romance" with one of the human trafficking victims.

"This is—" Theo couldn't finish. His hands tightened, crumpling the paper's edges.

"Complete garbage," his father finished. "That's why I've been talking to Jim Harlow about legal options. You have a right to privacy."

Theo stared at the distorted version of himself on the page. The person they described wasn't him—just a character they'd created to sell papers. The real story lived in his nightmares, in his healing shoulder, in quiet moments when marsh sounds echoed in his memory.

"They don't get to own this," Theo said finally, crumpling the paper completely. "They don't get to own me."

Evening light slanted through the venetian blinds, casting striped shadows across the community center's worn carpet. Five people sat in a circle of mismatched chairs, with a sixth chair—deliberately empty—positioned between Theo and a middle-aged woman named Diane. The empty chair had remained unoccupied for the past three sessions, its presence a silent acknowledgment of loss that permeated the room.

Dr. Loretta Jenkins, the group leader, glanced at her watch. "We have about twenty minutes left. Would anyone else like to share tonight?"

Silence settled over the group. Paul, a former firefighter, studied his hands. Diane adjusted her scarf. Marcus, who'd survived a hurricane that had taken his wife, stared at the empty chair. Eliza, the youngest besides Theo, picked at a thread on her sleeve.

Theo felt something shift inside him. Three months since his rescue, and he'd said little during these sessions, preferring to listen as others excavated their pain. But tonight, the empty chair seemed to pull words from somewhere deep within.

"Miguel would have been twenty-four next month," Theo said, his voice startling everyone, including himself.

Dr. Jenkins nodded encouragingly. "Tell us about Miguel, Theo."

"He was part of the village near the delta. He helped me when I was trying to disrupt the smugglers' operation." Theo's eyes fixed on the empty chair. "He had this laugh that seemed too big for his body. Even when we were setting traps or planning diversions, he'd find something to laugh about."

The group watched Theo with quiet attention, the usual shuffling and fidgeting suspended.

"He wanted to save enough money to send his sister to university in Monterrey. Engineering. He said she could build bridges that would last centuries." Theo's voice caught. "But he never made it out of the delta."

Dr. Jenkins leaned forward slightly. "What happened to Miguel, Theo?"

"We were creating a distraction so some of the captives could escape. Miguel was supposed to circle back to the eastern meeting point." Theo's hands trembled slightly. "He never showed up. Three days later, one of the fishermen found his body in the marsh. He'd been shot trying to help a family that had gotten separated from the main group."

The room absorbed his words. No one spoke.

"I keep thinking about those bridges his sister will never build," Theo continued. "All those people who won't cross rivers because Miguel died helping strangers."

"It sounds like Miguel made choices based on his values," Dr. Jenkins observed gently.

Theo nodded. "He did. But I was the one who came up with the plan. I was the one who—"

"Who survived," Marcus finished for him, his voice carrying the weight of his own losses.

"Yes," Theo admitted. "And sometimes that feels like the worst betrayal."

Dr. Jenkins gestured toward the empty chair. "That's why it's there, Theo. Not just to acknowledge absence, but to recognize that we carry others with us."

"I've been carrying him like a weight," Theo realized aloud. "Like I owe him my life because he lost his."

"And how might Miguel want to be carried?" Dr. Jenkins asked.

Theo considered this, remembering Miguel's laugh, his determination, his unwavering belief that things could be better.

"Not as a weight," Theo said finally. "Maybe as a bridge."

The evening light had faded now, leaving the room in the gentle glow of wall sconces. In the softened light, the empty chair seemed less an accusation and more a possibility—a space where absence and presence could somehow coexist.

The Mercer family dining room existed in a state of suspended animation. The same faded wallpaper with its pattern of blue sailboats, the same cherry wood table with its constellation of water rings hidden beneath a lace tablecloth, the same framed cross-stitch that read "Bless This Mess" hanging slightly askew. Four months after Theo's return, the room remained stubbornly unchanged while everything else had transformed.

"More potatoes, honey?" Linda Mercer hovered beside Theo, the serving spoon already poised over his plate. Her eyes darted across his face, searching for signs of improvement or decline.

"Mom, I've had two helpings already." Theo tried to sound light-hearted.

"You're still too thin," she insisted, depositing another mound before moving back to her seat.

Robert Mercer cleared his throat. "Astros are looking good this season. Pitching staff really came together after that rough start."

Theo nodded, grateful for the attempt at normalcy, though he could feel the effort behind it. His father's knuckles were white around his fork, his casual tone meticulously rehearsed.

Emma, sixteen and unyielding, watched from across the table. Unlike their parents, she hadn't adopted the careful script of avoidance that had characterized Sunday dinners since his return.

"Were you scared?" she asked suddenly. "When you were out there?"

The question landed like a stone in still water. Linda's fork clattered against her plate. Robert froze mid-chew.

"Emma, we don't need to—" Linda began.

"It's okay, Mom." Theo met his sister's direct gaze. "Yes. I was terrified most of the time. But fear kept me alert. It probably saved my life."

Emma nodded, absorbing this without flinching. "I would've been scared too."

Something shifted in the room's atmosphere—a loosening, like a knot finally working free after months of tightening.

After dinner, Emma tugged Theo's sleeve. "Come see something." She led him to her bedroom, where a large poster board leaned against her desk. "It's for my biology class. Marine conservation in the Gulf."

The board displayed carefully researched information about coral reefs, pollution impacts, and conservation efforts. In the corner, a small note: "Dedicated to my brother Theo, who survived the Gulf and came back to tell its story."

Theo felt something crack open inside him. "This is amazing, Em."

"I thought maybe," she said hesitantly, "you could come talk to my class about it someday. When you're ready."

For the first time in months, Theo felt the weight on his chest lighten just a fraction. "I'd like that."

The autumn breeze carried salt and promise across Magnolia Beach. Five months after his rescue, Theo knelt before a tide pool, his fingers hovering just above the water's surface. Unlike the marshy delta that had both imprisoned and sheltered him, this rocky coastline fifty miles north of Rockport offered neutral ground—a place without memories.

The morning fog had burned away hours ago, but Theo remained, transfixed by the miniature universe contained within the rocky depression. A tiny Sally Lightfoot crab scuttled across an outcropping, its bright orange carapace flashing in the sunlight. Near the pool's edge, sea anemones unfurled their tentacles in a lazy dance, while hermit crabs dragged their borrowed homes across the sandy bottom.

"That's a whole world in there," Theo murmured to himself, mentally cataloging each species—knowledge that had once been academic but now felt intimate, earned through survival.

"What's that?" A small voice startled him.

A boy of about eight stood a few feet away, pointing at something in the pool. His mother hovered several paces behind, her posture tense, eyes darting between her son and the stranger kneeling at the water's edge.

"That's a lined chiton," Theo answered, his voice softer than he intended. "See how it looks like a tiny armadillo? It can roll up to protect itself when the tide goes out."

The boy inched closer, dropping to his knees beside Theo. "Cool! What about that one?"

"Careful, Jamie," his mother called, taking a step forward.

Theo recognized the wariness in her eyes—the same look he'd seen countless times since his return. The newspaper stories had painted him as either a hero or a curiosity, neither quite human.

"That's a sea hare," Theo continued, keeping his movements slow and deliberate. "It's related to snails, but it can swim by flapping those wing-like parts."

"It looks like an alien!" The boy giggled.

Theo pointed to a cluster of purple-shelled creatures. "Those are aggregating anemones. They're actually animals, not plants. Each one has tiny harpoons in its tentacles."

"Harpoons? For real?" Jamie's eyes widened.

"Microscopic ones," Theo clarified. "They're called nematocysts. They shoot out to catch food or protect themselves."

The mother had drawn closer now, her caution gradually yielding to curiosity. "You know a lot about these creatures."

"I study marine biology," Theo replied, omitting the rest of his story. "This tide pool is like a perfect little ecosystem. Everything depends on everything else."

As he spoke, Theo realized he was smiling—genuinely smiling—for the first time in months. The familiar rhythm of scientific explanation felt like coming home to a part of himself he'd feared lost.

"Look how the hermit crabs use shells that other animals left behind," he continued. "And the algae creates oxygen for the fish. Nothing wasted, nothing without purpose."

For nearly an hour, Theo named each creature, explaining their adaptations and relationships. Jamie's questions came rapid-fire, his enthusiasm infectious. Even his mother eventually knelt beside them, pointing to a starfish and asking about its feeding habits.

When they finally stood to leave, Jamie waved enthusiastically. "Thanks for the science lesson, mister!"

As Theo watched them walk away, hand in hand along the shoreline, he felt something shift within him. The sea had nearly taken his life, yet here in this tiny pool, it had given him something back—a reminder that knowledge could be shared, not just hoarded for survival.

The tide was coming in now, water gently reclaiming the pool. Theo remained, watching the miniature world transform with each incoming wave, finding unexpected peace in the eternal rhythm of return.

Six months after his rescue, Theo stood in the hallway outside Lecture Hall B, his palms damp against the folder of notes he'd prepared. Students streamed past, some glancing curiously at him, others lost in conversation. Inside, Professor Abernathy's voice carried through the partially open door as she introduced the day's topic: Practical Applications of Marine Biology in Survival Situations.

"This should have been my classroom," Theo thought, picturing himself among the students, worrying about midterms instead of nightmares.

Professor Abernathy appeared at the door, her silver-streaked hair pulled back in its familiar bun. "They're ready for you, Theo."

Thirty pairs of eyes tracked him as he entered. Some students leaned forward with undisguised curiosity, while others shifted uncomfortably, uncertain how to react to the student whose ordeal had become campus legend.

"As I mentioned," Professor Abernathy addressed the class, "Mr. Mercer has firsthand experience applying oceanographic principles in extreme circumstances. His insights go beyond what any textbook can teach you."

The silence that followed her introduction felt leaden. Theo placed his notes on the podium, then abandoned them, stepping forward instead.

"Six months ago, I was sitting where you are," he began, his voice initially unsteady. "I thought I understood coastal ecosystems because I could label diagrams and recite tidal patterns."

A student in the front row nodded encouragingly.

"Then I found myself alone in a coastal marsh, and suddenly those academic concepts meant the difference between life and death." Theo gestured toward the whiteboard. "May I?"

Professor Abernathy handed him a marker, and Theo sketched the outline of the delta where he'd spent those harrowing weeks.

"When you understand how salinity affects plant distribution, you can find freshwater by identifying glycophytes." His hand moved with increasing confidence. "Knowing the feeding patterns of shore birds can lead you to fish. Recognizing how mangroves stabilize sediment tells you where it's safe to walk."

A young woman raised her hand. "Did you really use Spanish Needles as medicine?"

The directness of her question broke the tension. Theo smiled, rolling up his sleeve to reveal a faint scar. "This cut would have killed me without them. Professor Morales' ethnobotany course turned out to be surprisingly practical."

Laughter rippled through the room.

For the next forty minutes, Theo guided them through his survival techniques, explaining how understanding marsh ecology had provided food, medicine, and protection. The students' questions came rapidly now, their initial hesitation replaced by genuine engagement.

"The most important thing I learned," Theo concluded, "wasn't a specific technique. It was that knowledge isn't just theoretical. Everything we study in this room exists in relationship to everything else. That web of connections becomes visible when you have no choice but to see it."

As the session ended, students clustered around him, some sharing their own outdoor experiences, others asking about research opportunities. Professor Abernathy watched from her desk, a quiet satisfaction in her expression.

"That went well," she said when the last student had departed. "How did it feel?"

Theo considered the question. "Like... reclaiming something. Using what happened instead of being used by it."

She nodded. "The department is developing a field course on coastal resilience. We could use someone with your perspective."

"You're offering me a job?"

"An opportunity," she corrected. "To turn what you've lived through into something that serves others."

Outside the window, students crossed the campus green, their movements creating patterns like currents in a living sea. Theo watched them, feeling the first genuine stirring of purpose he'd experienced since his return.

"I'd like that," he said, surprising himself with how much he meant it.

Seven months after his rescue, Theo sat in a federal building conference room, the air conditioning set uncomfortably cold. The fluorescent lights overhead cast everyone in a pallid glow, making even the rich mahogany table appear lifeless. A water pitcher sat untouched beside stacks of manila folders, each labeled with case numbers and confidential stamps.

"Could you please state your full name for the record," said the court reporter, her fingers poised over the stenography machine.

"Theodore James Mercer."

Across the table, Assistant U.S. Attorney Cassandra Reeves arranged photographs in a precise grid. Beside her, AUSA Mark Thornton reviewed his notes, occasionally glancing up at Theo with calculated assessment. To Theo's right sat Diana Powell, his attorney, her posture straight and protective.

"Mr. Mercer," Reeves began, her voice clipped and efficient, "we appreciate your willingness to provide this testimony today. We understand this is difficult."

Theo nodded, remembering Dr. Mercer's advice about the deposition. *Focus on facts, not feelings. Breathe through the memories.*

"Let's start with your first encounter with Marcus Delgado. Please be as specific as possible regarding dates, times, and exact statements made."

For the next three hours, Theo methodically reconstructed his experiences. He described the dive boat preparations, Marcus's behavior, the abandoned vessel, and his subsequent discovery of the smuggling operation. The words came easier than he'd expected, clinical and precise, as if he were describing someone else's ordeal.

"The man who called himself Carlos—he later revealed his real name was Mendoza—maintained a separate command post here," Theo indicated a spot on the map spread before them. "The structure contained military-grade communications equipment and multiple weapons."

Thornton leaned forward. "You're certain about the weapons?"

"Four AR-15 style rifles mounted on the east wall. Three handguns in a locked case, which he opened in my presence. Ammunition stored in waterproof containers beneath the communications desk."

The court reporter's fingers clicked steadily as Reeves exchanged a significant look with Thornton.

"Your recollection is... exceptional," Reeves noted.

"I spent weeks planning my survival around their routines. I had to remember everything."

After a brief lunch break—during which Theo barely touched his sandwich—Reeves placed a series of photographs on the table.

"Take your time," she instructed. "If you recognize anyone, please indicate how you know them."

The first few faces were unfamiliar, but the sixth photograph made Theo's heart stutter. A heavyset man with a scar running from his left eye to his jawline stared back at him.

"That's Vince. He was Marcus's second-in-command at the compound. I observed him executing a prisoner who attempted to escape."

The eighth photograph hit harder. A thin man with hollow cheeks and cold eyes.

"This man shot Miguel." Theo's voice remained steady despite the surge of grief. "He was stationed at the northern perimeter. Miguel was creating a diversion so others could escape when this man fired three shots."

By late afternoon, Theo had identified eleven individuals and connected them to specific locations, dates, and actions. Diana squeezed his arm supportively as Reeves gathered the photographs.

"Mr. Mercer," Thornton said, closing his notebook, "your testimony today has connected three previously separate investigations across Texas, Louisiana, and Florida. The detail you've provided will be instrumental in dismantling one of the largest human trafficking networks on the Gulf Coast."

As the session concluded, Theo stood by the window, looking down at the city below. People moved along sidewalks, going about ordinary lives untouched by what he'd witnessed.

"You did well today," Diana said, joining him.

"Will it be enough?" Theo asked.

"Your testimony, combined with the evidence from the compound and the testimonies of those you helped rescue? Yes. It will be enough."

Theo nodded, watching a flock of pigeons rise suddenly from a nearby rooftop, their wings catching the late afternoon sun as they banked and turned as one.

Eight months after his rescue, Theo navigated the familiar hallways of the Marine Science building. The scent of formaldehyde and salt water wafted from the laboratories, once his second home. Students rushed past, backpacks heavy with textbooks and ambition, unaware of how quickly certainty could dissolve like salt in seawater.

Professor Lin's office door stood partially open, a chaotic symphony of papers and specimens visible through the gap. Theo knocked twice.

"Come in, come in," called a voice from within.

Professor Mei Lin sat surrounded by organized chaos—stacks of research papers threatened to topple from her desk, shelves overflowed with preserved specimens in jars, and three computer monitors displayed different data sets. A massive whiteboard covered the wall behind her, filled with equations and notes in multiple colors.

"Theo!" She rose, adjusting her glasses. "Wonderful to see you. You look..." she paused, studying him with the same analytical gaze she used for her research subjects, "different."

"I am different," Theo acknowledged, settling into the chair across from her desk.

Professor Lin had been his academic advisor since freshman year, guiding his course selections and research focus with precision and care. Her expertise in marine ecosystems had shaped his early academic path, and her recommendation had secured his spot on the ill-fated dive expedition.

"I've been reviewing your academic standing," she said, pulling a folder from one of the more precarious stacks. "With the incompletes from last semester resolved, you're in good position to resume your studies in the fall. I've drafted a schedule that would put you back on track for graduation by next spring."

She slid a proposed course list across the desk. Theo glanced at it—Advanced Marine Ecology, Phycology, Research Methods in Coastal Environments.

"I've been thinking about a different direction," he said.

Professor Lin's eyebrows rose slightly. "Oh?"

"I'd like to add Environmental Law as a minor."

The surprise on her face was evident. "That's quite a shift from your previous focus."

"Not a shift. An expansion." Theo leaned forward. "What I experienced in the delta—it wasn't just about survival. I saw firsthand how environmental degradation created opportunities for criminal exploitation."

He pointed to a map of the Gulf Coast on her wall. "The degraded wetlands provided perfect cover for smuggling operations. The same channels carved by oil companies became trafficking routes. The communities most vulnerable to climate change were the same ones targeted by people like Marcus."

Professor Lin listened intently, her initial surprise transforming into curiosity.

"The connections are there, if you know how to see them," Theo continued. "The science matters—it always will—but understanding the legal frameworks that either protect or exploit these ecosystems is just as important."

"And you want to work at that intersection?" she asked.

"I need to. What good is identifying a problem if I can't help fix it?"

Professor Lin sat back, a smile slowly spreading across her face. "You know, in twenty-three years of advising students, I've never had one come back from a trauma with such clarity of purpose."

She pulled a blank sheet of paper from a drawer. "Let's draft a new plan. Environmental Law will require summer courses, and you'll need to speak with Professor Jameson in Legal Studies. The cross-disciplinary approach will be challenging."

"I'm ready for challenging," Theo said. "The delta taught me that."

Outside the window, a flock of seagulls wheeled against the blue sky. Professor Lin followed his gaze.

"The university recently received funding for a coastal resilience initiative," she mentioned. "They're looking for research assistants with interdisciplinary backgrounds. The work involves both field research and policy development."

Theo nodded, feeling something settle within him—not the old certainty of youth, but something more durable. The path ahead wouldn't erase what happened in the delta, but it would give those experiences meaning beyond mere survival.

"That sounds perfect," he said.

Professor Lin began sketching out a new academic roadmap, her pen moving with purpose across the page. "Then let's make it happen."

Nine months after his rescue, Theo emerged from his tent well before sunrise. The coastal forest surrounding his campsite rustled with pre-dawn activity—nocturnal creatures returning to their dens, early birds stirring in the canopy above. He zipped his jacket against the morning chill and shouldered a small pack containing water, his journal, and a thermos of coffee.

The solitude that had once filled him with dread now wrapped around him like a familiar blanket. Each snapping twig and rustling leaf registered in his consciousness without triggering alarm. The darkness no longer concealed threats but possibilities.

Theo navigated the trail with practiced ease, his headlamp illuminating just enough ground ahead. The path wound through stands of live oak and loblolly pine before beginning its ascent toward the ridge overlooking the Gulf. His breathing deepened as he climbed, muscles warming with the effort.

The eastern sky had just begun to lighten when he reached the overlook—a flat outcropping of limestone that jutted from the forested slope. Below, the dark expanse of the Gulf stretched to the horizon, its surface rippled by the morning breeze.

Theo settled on a smooth section of rock and switched off his headlamp. The world transformed into gradients of blue—navy fading to cobalt, then to a pale cerulean where the sky met water. He unzipped his pack and extracted the thermos, pouring steaming coffee into the cup. The aroma mingled with salt air and pine.

"Perfect timing," he murmured to himself, watching the first sliver of sun breach the horizon.

The solitude that had once terrified him in the delta now felt like an old friend. He had returned to nature on his own terms, reclaiming what trauma had threatened to take from him.

As light spilled across the water, turning the surface to hammered gold, Theo removed his journal—a leather-bound volume with his name embossed on the cover, a gift from Aunt Clara to replace the one lost at sea. He opened to a fresh page and began to write:

The resilience of natural ecosystems mirrors our own capacity to recover from disturbance. Just as coastal marshes absorb storm surge to protect inland areas, we develop mechanisms to absorb trauma...

His pen moved across the page, thoughts flowing freely in the growing light. He wrote about adaptive cycles, about how disturbance creates opportunity for renewal, about the fine line between destruction and transformation.

The vibration of his phone interrupted his flow. Theo extracted it from his pocket to find a text from Emma:

Just checking you're still alive out there in the wilderness. Mom's pretending not to worry but keeps looking at the door.

Theo smiled, remembering how his family had hovered in the months following his return. Their concern had sometimes felt suffocating, but he understood its source.

Watching sunrise over the Gulf. All good. Tell Mom I'm fine.

He hesitated, then added: *Send her a picture.*

Theo snapped a photo of the golden horizon and sent it before returning to his journal. The text exchange reminded him of the delicate balance he was learning to maintain—between independence and connection, between solitude and community.

Another message arrived: *Beautiful. Stay safe. Love you.*

Love you too. Back tomorrow.

Theo set the phone aside but didn't turn it off. Nine months ago, he might have seen the interruption as an intrusion. Now he recognized it as a thread connecting him to home—one he could acknowledge without being tethered by it.

The sun climbed higher, casting his shadow across the limestone. Birds wheeled over the water, diving occasionally for fish. Theo sipped his coffee and continued writing, finding words for experiences that had once seemed beyond language.

In this moment, perched between forest and ocean, between past trauma and future purpose, Theo felt completely present—alive to both the solitude around him and the connections that awaited his return.

Ten months after his rescue, Theo stood at the university registration desk, watching as the administrator scrolled through his digital file. Morning light streamed through the high windows of the administration building, casting geometric patterns across the polished floor. Around him, other students waited in line, their conversations creating a gentle hum of normalcy.

"Mr. Mercer," the administrator said, adjusting her glasses. "I see there's a note here about your... special circumstances." Her voice lowered slightly on the last words, a well-intentioned attempt at discretion. "The university offers several accommodation options if you feel you might need them."

Theo noticed how carefully she chose her words, how the other staff members glanced his way with that mixture of curiosity and concern he'd grown accustomed to. His story had circulated widely, despite his family's efforts to maintain privacy.

"I appreciate that," Theo replied, his voice steady. "But I'm ready to move forward with a regular course load."

The administrator studied him for a moment, perhaps searching for hesitation in his expression. Finding none, she nodded and continued processing his enrollment.

"You're registered for Environmental Law 201, Marine Ecology 350, and the Coastal Resilience Practicum," she confirmed, handing him his schedule. "Professor Lin specifically requested you for her research team."

Theo accepted the paper with a small smile. "That's right. Thank you."

Outside, the September air carried the scent of freshly cut grass and possibility. Theo paused at the top of the administration building steps, taking in the sprawling campus before him. Students lounged on the quad's green expanse, some reading under trees, others tossing frisbees or huddled in study groups. The scene was utterly ordinary and, for that very reason, extraordinary to Theo's eyes.

He descended the steps and began crossing the quad, aware of how differently he moved through this space now. Before his time in the delta, he had navigated campus with the tunnel vision of academic ambition, seeing little beyond his next class or assignment. Now, he noticed everything—the way sunlight filtered through oak leaves, the varied cadence of conversations as he passed, the precise angle of a mockingbird's flight between buildings.

The world appeared simultaneously sharper and more connected, each element relating to all others in ways invisible to most passersby. Theo understood he occupied a unique position—fully present in this academic world yet carrying perspectives few here could comprehend. The realization no longer troubled him as it once had.

Near the science building, a young woman with an overloaded backpack dropped an armful of books, papers scattering across the walkway. Without hesitation, Theo knelt to help, gathering several volumes on introductory biology.

"First semester?" he asked, handing them back.

"Is it that obvious?" She blew a strand of hair from her face, looking embarrassed.

"The books gave it away," Theo replied with a gentle smile. "Plus the map sticking out of your pocket."

She laughed, accepting the recovered materials. "I'm still getting lost between buildings. Everything looks the same."

"It gets easier," Theo said, remembering his own disorientation as a freshman. "The pond behind the Life Sciences building is a good landmark—and they have the best coffee cart on campus."

"Thanks," she said, relief evident in her voice. "I'm Maya."

"Theo." He noticed her slight double-take at his name, the flicker of recognition. Rather than discomfort, he felt a calm acknowledgment. "Good luck with your classes."

As they parted ways, Theo continued toward the Marine Science building where Professor Lin waited to discuss their research project. The interaction left him with an unexpected sense of completion—a circle closing. Once, he had been the one in need of guidance, lost in unfamiliar territory. Now he could extend that same help to others, drawing from both his academic knowledge and his hard-won wisdom.

The campus clock tower chimed eleven, its resonant tones carrying across the quad. Theo walked on, his pace unhurried but purposeful. He moved forward not as someone who had escaped his past, but as someone who had integrated it—carrying both the weight and the gifts of his experience as he stepped into whatever came next.

Chapter 14

The morning sun painted Fisherman's Wharf in shades of amber and gold, transforming the weathered dock into something almost beautiful. Theo Mercer gripped the railing with white knuckles, his fingers betraying a tremor he couldn't quite control. Below him, the Gulf waters lapped against the pilings with hypnotic rhythm—gentle today, deceptively so.

Three dive boats bobbed in their slips, crew members moving with practiced efficiency as they loaded tanks and checked equipment. Their voices carried across the water, fragments of conversation punctuated by occasional laughter. The scene was painfully familiar, a perfect mirror of that morning eleven months ago when he'd stood in this exact spot, filled with anticipation rather than dread.

"Check the O-rings twice," a dive master called to his assistant. "Last thing we need is equipment failure out there."

Theo's mind flickered involuntarily to Marcus Delgado—the easy confidence in his instructions, the way his eyes had crinkled when he smiled, betraying nothing of what lay beneath. The memory sent a cold spike through Theo's chest, his breath catching as the past superimposed itself over the present.

A seagull landed on the railing beside him, tilting its head with that peculiar bird curiosity. Theo watched it, focusing on its movements to anchor himself in the moment, away from the undertow of memory.

"You don't know what's down there, do you?" he whispered to the bird. It blinked once before taking flight, abandoning him to his solitude.

On the middle boat, a young woman adjusted her wetsuit, laughing at something her companion said. For an instant, she was Martina, with her quiet competence and unexpected kindness. Beside her, a man checked his regulator—Danny's ghost, excited for the adventure ahead, unaware of what awaited them all.

Theo closed his eyes, feeling the salt spray on his face. He hadn't returned to Fisherman's Wharf since that day, had avoided even driving past the turnoff on his trips to Port Aransas. Dr. Mercer would call this exposure therapy, he supposed—confronting the source of trauma directly. But he hadn't planned this visit as therapy. He'd simply woken at dawn with the certainty that he needed to be here, to see the place where everything had changed.

The smell of diesel fuel and brine filled his nostrils, so familiar it ached. Beneath it lay the scent of the Gulf itself—that particular blend of salt and life that had sustained him during those desperate days in the marsh. His body remembered it all: the nausea on the boat, the cold shock of water when he'd jumped, the way his muscles had burned as he swam toward distant lights.

A charter captain strode past, nodding briefly at Theo before continuing down the dock. He wondered if the man recognized him from the news stories or the trial coverage. Probably not—he looked different now, leaner and harder, his eyes carrying a wariness that hadn't been there before.

The sun climbed higher, burning away the morning mist. Theo watched as passengers began boarding the dive boats, their faces bright with anticipation. They carried the same excitement he once had, the same innocent hunger for discovery. Part of him wanted to warn them, to explain how quickly wonder could transform into terror. But another part—the part that had survived—understood that their journey was their own.

Theo's hands finally stilled on the railing as he made his decision. He would return to these waters, not today but soon. The Gulf had nearly claimed him once, had changed him irrevocably, but it was also part of him now—teacher, adversary, and ultimately, the proving ground where he'd discovered his own capacity for survival.

Professor Lin's office embodied organized chaos—stacks of research papers formed miniature cityscapes across her desk, while shelves of marine biology texts lined the walls in a spectrum of academic spines. The mid-morning light filtered through partially open blinds, casting stripes across Theo's thesis proposal as he placed it on her desk.

"Human Trafficking Networks and Coastal Ecosystem Exploitation: A Case Study of the Texas Gulf Coast," Professor Lin read aloud, her fingers tracing the title. Her eyes lifted to meet Theo's, revealing both curiosity and concern.

Theo stood straighter, steadier than he had been at the wharf earlier that morning. "I've mapped the correlation between degraded wetland areas and smuggling routes," he explained, flipping to a color-coded chart. "Criminal organizations deliberately choose locations where environmental monitoring is minimal."

Professor Lin nodded, studying the data. Across campus, students hurried between classes, oblivious to the weight of the conversation unfolding in this small office. For them, the Gulf represented weekend excursions and marine biology field trips. For Theo, it remained both nightmare and classroom.

"Your methodology is sound," she said finally. "But I need to ask—are you certain you're ready to immerse yourself in this again? Academically and emotionally?"

The question hung between them, surrounded by the silent witnesses of academic tomes and research journals.

"I don't have the luxury of separating my academic interests from my experiences," Theo replied. "Every smuggler's camp I documented was strategically positioned where environmental regulations weren't enforced. They exploit these ecological blind spots."

Professor Lin removed her glasses, her expression softening. "You've transformed significantly since you first returned to campus. This proposal demonstrates remarkable academic rigor."

"I need to make it matter," Theo said simply. "Otherwise, it was just suffering without purpose."

Outside, a seagull called, momentarily drawing Theo's attention to the window and the glimpse of distant water beyond the campus buildings.

"The field research component will require you to revisit some difficult locations," Professor Lin noted, turning to the methodology section.

"I know." Theo's voice remained steady. "But I also know those waters better than anyone. The delta showed me its secrets once to help me survive. Now I need to use that knowledge to protect others."

Professor Lin replaced her glasses, decision made. "Then let's ensure your voice is heard where it matters most."

Chlorine-scented air hung over the university pool's surface, the afternoon sun casting rippling patterns through the high windows. The facility stood empty except for two figures—one in the water, the other perched at the pool's edge, legs dangling in the clear blue.

"Deep breaths, Theo. Focus on my voice, not the memories," Jake Morrison instructed, his tone calm but firm.

Theo floated on his back, regulator out of his mouth, eyes fixed on the ceiling. His chest heaved with rapid, shallow breaths. The wetsuit felt suddenly constricting, a sensation that had triggered his panic attack underwater moments before.

"I don't understand," Theo managed between breaths. "I lived in water for weeks. The Gulf became my home."

Jake nodded, understanding flickering across his weathered face. "The open water didn't trap you. This pool does."

Around them, the university's Olympic-sized pool stood in stark contrast to the wild, unpredictable Gulf. Here, every surface was manufactured, every depth measured and marked. The very control that made it ideal for beginners had become Theo's prison—reminding him of that desperate night escaping the dive boat, the crushing pressure of limited air, the terrifying confinement of the water's embrace.

"When you were submerged just now, where did you go?" Jake asked, his voice gentle but probing.

"Back to the boat. Back to the tank with forty minutes of air and five miles to shore." Theo closed his eyes. "I felt the weight of the water above me, just like then."

Jake had worked with veterans, survivors of boating accidents, and now Theo—people whose relationship with water had been fundamentally altered by trauma. He recognized the distant look in Theo's eyes.

"Let's try something different," Jake suggested, sliding into the water beside Theo. "We'll start at the surface. Feel the air on your face while your body experiences the water. Your brain needs to relearn that water and panic aren't the same thing."

Theo nodded, grateful for Jake's patience. His thesis research required underwater observation—there was no path forward without conquering this hurdle.

"The water saved you once," Jake reminded him. "It can be your ally again."

As they began the modified exercises, Theo felt something shift slightly within him. The water surrounding his body wasn't his enemy. Like the marsh that had both challenged and sheltered him, it was simply a force to be understood and respected.

"I need this," Theo whispered, more to himself than to Jake. "The answers I'm looking for are down there."

Jake nodded. "And we'll find them. One breath at a time."

Theo stood in the equipment room, methodically rinsing his mask under the tap water. The rhythmic sound of droplets hitting the metal sink echoed against the walls lined with tanks and hanging wetsuits. The familiar smell of neoprene and saltwater permeated the air as evening shadows lengthened across the floor.

"Surprise." A familiar voice cut through his concentration.

Theo turned to find Emma standing in the doorway, her hair pulled back in a ponytail, holding a dive certification card between her fingers like a prize.

"What are you—" Theo began, confusion etching across his face.

"Three months of lessons," Emma announced, stepping into the equipment room. "Every Tuesday and Thursday after my environmental science lab. Just finished my certification dive today."

Jake leaned against the doorframe behind her, arms crossed with an approving smile. "Your sister's a natural, Theo. Buoyancy control like she's been diving for years."

Theo set his mask down, water dripping from his fingers. "You never said anything."

"I wanted to be sure I could do it first." Emma moved closer, examining the regulator hoses hanging nearby. "Didn't want to get your hopes up if I freaked out underwater."

The fluorescent lights hummed overhead as Theo processed her revelation. His sister—who had once been afraid to put her face underwater in the swimming pool—had learned to dive. For him.

"Your research matters," she continued, voice softening. "And I thought... maybe it would be easier if you weren't alone down there."

Theo felt conflicting emotions collide within him—gratitude for her support, warmth at her dedication, but also a sharp spike of fear. The Gulf had nearly claimed him once. The thought of Emma in those same waters sent a chill through him that had nothing to do with his damp wetsuit.

"That's..." he searched for words, "incredible, Em. But you don't have to—"

"I want to," she interrupted firmly. "Besides, I'm majoring in Environmental Science, remember? Field experience looks good on grad school applications."

Jake watched their exchange with quiet understanding, recognizing the protective instinct that flashed across Theo's face.

"She's got solid skills, Theo," Jake offered. "Follows protocols to the letter."

Emma stepped forward and squeezed Theo's arm. "You're not the only Mercer who belongs in the water."

Theo nodded slowly, realizing that while he'd been fighting his own battles with the sea, Emma had been preparing to face it alongside him. The water that had once isolated him now offered an unexpected connection.

"Just promise me one thing," Theo said finally.

"What's that?"

"You stay within sight. Always."

Late morning sunlight danced across the water's surface, fracturing into golden rays that penetrated thirty feet down to where Theo hovered above the shallow reef. The conditions were perfect—visibility extended at least sixty feet in every direction, the water temperature a comfortable seventy-eight degrees, and the gentle current barely noticeable. Jake had chosen this site specifically for its calm conditions and easy exit.

Theo's breathing echoed in his ears, rhythmic and controlled as he surveyed the colorful coral formations below. Small schools of fish darted between the outcroppings, unconcerned by the human visitors. Emma floated nearby, her eyes visible above her mask, crinkled at the corners in obvious delight as she pointed to a passing stingray.

Then, without warning, something shifted.

The filtered sunlight streaming from above transformed in Theo's mind. No longer was it the benevolent glow of a perfect diving day, but the disorienting moonlight from that desperate night swim when he fled the boat. His chest tightened. The regulator that had been delivering air smoothly now felt insufficient, each breath too shallow, too thin.

Emma noticed the change immediately. Her brother's body language had transformed—his movements becoming jerky, his hands clutching at nothing. Through his mask, she could see his eyes had widened, pupils dilated with fear.

Jake, monitoring from several feet away, recognized the signs of a panic attack and moved closer, making a calming gesture with his hands.

Theo's mind raced between past and present. The weightlessness that moments ago had felt liberating now mirrored the terrifying suspension of that night—alone, adrift, hunted. His breathing accelerated, bubbles cascading upward in chaotic bursts.

Emma positioned herself directly in front of him, deliberately making eye contact. She placed her hand firmly on his shoulder and made the "okay?" signal. When Theo didn't respond, she made the "up" signal, pointing toward the surface with her thumb.

Jake appeared on Theo's other side. Together, they guided him upward, ascending slowly to avoid injury, maintaining physical contact throughout the journey. Emma never broke eye contact, her steady gaze anchoring Theo to the present moment even as his mind threatened to drag him back to the past.

The water grew lighter around them, the surface drawing closer with each controlled breath. Theo focused on Emma's eyes, finding in them something the delta had never offered him during those terrifying weeks—the certainty that he wasn't alone.

Mid-afternoon sun penetrated the clear Gulf waters, casting light across the reef system twenty miles southeast of Port Aransas. After the morning's panic attack, Jake had suggested this alternative site—a protected area where diving was strictly regulated. Theo had agreed, determined not to let his earlier setback define the day.

Beneath the surface, Theo moved with renewed purpose. His breathing had steadied, each inhale and exhale through the regulator now a rhythm that grounded him rather than triggered memories. Emma swam several feet to his right, periodically giving him thumbs-up signals which he returned with increasing confidence.

Jake hovered at a distance, giving the siblings space while maintaining supervision. He noted the change in Theo's body language—no longer rigid with fear but fluid and observant, the movements of a scientist rather than a survivor.

As they approached the southern edge of the reef, Theo slowed. Something caught his eye—an unnatural pattern in the coral structure. Where healthy reef formations should have shown organic growth, he noticed a series of parallel gouges. He gestured to Emma, pointing toward the damaged area.

She approached, her brow furrowing behind her mask as she examined what he'd found. Theo reached for the underwater slate attached to his BCD and quickly sketched the pattern. Below his drawing, he wrote: "Anchor damage? Recent."

Emma nodded, then pointed to a section several yards away. Theo followed her gesture and spotted what appeared to be synthetic debris partially buried in the sand—fragments of rope and what might have been packaging material.

The scientific part of Theo's mind clicked into high gear, temporarily overriding the emotional associations with these waters. He swam closer, careful not to disturb the sediment, and began documenting with the underwater camera he'd brought for research purposes.

The damage pattern was distinctive—not the result of natural events or clumsy recreational divers, but consistent with repeated boat traffic. In protected waters where vessels should maintain strict distance from reef structures, this suggested deliberate disregard for regulations.

Jake approached, curious about their focused investigation. Theo showed him the slate and pointed to the debris. Jake's expression turned serious as he recognized the implications. He made a circular motion with his finger—continue searching.

For the next twenty minutes, the three divers systematically surveyed the area. Theo found additional signs that troubled him: more debris, a metal canister half-buried in sand, and a section of reef where the coral appeared chemically damaged rather than physically broken.

With each discovery, Theo felt a shift within himself. The waters that had been the setting of his trauma were revealing a new purpose. Where once he had been prey, he was now becoming a hunter of evidence. His experiences in the delta had sharpened his perception—he recognized patterns that others might overlook, understood the signs of human intrusion in natural spaces.

Emma touched his arm and pointed to her air gauge, indicating they should begin their ascent. Theo nodded, taking one final series of photographs before following Jake toward the surface.

As they broke through into the warm Gulf air, Theo removed his regulator, his mind racing with connections and possibilities.

"There's something happening down there," he said, treading water as he faced Jake and Emma. "That's not recreational damage. It's systematic and recent."

Emma pushed her mask up onto her forehead. "You think it's related to smuggling?"

"I don't know yet," Theo replied, "but those patterns match what I saw near Carlos's routes. Different location, same methods."

Jake looked toward the distant shoreline. "Whatever it is, you've got documentation now. This isn't just about your past anymore, is it?"

Theo shook his head, feeling a clarity he hadn't experienced since before his ordeal. "No. This is about making sure what happened to me doesn't happen to anyone else."

Three days after the dive, Theo's apartment glowed with the blue light of his computer screen. Outside, campus lights dotted the darkness as students made their way to late-night study sessions. Inside, Theo hunched over his desk, cycling through underwater photographs, his face illuminated by the images of damaged coral and suspicious debris.

The clock on his wall read 11:23 PM when his phone vibrated against the wooden desk. An unknown number with a Houston area code. Theo hesitated before answering.

"Hello?"

"Theo? It's Isabella." The voice carried both strength and wariness, immediately transporting him back to the delta.

Theo straightened in his chair. "Isabella? How did you—"

"Your aunt Clara. She helped me find you." A child's voice murmured in the background. "Miguel, go brush your teeth, please. Mamá will be there in a minute."

Theo swallowed hard. The sound of her son's name brought back the faces of others he'd known in the marsh. "Is everything okay?"

"We're safe. We're in Houston now. I work with a victims' advocacy group." She paused. "But that's not why I'm calling."

Outside, the wind picked up, rustling the oak tree branches against his window. Theo waited.

"Have you noticed anything unusual along the coast? Boat activity, places that feel wrong?"

Theo glanced at his computer screen, where the damaged reef was frozen in high-resolution detail. "Actually, yes. Three days ago, I found something while diving."

"I knew it." Her voice tightened. "We've been tracking patterns. Different players, same game. The networks didn't die with Carlos."

Theo's pulse quickened. "What have you heard?"

"Disappearances from coastal communities. Strange boat movements. We have people watching, but they don't have your... experience."

The room seemed to shrink around him as memories of the delta pressed in. "You think they're still operating trafficking routes?"

"I know they are. Different faces, same methods." A silence stretched between them. "You understand how they think, Theo. You survived them."

Theo's gaze drifted to the map on his wall, pins marking the locations of his research sites. "I've been documenting evidence for my thesis, but I didn't realize..."

"It's not over," Isabella said simply. "Not for any of us."

The weight of her words settled in his chest. Theo thought of Emma in the water beside him, of the damaged reef, of all the things that connected his past to this moment.

"What do you need from me?" he asked.

"Your eyes. Your knowledge." Isabella's voice softened. "And maybe, someday, your testimony again."

Outside, campus security lights swept across the parking lot. Theo made his decision.

"I'll help. Whatever you need."

Sunday evening settled over the Mercer home like a familiar blanket. The dining room table, polished oak that had witnessed twenty years of family meals, gleamed under the pendant light. Linda Mercer placed the final dish—a steaming casserole of her special mac and cheese—at the center of the table, completing the comfort food spread she'd prepared.

"Robert, could you call the kids?" she asked, adjusting the serving spoon.

Robert Mercer looked up from his phone. "They're adults now, Lin."

"They'll always be the kids to me," she replied with a soft smile.

The family gathered around the table, a ritual that had taken on new significance since Theo's return. Emma arrived first, hair still damp from a shower, followed by Theo, who carried a folder tucked under his arm.

"No work at the table," Linda reminded him gently.

Theo hesitated before setting the folder beside his chair. "Actually, Mom, I wanted to talk to everyone about something."

Robert served himself a portion of pot roast. "Everything okay at school?"

"School's fine." Theo exchanged a glance with Emma, who gave him an encouraging nod. "I've been diving again."

The serving spoon in Linda's hand froze midair. Robert's fork clattered against his plate.

"Diving?" Robert's voice dropped an octave. "After everything that happened?"

"It's part of my research," Theo explained, reaching for the folder. "I've been documenting damaged reef sites along the coast. There's evidence suggesting—"

"Evidence?" Robert's face flushed. "The only evidence I care about is that diving nearly got you killed last time."

Linda placed a hand on her husband's arm. "Robert, let him explain."

"There's nothing to explain." Robert pushed his plate away. "No son of mine is going back into that water."

Theo's jaw tightened. "I'm not asking permission, Dad. I'm telling you what I'm doing."

"You have no idea what we went through when you disappeared," Robert said, his voice rising. "Eleven days of hell, not knowing if you were dead or alive."

"I lived it, Dad," Theo countered. "I know exactly what happened."

Emma leaned forward. "He's not alone out there. I've been diving with him."

Linda gasped. "Emma, you too?"

"Someone has to watch his back," Emma said firmly.

Robert's fist came down on the table, rattling the silverware. "This is insanity! Both of you, risking your lives—"

"It's not just about research anymore," Theo interrupted, pulling photographs from his folder. "Isabella called me. The trafficking networks are still operating."

A heavy silence fell over the table. Linda's eyes widened in fear.

"All the more reason to stay away," Robert insisted. "Let the authorities handle it."

"The authorities don't see what I see," Theo spread the photos across the table. "These aren't random boat damages. They're using the same routes, the same methods."

"So you're what—some vigilante marine biologist now?" Robert's voice cracked with emotion. "We just got you back, Theo."

"You never really got me back, Dad," Theo said quietly. "The person who went into that marsh isn't the same one who came out."

Emma reached across the table, squeezing Theo's hand. "He knows what he's doing."

"This isn't about competence," Linda interjected, tears welling in her eyes. "It's about not being able to bear losing you again."

Theo looked at his mother, then his father, seeing the raw fear beneath their anger. "I understand that. But I can't live in a bubble. What happened to me—it gave me purpose."

Robert shook his head, struggling to find words. "There are other ways to find purpose that don't involve putting yourself in danger."

"Not for me," Theo said with quiet certainty. "Not anymore."

The family sat in tense silence, their dinner forgotten, as the weight of Theo's choice settled over them like an incoming tide.

Mid-morning sunlight streamed through the windows of The Coastal Brew, casting long rectangles of light across the polished wooden tables. The coffee shop sat three blocks from campus, far enough to avoid the usual student crowds but close enough for convenience. Theo had chosen the corner table deliberately—backs to the wall, clear view of both entrances.

Agent Daniels arrived precisely at 10:15, her dark blazer and practical shoes marking her as federal law enforcement despite her attempt at casual appearance. She carried a leather portfolio under one arm and scanned the room with practiced efficiency before approaching.

"You look better than the last time I saw you," she said, sliding into the seat across from Theo.

"Hospital lighting isn't flattering for anyone." Theo pushed a coffee toward her. "Black, two sugars."

Daniels raised an eyebrow. "You remembered."

"Some things stick with you."

The unspoken weight of their shared history—hours of debriefings, testimonies, identifications—hung between them as Daniels sipped her coffee.

"Your message said it was urgent," she said, setting down her cup.

Theo opened his folder, spreading the underwater photographs across the table. "These were taken at three different sites along the coast. Notice the propeller marks on the reef?"

Daniels studied the images, her expression hardening. "Consistent patterns. Deliberate routes."

"Exactly. And this—" Theo placed a small evidence bag containing fibers on the table. "Found caught in coral at the second site. Synthetic rope, not the kind recreational boats use."

Daniels exhaled slowly. "We've been tracking increased maritime activity in these quadrants for the past two months. Satellite shows unusual patterns, but we lacked concrete evidence until now."

"It's happening again, isn't it?" Theo asked, though he already knew the answer.

"Different players, same game." Daniels leaned forward. "After your testimony, we dismantled Mendoza's operation, but nature abhors a vacuum. Someone's stepped in."

Theo felt a familiar coldness settle in his stomach. "Isabella was right."

"Isabella Vega?" Daniels's eyes narrowed. "She contacted you?"

"She's working with a victims' advocacy group in Houston. Noticed the patterns before anyone else."

Daniels gathered the photographs, sliding them into her portfolio. "These are extremely valuable, Theo. But I need to be clear about something—you've done your part. Let us take it from here."

Theo met her gaze steadily. "We both know I understand these waters better than anyone on your team."

"And we both know what happened last time you got involved." Daniels's voice softened slightly. "Your family nearly lost you once."

"Some choices aren't about safety," Theo replied. "They're about who we decide to be."

The fluorescent lights of the dive shop cast harsh shadows across the equipment laid out on the metal preparation table. Outside, darkness had settled over Port Aransas, the tourist crowds long gone, leaving only the rhythmic sound of waves against the shore. Jake Morrison moved methodically among the tanks, checking each valve with practiced precision while stealing concerned glances at Theo and Emma.

"I still think this is a terrible idea," Jake said, tightening a regulator. "Night dives are challenging enough without adding potential criminal surveillance to the mix."

Theo didn't look up from his wetsuit inspection. "The Coast Guard can't be everywhere at once. Agent Daniels admitted as much." His fingers traced over a small tear in the neoprene, which he carefully sealed with a rubber adhesive. "If we wait for official channels, we'll miss whatever's happening out there."

Emma stood nearby, her normally playful demeanor replaced by quiet determination as she checked her dive computer. The tension between the siblings was palpable—neither willing to back down.

"I've memorized the reef layout from our last dive," she said. "And I've logged fifteen night dives in the past month. I'm ready."

Jake shook his head. "It's not about skill. It's about what happens if you encounter something—or someone—you shouldn't."

The dive shop fell silent except for the hum of the air compressor. Through the windows, moonlight glinted off the water, both inviting and ominous. Theo knew that same light would penetrate only the first few meters of the Gulf's surface, leaving the depths in impenetrable darkness.

"We stick to the plan," Theo said finally. "Observe only. No confrontation. If we see anything suspicious, we document it and surface immediately."

Jake placed three specialized dive lights on the table. "These have red filters. Less visible from the surface, but they'll limit your vision range."

Emma checked her underwater camera, ensuring its waterproof housing was properly sealed. "Thirty minutes maximum bottom time," she recited. "No separation, no exceptions."

As they loaded the equipment into Jake's truck, Theo felt a familiar tightness in his chest—not panic, but purpose. The Gulf had nearly claimed him once. Now he was willingly returning to its darkest reaches, not as a victim, but as a witness.

"You don't have to do this," he told Emma quietly as Jake started the engine.

She met his gaze, her eyes reflecting the determination he recognized in himself. "Neither do you. But here we are."

The truck pulled away from the dive shop, headlights cutting through the coastal fog as they headed toward the marina where Jake's boat waited. Above them, clouds drifted across the moon, casting the world into deeper shadow.

Forty feet beneath the surface, darkness enveloped them like a living thing. The moon's influence ended mere meters below the surface, leaving Theo, Emma, and Jake floating in a void broken only by the narrow cones of their red-filtered dive lights. The water pressed against Theo's wetsuit, cool and insistent, a constant reminder of where he was and what had happened here months before.

The reef below them was a different world at night. Creatures that hid during daylight hours now emerged—brittle stars crawled across coral heads, octopuses slipped between crevices, and the occasional predatory fish darted through their light beams.

Theo checked his dive computer: 12:14 AM. They'd been submerged for seventeen minutes, floating motionless above the reef, their bodies arranged in a triangle formation. Each diver faced outward, scanning different sections of the water column, waiting.

Emma tapped her tank twice with her dive knife—their pre-arranged signal. She pointed upward, where the faintest shadow passed overhead, momentarily blocking the dim ambient light from above. A boat had arrived.

The three divers extinguished their lights simultaneously, relying on their night-adjusted vision. Theo felt his heartbeat quicken but focused on his breathing—slow, deep pulls from the regulator, just as Jake had taught him during their recovery dives. This was different. This time he was here by choice.

The boat's engine cut to idle, then stopped entirely. The silence underwater intensified, broken only by the rhythmic release of their exhaled bubbles. Minutes stretched like hours as they waited, suspended between the reef and the surface.

A splash broke the stillness—then another, and another. Cylindrical packages descended through the water column, weighted to sink quickly. Theo counted eight before they stopped. The packages settled on the reef, some wedging between coral formations, others disappearing into crevices.

Jake made the hand signal to activate their cameras. Theo switched his light to its dimmest setting and directed it toward the nearest package while Emma recorded. The plastic wrapping was professional-grade, watertight and secured with zip ties—identical to what Marcus had used.

The familiar sight sent a chill through Theo that had nothing to do with the water temperature. This wasn't some new operation; it was the same network, continuing despite Marcus's arrest. The system had survived its decapitation.

A sudden bright light cut through the water from above—a powerful spotlight from the boat scanning the area. Theo froze, his body rigid with tension. The beam swept past them, then returned, lingering. They'd been spotted.

Jake signaled frantically: *Lights off. Stay down. Don't move.*

The three divers killed their lights and pressed themselves against the reef, seeking shelter among the coral formations. Emma's eyes found Theo's in the darkness, wide with fear but steady. Above them, the spotlight continued its methodical sweep.

A new sound penetrated the water—the metallic click and clank of something heavy being prepared. Theo recognized it instantly: someone was readying a speargun.

The boat's engine roared back to life, and a moment later, something pierced the water nearby—a weighted line descending rapidly. Not a spear, Theo realized with mounting horror, but a grappling hook. They were trying to retrieve the evidence.

Jake gestured urgently toward a depression in the reef twenty feet away—their escape route. But to reach it, they would need to cross open water, directly through the spotlight's path.

Theo's mind raced. They could wait, hoping the boat would leave, but that meant abandoning the evidence. Or they could make a break for it, risking detection and whatever waited above.

As the grappling hook snagged the first package and began to rise, Theo made his decision. He reached for Emma's arm and pointed toward the depression, then to Jake. His sister nodded, understanding passing between them without words.

Whatever came next, they would face it together.

Theo broke the surface first, Emma and Jake emerging seconds later on either side. The night air hit their faces as they spit out their regulators, but before they could speak, blinding light engulfed them from all directions.

"Don't move! Hands where we can see them!"

Multiple spotlights created a cage of light around the three divers. The beams came not from one vessel but from three—larger than the boat they'd observed from below. Theo raised his arms instinctively, his dive computer still strapped to his wrist. Emma followed suit, her eyes wide but determined.

"Identify yourselves!" The command echoed across the water.

"Theo Mercer!" His voice cracked from the salt water. "With Emma Mercer and Jake Morrison!"

A moment of silence followed, then: "Mercer? Did you say Mercer?"

The spotlight dimmed slightly, and Theo made out the unmistakable profile of a Coast Guard vessel. Relief flooded through him, quickly followed by confusion.

"Stand by," the voice ordered.

Jake treaded water closer to Theo. "Coast Guard," he whispered. "What the hell?"

Before Theo could respond, a familiar figure appeared at the railing of the nearest vessel.

"Mr. Mercer," Lieutenant Commander Wilson called down. "I believe we discussed you leaving this investigation to the professionals."

Theo blinked against the light. "Commander Wilson?"

"The same." Wilson gestured to his crew. "Get them aboard."

Minutes later, wrapped in thermal blankets on the deck of the Coast Guard cutter, Theo watched as officers secured a smaller vessel fifty yards away. Men in civilian clothes sat handcuffed on its deck while Coast Guard personnel cataloged packages identical to those Theo had seen underwater.

"We've been monitoring this drop point for three weeks," Wilson explained, handing them each a steaming cup of coffee. "Thanks in large part to the intelligence you provided after your ordeal."

"You knew about this?" Emma asked, her voice a mix of accusation and admiration as she looked at her brother.

"I filed reports," Theo said. "But I didn't know they were acting on them."

Wilson nodded. "Your detailed descriptions of Marcus's operation gave us the patterns we needed. When similar activities appeared in this sector, we connected the dots."

"It's the same network," Theo said. "The packaging, the drop method—it's identical."

"Different players, same playbook," Wilson confirmed. "Marcus's arrest created a vacuum. These men work for his replacement." He gestured toward the apprehended boat. "Or they did, until tonight."

Jake shook his head. "So while we were down there documenting evidence—"

"We were up here, waiting to catch them in the act," Wilson finished. "Though you three nearly compromised months of surveillance."

Emma straightened her spine. "We didn't know you were watching."

"Clearly." Wilson's expression softened. "But your presence actually created a distraction that worked in our favor. When they spotted your bubbles, they panicked and made mistakes."

Theo looked across the water where Coast Guard personnel were securing evidence from the smaller vessel. "Did you get them all?"

"The local cell, yes. The higher-ups are still out there." Wilson placed a hand on Theo's shoulder. "But tonight's arrests will disrupt their operations for months, possibly years."

Theo nodded, feeling a complex mixture of emotions—relief, vindication, and a strange sense of completion.

"You know," Wilson said, "we could use someone with your knowledge of the coastline and these operations. There are civilian consultant positions—"

"I need to finish school first," Theo interrupted, surprising himself with his certainty. "But after that..."

Emma bumped her shoulder against his. "After that, the bad guys better watch out."

As the Coast Guard cutter began its journey back to port, Theo stood at the railing, watching the spot where the reef lay hidden beneath the waves. The Gulf had taken so much from him, but in return, it had given him purpose. The circle was complete.

Behind him, the rising moon cast silver light across the water, illuminating the path home.

Epilogue

The afternoon sun cast a golden glow across the Mercer family's backyard, where tables adorned with blue and white tablecloths—the university colors—dotted the lawn. A banner stretched between two oak trees read "Congratulations Graduate & Hero." The dual celebration marked not only Theo's graduation with honors in Marine Biology and Environmental Law but also recognized the commendation he had received from the Coast Guard for his role in dismantling one of the largest trafficking networks along the Gulf Coast.

Aunt Clara moved among the guests, refilling glasses and sharing stories of Theo's childhood fascination with coastal plants. Emma, now in her second year of Environmental Science, proudly showed Professor Lin photos from their most recent research dive. Jake Morrison chatted with Lieutenant Commander Wilson near the grill, their professional relationship having evolved into friendship over the past year.

At the center table, Theo sat beside his father, Robert, whose initial resistance to Theo's return to diving had gradually transformed into reluctant acceptance and, finally, unmistakable pride. The journey hadn't been easy for either of them.

"Remember when you used to take me fishing at dawn?" Theo asked, watching his father slice into the grilled redfish on his plate.

Robert nodded, his eyes crinkling at the corners. "You were always more interested in what was swimming beneath us than what we might catch."

"You taught me to respect the sea," Theo said quietly. "That saved my life more than once."

A shadow passed over Robert's face—the memory of those weeks when Theo was missing, when they'd feared the worst. Linda, sensing the shift in mood, reached across the table and placed her hand over her husband's.

"When I got that call," Robert said, his voice dropping so only Theo and Linda could hear, "that they'd found you alive... I made a promise." He cleared his throat. "I promised I'd never stand in your way again, no matter how afraid I was."

Theo's throat tightened. "Dad—"

"Let me finish," Robert insisted. "I broke that promise when you started diving again. I was terrified of losing you twice." He looked up, meeting his son's gaze directly. "But watching you these past two years—the way you've turned what happened to you into something that helps others—I've never been more proud of anyone in my life."

Around them, the celebration continued, voices rising and falling like the tides. Agent Daniels arrived late, presenting Theo with a small, official-looking envelope. Isabella and her son, now thriving in their new life, brought a homemade cake. Even Professor Harmon made an appearance, gruffly congratulating his former student.

As evening approached, Theo found a moment of quiet near his mother's garden. Emma joined him, bumping his shoulder with hers—their familiar gesture of solidarity.

"You okay?" she asked.

Theo nodded, surveying the gathering. "I never expected this," he admitted. "When I was out there, in the marsh, I thought I'd lost everything."

"Instead, you found something," Emma observed.

"More than that," Theo said. "I found my way back—not to who I was, but to who I could be."

The sound of laughter drew their attention. Robert was telling a story, his hands animated, while Linda watched him with affection. Aunt Clara nodded approvingly as she passed a plate of her famous biscuits.

In that moment, surrounded by the people who had supported him, challenged him, and ultimately accepted the person he had become, Theo understood that his journey through darkness had not only transformed him—it had strengthened the bonds that held his family together. What began as survival had become something more profound: a homecoming in the truest sense.

About the Author

Born in Little Rock, Arkansas, at the start of World War II, Wallace Berry grew up on a farm in the Arkansas countryside. His childhood, steeped in the rustic simplicity of farm life without modern conveniences, deeply rooted in him a love for the wilderness. The surrounding forests and hands-on experiences of rural living profoundly shaped his appreciation for nature and a life outdoors. As an adult, Wallace made the Texas Gulf Coast his home, carrying with him the values and passions developed during his formative years.